# Dark Angel

*Also by Eden Maguire:*

BEAUTIFUL DEAD
1. Jonas
2. Arizona
3. Summer
4. Phoenix

*Coming soon*
Twisted Heart


*Also by Hodder Children's Books*


Dark Heart Forever
Dark Heart Rising
*Lee Monroe*


Sisters Red
Sweetly
*Jackson Pearce*

# Dark Angel

## Eden Maguire

Hodder
Children's
Books

A division of Hachette Children's Books

*For Caroline, for all the years of support and friendship.*

So farewell Hope, and with Hope farewell Fear,
Farewell Remorse: all good to me is lost;
Evil, be thou my good.

John Milton, *Paradise Lost*, Book 4

# 1

Out here, fire eats up the forest. Tongues of flame lick the trees and dance like devils across the land. They swirl through valleys and jump rivers, carried by the wind. We're talking total inferno.

Bobby Mackey, a smokejumper for twenty years, tells us how it is. 'We bring in air tankers to drop the retardant, three thousand gallons at a time, plus Sikorsky Sky Cranes. They can douse a hotspot with two thousand gallons. Then the ground crews form fire lines to contain the blaze. If that doesn't work, they drop more guys from choppers. That's where I come in.'

A smokejumper makes a living by parachuting from a plane into forest fires. How crazy is that?

Sure, I've seen the tree canopy catch alight, watched the wind shift and send a wall of flame roaring down the valley – all from a safe distance. But jumpers get caught in the thick of it without shelter and in a sudden blowup it can all be over in the space of five minutes.

Bobby says, 'Those guys about to die – I know what they're thinking. You can't breathe, it's so hot. The fire is sucking in the air around you, there's no oxygen. Your clothes and hair vibrate with the air rushing by you. Breathe, breathe, breathe. At the last moment you're not thinking about fire, you're thinking about air.'

What can you say? Men die. Rocks stay red hot for days. They slide down the mountains in clouds of ash. Burned branches fall on your head. You hear them thump to the ground and you don't know which way to run.

Red, orange, yellow – I've watched a night-time finger of fire race down from Black Rock, small spurts of flame sneaking out of underground lairs days later. That's wildfire. That's how it is in the mountains where I live.

I tell you this because my house is built in the middle of a burnout. Eighteen years ago, the year I was born, fire ate up this place. That's why there are no trees taller than the roof of a single-storey building, why all the homes are contemporary design and open plan, with clear views of Prayer River and Turner Lake out beyond the old historic centre of Bitterroot.

Smokejumper Bobby wore his yellow firefighter's

jacket, helmet and goggles to shock-jock us high-school leavers into seeing the dangers of setting fires during the dry season, telling us he never wanted to experience a repeat of August 2000 when blazes burned out of control in sixteen states. His skin looked like flames had creased and singed it, like smoke was ingrained in the lines under his eyes and down either side of his mouth. 'Next time you kids camp out by the lake, observe to the letter those Red Flag fire hazard warnings – no campfires, no smoking cigarettes. Remember those pinon pines and junipers may take hundreds of years to regenerate.'

I was listening but my mind was drifting off. Personally I didn't care too much about trees burning; more about the million rabbits, raccoons and porcupines too slow to take cover, and anyway where would they run?

And I was still picturing air being sucked out of my lungs – a whoosh, a wall, a swirl of flames engulfing me.

'Tania?' Grace pulled me to my feet at the end of the lecture.

Bobby was sitting in his yellow jacket at the front of the room, signing copies of *Smokejumper*, his recently reprinted autobiography, for a line of maybe fifteen or twenty students, mostly guys. If the girls were anything like me, they were too freaked out to invest the necessary twelve dollars.

3

'Are you OK?' Grace asked.

I nodded and stood up. Why did getting air into my lungs suddenly seem problematic? I took short, shallow breaths; could almost feel flames scorch my skin.

I should tell you. On the plot of burnout land where my dad built our house there was once a home where three people died – a husband, wife and baby girl. On the neighbouring plot, the fire cornered a widow in her sixties. She never made it through the smoke and flames.

In the three decades he'd been on this earth, Dad's family had already been through so many hard times, both back home in Romania and here in the land of the free, that he claimed he didn't ever feel queasy about building our house there on that plot – like a phoenix rising from the ashes, he said.

I didn't learn about the fatalities until I was eight, when I was already having regular nightmares. The facts on the forest fire hit me hard. I was eight years old and having bad dreams about suffocating, struggling to draw breath and waking up in a cold sweat, screaming for my mom.

'Who told Tania about the wildfire?' she demanded, ready to blame Dad.

Nobody. I'd learned it from Bobby Mackey's book in

the town library, straying one Saturday afternoon from kids' fiction into the adult section, where I'd found the smokejumper's autobiography in the new book display. Glossy pictures of orange flames and black plumes of smoke rising above the green tree canopy drew me in, leading me to read details about the people who had died. Mrs Dorothy Earle, Karl and Maia Witney and their baby girl.

'You're sure you're OK?' Grace checked.

A branch falls among smouldering embers. Sparks leap into choking, smoke-grey air. Burned trunks rise like black pillars as far as the eye can see.

'I need some air,' I told her, walking quickly from the building.

'Lighten up.' Holly Randle's advice had mixed motives. On the one hand she has genuine worries about my obvious mood dips, on the other she judges me for being way too thin-skinned and hypersensitive, which was what was behind her 'lighten up' lecture on this occasion.

We were driving home in her car after Bobby's lecture. Holly lives in the house next door to me, in Mrs Earle's plot on Becker Hill. She claims she has no dreams about the widow who lived there before the fire.

'That guy really got to me,' I explained. 'Did he have to go into graphic detail?'

'I guess. Shock tactics and all.'

'I'm shocked,' I conceded, leaning out of the car to gaze up at the clear blue sky. 'I was there, living every last moment of those trapped firefighters.'

'You looked awful, believe me – like you were going to pass out. If Grace hadn't hauled you out of there, I'd have stepped in and done it myself.'

'Thanks – I think.'

'No, really. Your face turned whiter than my bedsheets; your breathing was bad. I've seen you do this a hundred times – someone paints a picture and your imagination goes into overdrive.'

'My imagination,' I echoed. 'And thanks again.' I sighed, shifting so that I sat upright in my seat. 'But I already have a mother.'

'Sorry for caring,' Holly muttered, climbing the hill between the baby pine trees lining the sides of the road. 'Anyhow, where's the hottest guy on the planet when you really need him?' Holly is also jealous of my relationship with Orlando and so always refers to him with lashings of sarcasm – did I mention that? Orlando, the hottest boy in Bitterroot, no contest. He looks like he works out daily but actually not true. Plus he can turn on that wide Irish smile and kill with a glance.

My boyfriend's parents had flown with him to Dallas to check out the college campus. He would be away for three days and I was already experiencing withdrawal symptoms. It happened before when they took him to Chicago and left me for an entire weekend in a tactile desert – no touching, no kissing. 'He's in Dallas,' I muttered as Holly stopped the car and I got out.

'But he'll be back Friday?' she checked.

'What's Friday?'

'The party, stupid!'

'Yeah, the party – he'll be back.'

'Does he have his costume?'

'No. Does Aaron?'

'Yeah. My mom made it. And mine too. Do you even have yours?'

'Not yet.' I'd been thinking about the costume but not doing anything, which was normal for me. Think, think, think – no action. I mean, how hard could throwing together a party costume be?

'No costume – no entrance through heaven's gates,' Holly warned.

What she meant was, I wouldn't get to meet the living god, the rock legend that was Zoran Brancusi. He was our party host. The invites, sent out to every teen in

Bitterroot, stipulated a theme – 'Heavenly Bodies'. It was wide open to interpretation, but Holly had already settled on a fittingly divine outfit for her and Aaron. Likewise Grace and Jude.

'No problem,' I called after Holly as she swung into her own driveway. 'My costume will be spectacular. It's in my head – every last detail.'

'Liar!' she yelled back. The garage door rolled open and her car disappeared inside.

'You know me so well,' I muttered, taking out my phone, hoping for a message from Orlando – Missing u. Can't w8 4 Friday. xox type of thing. No new messages, my phone told me.

Sometimes I sit inside my house and wonder, what was the baby's name – Katie? Jordan? Mollie? Which room did she sleep in? Bobby Mackey's book tells you only that she died in the fire on her first birthday and that her parents ran back into the house to try and save her – first the mom then the dad, both in vain.

I sit in my room and listen. The breath of a sleeping baby is silent, eyes closed, lashes curled, its tiny chest rising and falling.

'Hey, Tania. How's the costume coming along?' It was

Grace on the phone, checking up on me.

'I made a few sketches,' I lied.

'I need details. Are you doing the angel thing – wings and all?'

'Seriously, I'm not that into the Heavenly Bodies theme.'

'So I heard. What's wrong with you?'

'Angels are all played out.' Gauze and sequins, plumage, shimmery silver body paint. Been there, done that.

'So surprise us – come up with something original. Paint yourself red all over, show up as a Martian.'

'Thanks for that suggestion, best buddy of mine. Very attractive.'

There was a pause while I heard Grace turn on the shower. 'You and Orlando *will* be there Friday?' she checked.

'You betcha.'

'Cool. Gotta go now, hon. I'm meeting Jude in five.'

Beep went the phone. End of conversation. I sat on my bed and doodled a couple of sketches, but my angels came out as devils, with horns and forked tails. 'Hmmm . . .' I said.

'Interesting,' Mom said when I went downstairs and showed her the fruits of my labours. She was taking laundry from the machine, breathing in the scent of meadow flowers. 'I can definitely see Orlando as a devil.'

'Nice. I'll tell him.'

Mom folded towels, hung shirts on hangers. 'How's Dallas? Did he text you?'

'No. I guess he's busy.'

'When does he get back?'

'Thursday. These costumes are driving me nuts. I think we won't go.'

Mom smoothed the neat pile of towels. 'Go,' she urged. 'It's a big event. Maybe you'll even get to meet the man himself.'

Eighteen months back, Zoran Brancusi had quit the rock scene at the height of his fame. His last album, entitled *Heavenly Bodies* – so no surprise about the party theme – went global. He did the world tour then got badly injured in a car crash and dropped out of sight. A year later he turned up in Bitterroot. Not in town exactly. To be clear, he bought twenty thousand acres of land, including half a mountain covered in pine forest. He built a house out there, in Black Eagle Canyon. The upcoming party looked like his way of saying hi to a thousand new neighbours – the entire teen population of Bitterroot.

'He's planning a comeback,' Mom predicted as she carried the towels into the bathroom. 'There'll be a host of celebs at the party, a deal with a gossip magazine – photographs, a full-length feature. You wait and see.'

Orlando called me at midnight from Dallas. I pictured him hunched over his phone, long legs resting on a coffee table, dark hair flopping forward. I totally wished I was there.

'Bird of paradise,' he suggested for my costume.

'Really?' Technically it wasn't a heavenly body; it actually existed. I explained the subtle difference to my absent boyfriend.

'Why so literal all of a sudden? The clue's in the name – bird of *paradise*. Garden of Eden, all that stuff.'

'I'll think about it.'

'It'll be cool, Tania. I see you as a bird, a delicate, exotic bird – turquoise plumage, orange and gold.' He's applying for fashion design courses at college so he says stuff like this without blushing. 'Make a mask, a headdress with feathers. You're creative – you can do it.'

'I'll think about it,' I said again. Say you miss me, tell me you can't wait to hold me in your arms. Insecurity was seeping out of every pore.

'I went to a seminar, got introduced to two potential course tutors – Julian Sellars and Mimi Rossi. They were both amazing,' he tells me, fast and enthusiastic.

'Oh, and by the way, I won't be there.'

'What do you mean, you won't be here?' Explosion into uncontrolled panic; I can't keep it out of my voice.

'I won't make it back in time,' he explained calmly. 'Mom plans to visit a cousin here in Dallas. The trip is extended till Sunday.'

I go into freefall and Orlando puts up a barrier. He plays it deliberately cool, doesn't give the needy version of me any space. It's a pattern we've gotten into.

What he likes is me when I'm creative – sketching, painting. This bit he understands and admires.

'You're so gifted,' he tells me. 'You don't know how talented you are.'

Me and a million other wannabe Warhols, I think, standing back from my latest canvas – a silkscreen portrait of a rainbow-coloured woman with the eyes blanked out, no window into the soul.

'And beautiful,' he insists, loosening my long black hair and watching it slide down my back. I'm his trophy girl, up there on a pedestal.

'I don't feel it,' I sigh, knocking back each and every compliment. It's a plea for him to understand what goes on beneath the surface, how I feel inside my so-called beautiful skin.

Up goes the wall. Orlando rolls his eyes and talks basketball, which he knows I hate.

This sounds like the perfect relationship, right?

I was in school the next day, still dark and moody, sitting between Grace and Jude after classes had ended.

'So come with us.' Grace took in the latest news from Orlando and jumped in with her offer. 'This doesn't mean you're off the party hook,' she warned.

Take Grace and Jude as a more finished version of me and Orlando. Jude of the perfect teeth, jaw line and long neck, the Afro-American shaved head and curling lashes. Flawless, blonde Grace Montrose with long, slim fingers and wide blue eyes. She has no insecurities for Jude to ignore.

'We'll call for you,' he told me. 'We'll drive out to Black Eagle together.'

I was still hurting from last night's argument. 'Did you forget the party?' I'd asked Orlando, trying not to load my tone with accusation and failing.

'No I didn't forget,' he'd replied. By now his feet would have been off the table, his eyelids would be half shut and his oh-so-kissable mouth wouldn't be smiling. 'Like I said, Mom plans to visit her cousin. What do you want me to do – sprout wings and fly home on an air current?'

'Try a conventional airplane,' I'd suggested.

'Ha-ha. Where will I find the cash?' There was a pause filled by a sigh, followed by an attempt to soften the blow. 'Listen, Tania, it's only three extra days.'

'That's not the point – it's the party!'

'Oh, sorry – The Party! Well, what do you know, I didn't mark that down as the pinnacle of my social diary this summer. I'm kind of busy looking for a college place for the fall.'

He'd turned it around and put me in the wrong, made me feel so bad. I'd apologized and went to bed hating myself, wondering when exactly I'd begun to press the destruct button on our relationship.

'Tania, we'll drive you out to Black Eagle Lodge.' Grace broke my dark thoughts to repeat the offer. 'And tomorrow night I'll come to your place to help with your costume. What was it again – bird of paradise?'

My dad came home that night with news that should have solved the costume dilemma plus the going-to-the-party-solo problem in one fell swoop.

'Forest fire,' he reported as he flung down his flight bag and kicked off his boots. 'Out at Black Eagle Canyon. I saw Forest Service pumper heading out there to join county fire crew.'

'How bad?' Mom asked.

I was half elated that the party would now be cancelled, half spooked by the news of a fresh forest fire. It ended in a shiver right down my spine.

'Plenty of smoke heading down mountain. Couldn't see flames.' Dad was tired – he'd been out of state on a construction project in the Utah desert, sleeping in camp for three nights. At the best of times he chops his English into short, sharp bursts, ignores details like the definite article, the personal pronoun. Exhaustion exaggerates the habit.

Mom jumped on the news. 'How did it start?'

'Fuel accumulation at ground level – deadwood. Lightning strike, no rain.'

'Let's hope it stays low, doesn't get into the canopy,' Mom said. Round here everyone is a wildfire expert. 'Wind's coming in from the north, which means the flames should push towards Turner Lake and fizzle out.'

We all thought but no one said, What about our retired rock star's multimillion-dollar spread? Did the flames engulf the house?

'Untouched,' Holly reported next morning. We could smell smoke in the air, even from a distance of ten miles. Everyone gathered at the school entrance, picking up

15

snippets of news. 'The flames leaped from one side of Black Eagle Canyon to the other; left the lodge unscathed.'

'It's a miracle,' Jude said. 'But I guess the party's off.'

'No way,' the fountain of all knowledge insisted. 'Zoran already put it on his blog – attendance of heavenly bodies required, his place, eight p.m. tomorrow.'

Smoke still hung in the air during lunch break. We breathed in acrid fumes, felt it catch at the back of our throats.

I picked up a text from Orlando: 'Sorry,' he said. That was all. It was enough. 'Me too,' I texted back. 'Luv u.'

Grace was rechecking Zoran's updated blog. 'The flames stayed low on the ground,' she reported. 'The fire crew graded it low intensity, surface fire. Trees, house, outbuildings are all OK.'

'Cool,' everyone agreed.

But then Jude brought the mood down. 'The way I heard it, a guy from the forest service got caught on the mountain without a shelter.'

'No way. What happened to him?' Leo Douglas asked. He'd been sitting next to me, watching me text Orlando and I'd been about to tell him how his best buddy was delayed in Dallas and wimping out of the biggest party of the decade.

'They didn't find him yet,' Jude told us. 'He's been missing since four p.m. yesterday.'

'How do they know he didn't have a shelter?' Leo again.

A shelter is a foil tent that a firefighter shakes out and climbs into while the flames sweep through. The way Bobby Mackey tells it, it's a total life saver.

'It was still in the truck with his name on. Marty Austin found it and tried to locate the missing man by two-way radio. No reply. The guy is twenty-four years old, with a wife and a baby.'

'So how come it's not on Zoran's blog?' Grace didn't want to believe Jude. She finds it hard to absorb bad news.

I was in freefall again, smelling smoke, hearing the deadwood crackle, shielding my face from its orange blaze. Sparks rise and dance in billowing white smoke, way above the treetops.

'I guess he won't want to talk about it – not until it's been confirmed,' Holly suggested.

What followed was one of those uneasy silences that no one found a way to break. We were all thinking maybe our rock star shouldn't go ahead with the party out of respect, or maybe they would find the missing guy safe and well.

But I remembered the time last fall when a woman hiker in her early thirties went up Black Rock alone. It was a normal day, no weather warnings. She never came back. They went over the whole area with a fine-tooth comb – nothing. In the end they came up with two strong possibilities. Either the lone hiker had fallen into a sink hole caused by an old forest fire – the kind of hole that opens up when flames have burned underground for weeks, gobbled up tree roots and hollowed out big, unseen caverns. Or else she'd *wanted* to disappear, i.e. she'd planned the whole thing in order to flee from her family. If you run with this story, she and her secret lover are currently running a beach bar in Barbados, Bermuda, Bali . . . you choose. Personally, with my apocalyptic sensors on full alert and given the many and lethal dangers up on Black Rock, I lean towards the sink hole option.

As you can see, I'm the complete opposite of my best friend Grace.

'Are you OK, Jude?' she asked as we gave up speculating and headed indoors for afternoon class. The two of them hung behind. He was searching through his pockets for something.

'Inhaler,' he mumbled.

I noticed he was short of breath, trying to draw air into clogged lungs.

Luckily Grace always carries a spare. She dug it out of the bottom of her bag and handed it to him. 'Is it the smoke?' she asked.

Jude nodded, inserted the mouthpiece and sucked hard. I heard the light mechanical whir of the tiny device.

'Slow down, breathe deep,' Grace instructed, so accustomed to Jude's asthma attacks that she didn't miss a beat.

'You want to take him to a doctor?' I asked.

She shook her head. 'Give him five minutes, he'll be cool.'

'Sure?' Jude didn't look cool. His breaths came short, shallow and sharp, his head was tilted back and his mouth was pursed into an 'O'.

Grace nodded. 'Go ahead, Tania. I'll see you later – costume, remember?'

'My place?'

'Seven thirty. See you.'

I went inside and sat through classes, living with a shaky feeling that the blaze out at Black Eagle Canyon, the missing firefighter, even Jude's asthma and Orlando not being here were all bad signs that combined into some kind of warning not to attend the party, a message in the ether.

'Even for you that's total bullshit,' tell-it-like-it-is Holly

19

informed me on our drive home. 'Quit the superstitious crap, Tania, for chrissakes.'

I didn't argue with Holly. I never do.

Time to join dots, I guess.

Holly Randle doesn't suffer fools. She spits out tough opinions, no softening, no compromise. She has the mind and body of a professional athlete, a tennis player serving 120mph balls straight at your body. Her total focus is on winning every argument, holding the advantage, psyching out the opposition. Physically she conforms to type too – she's tall, tanned and wears her blonde hair tied high on her head, like those Eastern European Amazons who blast their opponents off the court, whose legs go on for ever and whose names begin with an impossible collection of hard consonants all rattling together and ending in 'ova'.

If Holly hadn't lived next door to me all our lives, I know for sure we wouldn't be buddies.

'Costume time!' Grace announced, knocking at my door an hour later than planned.

I checked my watch. Eight thirty.

The single organizational skill Grace possesses is the ability to produce an inhaler for Jude whenever he has an asthma attack. Otherwise she floats blissfully through total chaos.

'How's Jude?' I asked as I let her in.

'Not so good,' she frowned. 'His dad took him to the ER.'

'What did I tell you!' I yelped. 'I said he needed to see a doctor.'

'The hospital is keeping him in overnight. They say the smoke from Black Rock is definitely making him worse.'

'See!'

'Yeah. Honestly, Tania, this happens so much. I guess I've become a little blasé.'

'Gotcha.' I backed off, sensing that Grace had already done the *mea culpa* routine on herself. 'You're sure you want to be here? Shouldn't you be at the hospital?'

She shook her head. 'You mean, with Dr Medina standing guard, bedside?'

'I hear you.' Everyone in the world loves golden, gentle, generous Grace – everyone except Jude's family. What's not to love? She's a people magnet, the most popular girl in our year with both students and teachers. You're naturally drawn to the way she always makes time and space for you; you bask in the sunshine of that laid back, effortless smile.

'So show me the sketches,' she insisted, and I had to admit that I hadn't made any yet and Grace sighed and made me sit down and focus until I developed the bird of paradise idea into something that could be scrambled together in the space of twenty-four hours – basically a turquoise one-piece bathing suit from my closet, draped with petals of gold foil to mimic plumage and topped with an elaborate bird mask with a high purple crest.

'We need Orlando,' Grace sighed as we discussed details. 'He'd know how to do this.'

I need Orlando, period, I thought. God, I was missing him, and how come minutes stretched into hours, hours into days when he was away?

At ten pm Grace got a message from Jude in the hospital.

Out of my mind, crazy bored. When can u visit?

Early 2moro. Get some sleep xox

Bed is lonely without u.

Sleep! Grace's finger trembled over the Send button and she sighed as she pressed it.

'Go home,' I told her. 'He'll be OK in the morning; they'll let him out of the hospital, you'll see.'

When I finally went to bed it was past midnight and my room was a mess. Scraps of gold foil and stray feathers from my mom's old feather boa littered the carpet. Before I could slide under the sheet, I had to clear cans of paint and glue from my bed. Then I opened the window to disperse the fumes. As I sank my head against the pillow, though my costume was almost complete, I still had the sickening feeling in my stomach that I really, truly didn't want to go to the party on Black Rock.

Eventually though, I quit worrying about who I would talk to and would anyone even want to dance with me and I drifted off in the darkness.

I drifted, then jerked awake, turned on to my side, drew my knees up to my chest, tried to sleep. It was no good. I turned again, stretched my legs, pulled the pillow over my head to cut out the distant sound of a siren wailing along a deserted highway.

I don't know if I was asleep or awake but I smelled woodsmoke. It's unmistakable; not unpleasant, especially the sweet scent of burning pine resin. I breathed it in, began to wonder, where is this fire – on the mountain or inside my head?

*Suddenly I feel the wind. It's so strong it almost lifts me off my feet. And I see the first orange firebrands in the dark sky, flung into the air ahead of raging flames, then the fire itself, heating the mountainside so that trees burst into flames, turning to ash, and the flames jump gorges and rampage on.*

*I raise my head, try to get out of bed but smoke is filling my lungs, a blast of red-hot wind forces me back.*

23

*Live embers drop on my flesh, fade and die. Though the fire has found its own direction and is running towards me, I can't move. Flames are sweeping down Black Rock, trees are twisting and cracking – sharp explosions all around, the sound of branches crashing to the ground.*

*The head of the fire sweeps over the ridge on to Becker Hill. It hits an old-style log cabin overlooking the lake and explodes into a wall of flame; now it's arching over the next house in its path, leaping over the roof, leaving it untouched.*

*The hot wind blasts down the hill, tearing at doors and shutters, flinging those firebrands into porches, shattering windows.*

*I'm trapped in my bed, feeling the searing heat. My heart is thumping through my ribs. I hear a baby cry, a woman scream. The flames arch again in a fantastic riot of yellow and red. Someone is praying; a figure runs straight into the flames without looking back, then a second person – straight into the inferno – and the cries stop and the only sound is wind sucking around corners, whooshing through the room, and roof timbers cracking in the roaring flames.*

*And me sitting up and sobbing.*

Someone ran into the room and turned on the light. Mom held me and promised it would all be all right, that it wasn't real, only a nightmare – the same way she'd soothed and comforted me through all the years.

\* \* \*

24

I knew not to share with Holly, or Aaron or Leo. Instead I chose Grace, once I'd checked with her that the medics had given Jude the all-clear.

'He's home,' she'd told me when we met at the school gates. 'They gave him new medication and warned him to stay inside until the smoke clears from the valley.'

'I don't get it,' I told her as we headed for class. 'Why do I always dream the same thing – the fire, the people burning to death? How come I believe I'm actually there?'

'I have no idea. I never even remember my dreams, let alone relive them the way you do.'

'So that's it? It's a recurring nightmare, end of story.'

She nodded. 'What else?'

'You don't think it's a kind of sixth sense – something weird and extra sensory that most people don't know they have?' I almost apologized as I said it, knowing how crazy it made me sound.

Grace wasn't willing to give the idea any space. 'Think about it. Make the link with the specific history of your house – not the actual house, but the plot it stands on – the fire, the tragedy.' She hesitated, obviously not wanting to continue and hurt my feelings.

'Go ahead – you're planning to be the psychology major,' I sighed.

'Somehow that event has taken hold of you, deep down in your subconscious. Then yesterday, when we were discussing the latest fire out at Black Rock, it lit up those dark corners of your brain, and there you go again – classic nightmare build up.'

So Grace was a rationalist, a budding scientist who didn't believe in the paranormal – I already knew that.

'Something new happened – I heard the baby crying,' I confessed. And I feel connected; it feels like it's happening to me.

'Only in the dream,' she insisted, blocking my way into the noisy classroom. 'You hear me, Tania – *only* in your imagination.'

'OK, yeah.' I stopped there, didn't press on to describe the link I felt to that long-gone child – the love and the pity, the helplessness when I heard her cry.

Dad was home for a week after working two weeks on the Utah site. During his down time he likes to hike in the forest, fish in white-water rapids and read biographies of dead American presidents. This is down to his immigrant background. In Romania he and his family lived on the breadline in a tiny apartment on the tenth floor of a cement tower block in Bucharest. His dad traded black-market Levi jeans until 1986 when he fell foul of the Communist regime and the entire Ionescu family had to flee the country by stowing away in a shallow compartment concealed under the floor of a truck.

And I guess while I'm on the subject of parents, you may have the wrong idea about my domestic goddess mom with the stack of sweet-smelling laundry and the ever-hugging arms. She's also a commercial property lawyer working for a multinational energy company, renting office space all over the world. I'm serious – she's a legal hotshot, so she was currently on a plane to Russia and Dad was on the couch with JFK.

'They found firefighter guy,' he told me, deep and staccato, when I walked in the house after school. 'He took shelter in old mine.'

'Is he OK?' I asked.

Dad shook his head. 'Didn't make it. They told family in Irvine County. Brother lives here in Bitterroot.'

So I went straight on to Zoran's blog, expecting and probably hoping to see 'Cancelled' written all over the invite to his party. But no, he'd updated everyone with the sad news and decided in spite of the tragedy that the Heavenly Bodies event would go ahead: 'Our doors are still open, the band is here. We're ready to party.'

'Look at this,' I said to Dad. 'Don't you think he would cancel?'

'Lot of money, lot of time getting ready,' he shrugged. 'Live music, caterers. Anyhow, celebrities don't think how we do.' And he went back to the Cuban missile crisis and how the president was rumoured to have taken his eye off the threat of nuclear war to admire the curvaceous charms of Marilyn Monroe.

So when Grace called to tell me that Jude still couldn't leave his house, I was more than ready to call a rain check.

'Let's stay home, girls together,' I suggested. 'Play some music, read magazines.'

'And miss the big event?' she argued. 'Tania, *everyone* will be there!'

'But you can't leave poor Jude.'

'What am I gonna do? Hammer at the door pleading with the parents from hell to let me in?'

'OK, but how's he going to feel knowing you're out partying?'

'Don't do that to me,' she warned. 'Jude knows how much I've been looking forward to this, so he's fine with it. What does Orlando want you to do – stay home and mope?'

'Actually, he said for me to go party.'

28

'Exactly my point! And the costumes, Tania – we made a lot of effort.'

I stood with the phone to my ear, gazing out of the window at the sun sinking behind Black Rock. It looked like a gold coin with a red rim melting on to the dark horizon and turning the sky violet. 'Why don't I want to go?' I sighed.

'Because deep down you're an antisocial loner with depressive inclinations and I see it as my duty to rescue you from yourself!' Grace declared in doctor–patient tones. 'I'll be over at your place in thirty minutes, dressed and ready to party.'

## 2

It was time to go, Grace told me.

There she was at my door, dressed as an angel, totally convincing. Whatever image you have in your head, double it for the effect Grace made in her costume, all gauzy and ethereal with her smooth pale skin, soft, full lips and shining, clear grey eyes. Long, fair curls hung loose. She wore fine silver and gold cord wrapped around her torso over thin white chiffon folds like a Botticelli Venus, showing the curves of her breasts and the lean lines of her thighs. And white feathered wings spread wide behind her.

'Can I get a ride?' Holly called over the fence. Her version of angel was bolder, more warrior archangel – with her physique how could she help it? Her blonde hair was invisible under a silver headdress shaped like a helmet, there were no soft folds to her metallic tunic and she wore shiny wristbands and open gladiator sandals, also in silver.

'Sure,' Grace told her. 'Just throw your wings in the back.'

Holly frowned as she strode up the drive. 'I don't do wings the way you do wings,' she said, showing us the two small silvery ones attached to the heels of her sandals. Mercury, messenger to the gods – that was who she was.

Grace and I paused then grinned our approval.

'Where's Aaron?' Grace wanted to know.

Holly shrugged. 'We had a fight over who would drive. Now he says he won't go to the party. Do I look like I care?'

'Poor Aaron.' I said this deliberately. We all do, as a kind of joke – 'Poor Aaron' – every time Holly throws her weight around. Example: she leaves this incredibly gorgeous guy standing outside the music store in town for a whole hour then doesn't even say sorry when she shows up. Poor Aaron. Or she beats him at tennis then makes sure everyone knows. Poor Aaron again. But he grins and doesn't seem to care. I guess that means they're in love.

'Get in the car,' I told Holly. 'And don't squish my mask.'

For once, Holly did as she was told. 'Hey, Tania,

31

you rock,' she told me as she assessed my turquoise and gold splendour with a cool eye.

Compliments from Holly are rare. 'Did I just hear her say something positive to me?' I muttered to Grace.

'Get in the car too,' Grace told me, glancing at her wrist and remembering that angels don't wear watches. 'I'm sure we're gonna be late.' Pot, kettle, black.

'Bye, girls,' Dad said, coming around the side of the house carrying JFK. He wouldn't put the book down, wouldn't eat or sleep until he'd read all eight hundred conspiracy-laden pages. 'Say hi to Zoran Brancusi from me.'

Grace released the handbrake and slid down the drive.

'Awesome. Does your dad actually know Zoran?' Grace was surprised. I find she usually takes stuff too literally.

'Like, yeah!' Holly laughed from the back seat. 'There are only a million Romanians living in the United States as we speak!'

'Be back before midnight!' Dad called after us.

So we set off down the road, three little Cinderellas totally thrilled to be going to the ball.

\* \* \*

Holly demanded music. Grace played a CD by a girl singer she'd just discovered. She was only the same age as us but she sang wise, soulful songs about her boyfriend leaving, the world lying at her feet in fragments but finding the strength to carry on. The album title track was called 'Out of the Ashes'.

'I thought it was Tania who was fixated on things burning!' Holly sighed.

'Listen, I just like her voice, that's all.' Grace drove through town, along Main Street, already in deep shadow, out along the tourist route up towards Black Rock.

'I'm not fixated,' I protested.

'Yeah, you are,' they chorused.

'I don't like the word "fixated".' Meaning, I personally think my preoccupation is justified even if they don't. I pointed to the mountain looming ahead of us. 'Look around – what do you see?'

'Smoke,' Grace admitted.

'My point exactly.'

We were entering burnout territory from a small forest fire two years earlier, where you get those weird, blackened tree stumps pointing like crooked, witchy fingers towards the sky, with toppled trunks criss-crossing the hillsides and green grass just returning. Beyond that we could see a heavy cloud clinging to Black Rock, backlit by the setting sun so that grey turned to white at its fluffy rim.

'I cried the day you left me.' Grace's singer had a broken voice to match the message. 'Tears fell like rain.'

'Jesus!' Holly groaned as she reached over my shoulder to press a button and change the disc. She tilted her silver helmet back from her face. 'I thought we were supposed to party.'

'We will when we get there,' Grace promised. The Botticelli angel was driving fast into the white-rimmed smoke cloud, through the burnout, on up into the mountain towards the blue peak when a line of guys in helmets and yellow jackets hiked wearily along the side of the road towards us.

'Here come the firefighters,' Holly pointed out.

There were about twenty of them in single file, some with goggles strapped to their helmets, most carrying a pickaxe or a shovel, all wearing backpacks and all dog tired after twenty-four hours on Black Rock. As we approached, someone gave an order to halt and wait for transport. Silently unslinging their packs, the men sank on to the sloping grass verge.

'Poor guys,' Grace muttered, remembering their dead colleague. 'Does anybody know how the fire started?'

Holly and I shook our heads. The missing firefighter.

No shelter, a wall of flames a hundred feet high, what hope did he have? I felt my own throat constrict and my lungs struggle to suck in air.

'It makes you feel kind of guilty,' Grace went on, glancing down at her fancy-dress costume.

It was time for my told-you-so moment and, passing those slumped, worn-out figures, I was about to rub this in – 'I said this earlier, but did anyone listen to me?' – when Holly got there first.

'Life goes on,' she insisted. 'They got the fire under control, didn't they? They did their job.'

We coasted by and were silent until we drove right into the smoke, which had risen in a column then spread out into a mushroom cloud to descend towards us. Grace took her foot off the accelerator pedal. 'It's a good thing Jude didn't come along,' she muttered. 'It's hard enough trying to breathe enough oxygen with a normal, healthy pair of lungs.'

Suddenly red brake lights winked on the road ahead. 'Watch out!' I warned.

She braked and we joined a slow crawl of traffic.

Holly lowered the window to peer out. 'What do you reckon – are all these people going to the party?'

'Where else?' Grace knew the road up Black Rock didn't go anywhere except Zoran's place. 'Let's hope the smoke eases before we get there.'

'Close the window,' I told Holly. Fumes had filled the car and caught in the back of my throat. Last night's nightmare began to play out in my head again. I wondered what I would do if ever I had to face the choice the Witneys had faced and knew instantly that I and ninety-nine point nine per cent of parents would do what they had done, regardless.

Grace glanced sideways at me. 'You OK?'

I nodded and stared out at the burned hillside. Yesterday's tragedy jostled for my attention and shouldered the Witneys to one side – a guy alone on the mountain without shelter, facing a hundred-foot wall of flame, putting all his effort into a hopeless, breathless sprint towards the entrance of an old mine shaft – then oblivion.

'Cool. The smoke's lifting – see.'

Sure enough, we were driving clear of the aftermath of the fire, able to see the steep road rising ahead of us, plus the smoking ruins of ponderosa pines to either side. They rose from the rocky ground, jagged and charred, with smoke tendrils still curling at their feet. The smoke spilled over cliffs and snaked its way along a lower ledge, and down again towards the town.

'Has anyone seen Zoran's place before?' Holly looked

eagerly ahead for the first sign of the rock star's spread. 'I hear it's spectacular.'

'Leo was skiing up here last winter,' Grace reported. 'He saw the place under construction but only from a distance. There was big security even then, and that was before we knew who'd bought the land.'

'Swimming pool, jacuzzis, a tennis court.' Holly listed the amenities we'd all read about in the local newspaper. 'A private gym, staff quarters for fifteen people, a self-contained guest wing, his own recording studio even though he's officially stopped making music . . .'

'Helipad?' I asked in a voice dripping with cynicism. I mean, how come a guy who wanted to put his starry past behind him and become a mountaintop recluse put out all this information? And why this party? I agreed with Mom – the rock god was preparing a comeback.

'Yes, helipad.' Holly went tight-lipped on me.

'Zoran is seriously loaded,' Grace sighed. 'Think of the royalties and the cover versions.'

'The advertisements, the merchandising, the modelling contracts . . .' Holly was talking to Grace, not to me. 'It was about two years ago, just before he released his final album, that his brand went beyond global into the stratosphere, which proves something.'

'What?' Grace asked.

'That retirement was his best move ever.'

'Smart,' Grace agreed. 'Leave your fans begging for more.'

'But what do you do afterwards?' I wondered. 'After you stop being famous?' It was a question I asked myself when I saw kids my age explode on to the music scene. The same with sports stars, I guess. They shine and burn out way before thirty.

Holly shrugged. 'Anything you want.'

'But *what*? You're way up there, an A-lister – everybody wants a piece of you. Being in the public eye, dealing with fans, the press, all that crap – it's full on. Then suddenly you step back, close the door and what you get is silence, day after empty day.'

'How do you know?' Holly demanded. 'Maybe Zoran had a game plan in place – something more than a few rounds of golf and buying an island in the Caribbean.'

'Yeah, I don't see him in a golf buggy,' Grace agreed. 'Or in an infinity pool overlooking the ocean.'

'He built this place instead. He must have had a reason.' Holly was still eagerly looking for signs of civilization.

'First, it's breathtakingly beautiful. Second, it's breathtakingly—'

'I hear you. Maybe he wants to adopt a bunch of cute

kids from Africa and let them live the American dream.'

'Or maybe he actually, genuinely likes silence,' Grace suggested.

'Again – why this party?' I wasn't enjoying this trip and didn't care if it showed.

'What was that?' Holly asked from the back seat. 'Did our little ray of sunshine just make a contribution?'

'No. Forget it.' In fact, I was the first to spot the split in the road and the cars ahead taking the dirt track up to Black Eagle Canyon. Grace swung a left and we rumbled on to the rough surface, stones spitting out from under the tyres as the car's suspension took a beating. 'Anyone scared of heights?' Grace asked, glancing at a sheer drop into a rocky ravine. Down in the depths, white smoke had settled over the winding creek that wound on through the valleys until it joined Prayer River out beyond Bitterroot.

Yeah – me. I gripped the wheel and stared ahead. I'm scared of heights. What a bag of neuroses and phobias, you're thinking. Flames and fear of falling are just two of the terrorist snipers lurking inside my head.

'We're here!' Holly leaned forward to point at the ranch-style entrance to Zoran Brancusi's spread. It was constructed in traditional style, as a square archway of rough poles topped with a sign that spelled out the words

"Black Eagle Lodge" in lettering burned into the pale wood and giving no sign of the luxury that lay beyond.

It was Grace's turn to lower her window. 'I hear music!' she announced.

We'd reached the point in the evening where the sun had sunk below the horizon but before darkness falls. It's light without shadows, flat and still, when pale colours shine, white looks whiter and a summer tan darkens.

'Magical!' Grace whispered.

We parked the car and walked side by side with a hundred fantastical creatures dressed in feathers, face paints and glittering silver, all drawn towards the open-air stage erected in the base of a natural amphitheatre surrounded by rocky slopes. Following the dreamy, mesmeric notes that floated skywards, we three heavenly bodies crowded together with a thousand others and stood gazing up at two guitarists and a drummer playing soft and slow.

I saw angels everywhere, eyes shining in the dusk light, mouths parted, bodies swathed in white, silver, gold. The sky darkened to indigo.

'So cool!' Grace began to sway to the music. I heard her gasp as a switch was flicked and the musicians stood suddenly in pools of purple light, while pinpricks of silver laser beams swept across the stage and over the black hillsides. I saw Holly's face soften and her eyes half close as she tilted back her head and drank in the sound.

'Hey, Holl.' Aaron was at her side out of nowhere but he must have seen us arrive. Adonis put his arm around the waist of Mercury girl.

'Hey,' she whispered back, their fight instantly forgotten.

'Have fun,' Grace told Holly and Aaron as they disappeared into the crowd.

And now, Grace and I were *two* lonely Cinderellas looking for our prince.

The music grew louder, faster. Arms were raised above heads, bodies swayed. Dizzy lights spun over our heads.

Beside me, a girl wore a mask that totally covered her face. It was flame-coloured, fringed with gold. Her red and golden butterfly wings shimmered as the laser beams danced. Beyond her, another girl was dressed all in white and just ahead, a tall, dark-haired guy stood stripped to the waist. He had scrolling patterns painted across his broad shoulders and dreamcatchers tied to his belt, feathered and beaded. He wore pale, fringed trousers and when he turned his head I saw that his face was streaked white and crimson.

Grace saw him too and she glanced at me, wide-eyed.

41

'Who's that?' she mouthed. 'Do you recognize him?'

I shook my head and shrugged, swallowed hard as shaman-guy spotted us, turned his back to the stage and seemed to head our way.

'That sure is one heavenly body!' Grace giggled. Semi-naked, smooth-skinned, muscular and covered in war paint, he had dark eyes and wide, full lips. It's amazing how much information your brain can process in the space of a few seconds when you really focus.

I grinned nervously, glad when someone stepped across his path to yell into his ear. He listened, nodded and walked off in another direction.

Grace though was disappointed. 'Aaw – I wanted to ask him about his costume.'

'Yeah, his costume!'

'I'm serious. Is he the Great Spirit in the Sky, or what?'

'He sure is taking the party theme seriously,' I admitted, switching my attention back to the stage, beginning to wonder when Zoran would grace us with his presence. By now the three musicians were deep into a long instrumental, heads bent and eyes closed in concentration, guitars and drums gleaming under the overhead lights. The pace quickened, excitement was building to a high whine of guitars, a pounding of drums, a flicker of lights, and all under a vast dark sky, surrounded by mountains.

'So cool!' Grace sighed as the piece reached a climax. Our arms were still raised, we were swaying rhythmically, getting lost in the music, totally in the moment.

Then suddenly, silence. The two guitarists stepped back out of the light. We waited.

There was no corny drum roll, no announcement, just Zoran walking on to the stage and up to the microphone.

We went wild. We yelled, cheered and clapped. The sound rolled round the amphitheatre and came echoing back. Zoran stood and took the applause, perfectly still and resting in the knowledge that he was the centre of it all.

Over the years I've seen Zoran Brancusi on TV, I've watched his videos but I've never seen him in the flesh. I know he takes your breath away just to look at him. It isn't easy but I'll try to explain why.

It's not that he's perfect to look at like the Spirit in the Sky guy – Zoran's no athlete, no bodybuilder. In fact he's skinny and his face is drawn and shadowy, more so as he gets older. And he doesn't do macho – more a weird kind of cross-gender, mostly around the eyes and lips, which are full, and especially when you see close-up pictures of him wearing mascara and a diamond in his ear. But he holds himself tall, without that usual rock-star slouch. He's at ease with the camera on him, knowing we love to look at him. In fact you can't help yourself; you just want to follow every move.

And when he moves, he's like liquid – smooth, sinewy, flowing across the stage, gliding under the lights. He moved now under multicoloured lights, took the microphone from the stand, walked the width of the stage, nodded at the lead guitarist and started to sing.

They talk about the voice of an angel, and this is what it's like. Perfect pitch, perfect timing. He sings like he's singing just for you; the notes soar, the words enter your head and move you into an unreal space.

'Come with me,' he sings. And he means you, just you. 'Fly with me/ You're stardust, you're heavenly . . .'

Our hearts opened to him; we drank him in.

'Stay with me, I'll never let you go . . .'

Guitar notes surround you, that voice ensnares you. Zoran was onstage in a single spotlight of silvery light, dressed in plain black T-shirt and jeans; he floated, he twisted and turned.

'Forever in my arms, you're heavenly.'

All the guys in their costumes wished they could tell it to their girlfriends the way Zoran does. All the girls longed to hear it in real life, not just in the words of a song. It's pure and absolute; it's the way love should be.

When the song ends and you step back into the here and now, you leave a little piece of your heart with Zoran.

'Excuse me.' The set had ended, leaving us sighing. Zoran had made his exit but his backing group played on.

Grace and I turned towards the speaker – Spirit in the Sky, complete with war paint and dreamcatchers at his belt.

'I'm Ezra,' he told us. 'My job is to check names against the list of invites.'

God, even the party stewards were extraordinary. Not stubble-headed guys in black polo shirts who need to spend more time in the gym.

'Can you give me your names?'

'Grace Montrose,' Grace told him, overcome and almost stammering with embarrassment.

I was looking for an official guest list, not seeing it in his hand. 'Tania Ionescu,' I said with a frown.

Ezra registered the information with the slightest of nods. 'Cool. Can you please follow me?'

Grace panicked, afraid we were about to be thrown out. 'Did you bring the invites?' she hissed.

'They're in the car.' Personally I wasn't worried, though I did decide to follow Grace as she trailed after Ezra. I didn't even believe he was an official steward – more like this was his way of getting cosy with Botticelli Grace, who he'd worked out was probably the most beautiful girl there.

'It's OK, there's no problem,' he told us as he led us away from the crowd and down the side of the stage towards a high security barrier where two more conventional heavies stood guard. I saw them through the gloom – bare-armed and stocky, standing with feet wide apart and hands clasped in front of them.

'We left our invites in the car,' Grace began to explain. She misjudged the uneven ground and missed her footing, giving Ezra the chance to reach out and support her. He waited until she got her balance then walked on up to the nearest security guard.

'What are we doing?' I muttered, spotting a coil of cable and carefully stepping around it. 'Do we really want to follow him? I mean – do we?'

'He told us no problem.' Grace's white costume showed up in the dark, but I couldn't read her expression. 'Actually, it looks to me like he's getting us backstage passes!'

'No way!'

'Yeah – look.'

Security guy number one beckoned us then asked us to hold out our wrists while he stamped a number on to our skin. Grace's read twenty-two, mine was twenty-three. As soon as it was done, the guard stood aside to let us through the gap in the wire fence.

'Zoran would like to meet you,' Ezra told us but looking only at Grace. 'He asked especially.'

Confused didn't cover it. Dumbstruck maybe.

'I guess you have questions,' Ezra invited.

We hurried to keep up with his long stride. 'The main one would be "why?"' I was ahead of Grace, crossing an area of flat, smooth asphalt painted with a giant yellow circle – the famous Brancusi helipad. Why had the rock legend chosen to invite two unknowns into his inner circle?

Our native guide didn't answer this one, only strode on towards a cluster of dark, state-of-the-art buildings set into the steep, rocky hillside. 'Curious, huh?' he said over his shoulder. 'It took me a long time to find you among that crowd. I guess I asked two hundred girls for their names before I picked the right ones.'

'In what way "right"?' With Grace all set to follow Ezra between sliding glass doors into one of the main blocks, it was down to me to keep on firing the questions.

Once again he ignored me. 'I had most people's pictures off Facebook, but no one is easy to identify in costume, that was the problem. Especially you, Tania – the mask covers most of your face.'

'It's a bird mask. She's a bird of paradise,' Grace informed him sweetly, stepping through the doors into a hallway the size of a tennis court. The floor was white marble, the walls lined with floor-to-ceiling mirrors. 'Cool, huh? Her boyfriend gave her the idea.'

Ezra broke his stride. 'Boyfriend?' he checked.

'Orlando,' Grace explained. 'He's in Dallas. He couldn't make it.'

Our guide nodded and walked on. 'What about you, Grace? Did you come alone?'

'Jude's sick. He has asthma. Smoke really gets to him.'

'That's tough. Those guys are missing a big event.' We'd reached the far end of the hall, where Ezra pressed an elevator button. 'What did you think of the music?' he asked us.

'Out of this world,' Grace told him.

I was silent. More questions had crowded in. Or rather, new suspicions. True, I had no direct experience of the glam but tacky world of groupiedom. But I'd read about it in magazines since junior high and it felt like this was what we were being pulled into – big rock star uses a sidekick to select hot chicks for post-gig entertainment. Girls are more than happy to cooperate. If nothing else, they can sell their sordid story to the highest tabloid bidder.

'And you?' Ezra asked me.

'I was kind of surprised to see him onstage. And I was wondering – is this a dry run for Zoran's big comeback tour?'

Ezra raised his eyebrows. 'I'm only the messenger. What do I know?'

The elevator doors slid open and we stepped inside. There were no up buttons, only two to go down. The doors slid shut. My stomach lurched a little as we dropped underground.

'Did he ask you to bring other guests to meet him, or are we the only ones?' I checked. The lift stopped and I reminded myself to pay attention to the route we took, in case the need arose for a quick exit.

'You're special but not that special,' Ezra teased, appraising us at close quarters. He checked out my bird mask with its purple plumage, my body-hugging turquoise and gold feathering, then the silky cords bound around Grace's flimsy white shift, her flat gold sandals and bare feet.

'So is it a best-costume thing?' Grace asked, suddenly self-conscious. She's a sweet girl but I don't really see her making it to the top as a psychologist. Meanwhile, I suspected I might be showing too much upper thigh. And was there an unintentional bondage thing going on in Grace's costume? I saw for the first time that this was the way it might look. Realizing there was nothing to be done about the thigh problem, I did manage to hitch up my bodice to show less cleavage.

'No, it's not a best-costume thing,' Ezra said with an enigmatic smile. The elevator jolted to a stop. 'Follow me,' he instructed.

'Do we have a choice?' I muttered.

'Don't get lost.'

Actually, this was good advice. I mean, we were underground in a sort of dimly lit maze. There was a main corridor with identical passages leading off and really no chance of keeping track of where we were. Anyhow, there were distractions in the shape of amazing Jackson Pollock-style drip paintings on the walls, alcoves screened by gauzy drapes and glimpses through open doors of sitting rooms with animal-skin rugs, white leather sofas draped with fur throws, even a room with a giant cinema screen.

'Zoran built right into the mountain.' Ezra had stopped

checking us out and was transformed into the complete tour guide. He was so good at it that I even began to forget that he was dressed like Geronimo. 'He worked alongside the architect every step of the way. For instance, he specified special infrared lighting throughout to compensate for the lack of natural daylight. And of course building into the rock gives him maximum privacy.'

'Like Bill Gates.' Grace must have read that somewhere. 'His place is built into the hillside and it overlooks a lake.'

I doubted that Bill Gates had tracks from the *Heavenly Bodies* album piped through his entire house, which is what we were experiencing as a background to Ezra's tour. And I guessed that his taste in decor didn't include this row of primitive carved masks that scared the crap out of you with their staring eyes, bones through their noses and straggling black locks of real human hair. I shuddered as we walked on by.

'Bought from a museum in Mexico just before it closed down,' Ezra informed us, picking up my reaction. 'They represent Aztec gods. This is Tepeyolohtli, god of the interior of the earth. Appropriate, huh?'

I believed the Tepeyo . . . thing without question. Like I said, I was in a hurry to leave them behind.

We moved along the corridor and into a new track –

the one called 'Spirits', which made it to number one in the singles charts – about loving and losing and the power of the mind to keep love alive even after death. Zoran's final album contained more spiritual stuff than I'd realized. And this track used high woodwind instruments, probably Mexican or South American pipes, with the usual guitar and keyboard more in the background. Anyway, it was weird how they overlapped – the masks on the wall and this particular song.

'Are you ready to meet the great man?' Ezra asked, pausing at a glass screen through which we could see a small room with plain white walls and minimalist furniture, no rugs on a polished wooden floor and green-tinted strip lighting concealed behind cornicing that ran the length of all four walls.

I thought this was strange too – that a guy with all these millions should make his sitting room look like the interior of a hospital.

Grace nodded while I frowned. What in the world have we walked into? I still wondered.

'Nervous?'

Grace nodded. 'This doesn't happen. My head's spinning.'

'It's OK to feel that way.' Ezra did his best to ease us into the situation. 'Just try to mingle, wait for Zoran to make the first move.'

'Mingle?' Didn't it usually take other people to achieve this? And what kind of first move exactly? I peered through the screen at the clinical, empty room.

'This way.' Ezra took an unexpected turn right, quietly singing the words to 'Spirits' as we walked on – 'Love lives on, it never dies/ My love stays with you, there are no goodbyes . . .' until the corridor opened up to a vast underground room as different from the hospital waiting room as you can imagine.

For a start, this space was crowded with maybe thirty party-goers all in fancy dress, a mixture of boys and girls. And it was dimly lit by wall lights that glowed yellow from ornate gold brackets, so it took me a while to pick out Aaron and Holly. Actually, it was the silver helmet that did it.

'You too, huh?' She sped across the room on her winged heels. 'They picked you to join the inner circle!'

'How long have you and Aaron been . . . mingling?' I wanted to know, relaxing a little now that I saw normal guys from Bitterroot among Zoran's 'special' guests.

'Maybe fifteen minutes.' She pointed to Ezra, who had taken Grace to a small bar in the corner of the room and was offering her an iced drink. 'We were picked out of the crowd by the same guy as you. Look – the cool one who's hitting on Grace right now.'

'Don't worry, she already told him about Jude,' I said, practically biting my own tongue off when I realized how naive that sounded.

Holly's eyebrows hit her hairline then she passed quickly on. 'So, how unreal is this. This is a party within a party and we actually get to meet the host!'

'Totally weird,' I agreed. 'How did he choose his special guests, do you know?'

'Pretty much stuck a pin in the list – that's what I heard.' Holly's glance shot restlessly around the room. Like everyone else, she was holding her breath until the great man appeared. Meanwhile, her enthusiasm bubbled over.

'Have you *seen* the dudes he has working for him?'

'Besides the dreamy dreamcatcher? No.'

'So look over by the inner door. Check out the guy with the Aztec necklace and the eagle wings.'

I looked and saw another tall, semi-naked figure wearing a feathered cloak over one shoulder, a black loincloth and a collar of braided gold. 'I see him.'

'Lewis. He's the god of youth. See those football-player thighs. And the one over there, with the beaked helmet and eagle wings – Daniel. He's some kind of sun god.'

'Yeah, I get the theme,' I muttered, hardly bothering to

look. Zoran and his team obviously had a thing for Aztecs and Native Americans. I wondered if the man himself would be in costume when he finally made his big entrance. Meantime, I spotted Grace and Ezra moving away from the bar towards Lewis, the god of youth.

It was then, while I was looking in the opposite direction, that the inner door opened and Zoran appeared.

It was as if someone had flicked off the sound switch. Silence fell, and all heads turned towards the costumed figure in the doorway.

Here's my second in-the-flesh impression of Zoran Brancusi, this time from close up: he's even taller than you imagine, maybe six feet five inches, with hair cropped close to his skull and no spare flesh to soften the angles of his face and jaw. The skin is taut over the bones, the eyebrows flat and heavy over dark, glittering, heavily lashed eyes. So it isn't height, the smoothness of his skin, or even the headdress of black feathers rising like a Mohican plume over the smooth dome of his skull that holds your attention, but the strength of his gaze.

We stood transfixed, waiting for him to walk among us.

He worked the moment, looking sharply from one guest to another, unsmiling, eyes darting here and there. Like everything else about him, his costume was extraordinary – the black feathered headdress, the lithe, bare torso, the angel-wing tattoo on his left arm, the fringed leather trousers and bare feet.

Then low music broke the silence, Zoran took two steps forward and drew us towards him like iron filings to a magnet.

'Hi,' he said, still observant, only nodding his head as kids clustered round. 'Hey, how are you doing? Great to meet you. Hi.' He spoke but he was constantly on the lookout for members of his team who had organized the party within the party. When he spotted dreamcatcher Ezra, he gestured for him to bring Grace to his side and then he beckoned Daniel the sun god and apparently gave him the order to comb the room until he found someone in particular.

I wasn't prepared for that someone to be me and so acted pretty dumb when sun god eventually came to fetch me.

'There must be some mistake,' I mumbled, with Holly shoving me from behind.

'You're Tania Ionescu, right?' Daniel said.

'Yeah but Zoran doesn't know me. Why is he asking to see me?'

The go-between looked me straight in the eye and shrugged.

'OK, I get it – you're only the messenger,' I muttered. My heart was racing, my palms sweating.

'Just follow, OK?' As he turned, Daniel's eagle wings brushed my shoulder and for a split second I had the image of him actually soaring across a pure blue sky. I saw his cruel, curved beak, his huge wingspan, heard the beating of wings. I was his prey, cowering below. 'Follow,' he said again.

And sun god took me to meet Zoran.

# 3

It was a lonely walk, pulse racing, knees weakening. I felt like a moth metres away from a scorching flame.

'Tania Ionescu,' sun god said as he delivered me to the master then quietly backed out of range.

'Ionescu,' Zoran repeated.

'I-O-N-E—' My gut reaction was to spell my name, like always.

Zoran cut me off with a nod. 'You're from Romania.'

'My dad,' I corrected. 'I was actually born here.'

'A citizen of the United States.' The eyes were fixed on my face, the voice was mostly expressionless though I thought I picked up a small hint of amusement here. 'So where in Romania were your dad's family?'

'In Bucharest.'

'During the Ceauşescu regime?'

I nodded. 'Dad escaped with his family and came here in eighty-six.'

'And remained.' The gaze stayed on me, pinning me to the spot. 'I guess he could go back home now.'

'I guess.' The legend talked banal family stuff like anyone else – how bizarre – while fellow guests jostled for his attention.

A girl held out a pen, bared her arm and begged for an autograph. 'But he married an American?' Zoran asked.

I nodded. 'He says that here feels like home now. He reads American history.'

How many gawky, geeky, lame remarks can one girl make in the space of an evening? Keep on counting.

'I left the country when I was five years old,' Zoran told me. 'My family spent time in the former Czechoslovakia. After my dad was assassinated, my mom and I kept on moving west – Switzerland, Spain, eventually Mexico.'

Assassinated is not a word you expect to be dropped into casual party conversation. It throws you off balance and begs a thousand questions, which I somehow couldn't shape up into proper sentences. 'Jeez, I'm sorry,' I breathed inadequately.

He shook his head. 'It happened a long time ago. I don't really remember my father. And that kind of childhood – always moving on – it gives you an independence, a strength. I guess what I'm saying is that I learned early on not to need people.'

'I guess.' A few gossip-mag details flitted through my head – the fact that Zoran had a zillion rock chick girlfriends through the years but had never married or had children, that he owns homes in New York, Italy and the Bahamas.

'I'm a wanderer, born and bred. But the counter side of that is that I've developed a strong nostalgia for my homeland.' Zoran steered me through the crowd, ignoring the bustle and clamour around us, making sure his stewards kept the autograph hunters at bay.

Out of the corner of my eye I saw that Ezra and Grace were following in our wake.

'It's highly romantic and completely illogical,' Zoran continued. 'Here am I, living this rootless, privileged existence, achieving what everyone would recognize as the impossible American dream, but still yearning to be in contact with little old Romania, to be part of a big family, to know the language, the culture of my forefathers.'

I nodded, flattered by the confession, by his assumption that I was on the same wavelength, that I was even worth talking to. I mean, he was way up there; I was nobody.

By the way, unlike my dad's, Zoran's English was perfect. Maybe a little formal and quaint for a rock star, but grammatically right on.

'Which is why, the moment I saw your name on the guest list, I said, "Find that girl."' He stopped now, glancing over his shoulder to check that Ezra and Grace were close by. 'They tell me you almost didn't come.'

'To the party?' I stammered. How the hell did he know that? 'The fire – I guess it spooked me.'

'I'm glad you made it. And you know it wasn't an easy decision. I had my office contact Tony West's family – the firefighter who died – and they said to go ahead, Tony died doing what he loved and anyway that's what he would have wanted. I'm making a donation to the forest service so they can upgrade their equipment.'

I nodded, though I wasn't sure that a donation, however generous and well meant, balanced out the family grief quite the way Zoran implied.

'Not that one thing cancels out the other,' he added, looking me directly in the eye and making me feel as though he'd read my mind. A security guy opened a door for us and I found myself out of the main party gathering and in the cinema room I mentioned earlier. 'Do you believe in miracles, Tania?'

I assumed I was alone with him until I saw that Ezra

had brought Grace along too. 'I never thought much about it,' I confessed.

'But you're a sensitive person – I can tell that.'

How? How can you tell? Do I have the word "sensitive" tattooed on my forehead? Up went my defences and I turned to Grace for help.

'Tania's real creative,' she told Zoran unhelpfully. 'She's hoping to travel to Europe to study the history of art. But her big thing is painting. She's actually a great artist.'

'I see that. It comes through in your costume – you have a strong visual sense, an eye for colour. You're used to looking beneath the surface; you try to work out reasons.'

'That's still not the same as believing in miracles,' I argued.

'Watch this,' Zoran told me, turning towards the giant screen on the wall at the same time as someone, presumably Ezra, pressed the button for a video to play.

It was a home-shot sequence, filmed the previous day when the fire on Black Rock was at its height.

'It was shot on a mobile phone so these are not high-quality images. Also it was filmed from the helicopter and the pilot had trouble navigating through the smoke, which is why it's unsteady,' Zoran told us. 'See Turner

62

Lake in the distance? And that's the old burnout area, and the dirt track you just drove along. The summit of Black Rock is hidden behind the main smoke column.'

I held my breath as the video played out, hearing the chopper blades churn, seeing the images blur as they flew through smoke clouds.

'So now the pilot is steering upwind of the blaze – you can see the flames sweeping through the trees. That's Black Eagle Canyon, that's the house – see!'

All too clearly I saw the black pall of smoke, the flames racing across grassland and brush, travelling so fast it left trees only scorched but not consumed. And I spotted the one-storey modernist buildings set against the bare rock of the canyon, standing right in the path of the raging fire.

'Watch!' Zoran said.

A wave of flame approached the canyon. It ate up scrub and young aspen trees, reached the edge of the gorge and seemed to pause.

'Look at the direction of the wind, see how the flames leap clean over the house,' he murmured.

He didn't need to tell me; I was already hypnotized. Firebrands jumped skywards ahead of the inferno, streaking red and gold through the black smoke, clearing the gorge and landing on the far side, igniting the land beyond. Then the flames themselves leaped and arched, carried by a mighty wind. They left one side of the gorge and landed on the other, danced and raged on as before. Zoran's house was spared.

'Now do you believe in miracles?' he said.

'Tania hates fire. She has a kind of phobia,' Grace explained.

I must have passed out for a few seconds, gone blank, sunk to my knees, because Ezra was offering me his hand, my head whirled and I had trouble recalling exactly where I was.

I was so weak that the dreamcatcher guy had to hold me upright and lead me to a chair. Though the screen was blank, I could still hear the chopper blades churning above the whoosh and blast of furious flames.

Zoran was nowhere to be seen.

'Do you need water?' Ezra asked, leaning over me.

I nodded and he went away, leaving me and Grace alone.

'Don't do that to me, OK!' she murmured, taking the seat next to mine.

'What did I do?'

'You just dropped to the floor – I thought you'd had a brain seizure or something. One minute you're standing watching the screen, the next you're flat out. I thought you'd never open your eyes ever again and wondered how I was gonna go back and tell your folks!'

'Sorry.'

'It's OK, I understand. I told Ezra how it started – how you most likely connected it with the old fire on Becker Hill. He said Zoran had no idea you would get so spooked.'

'He seemed to know everything else about my life,' I muttered, remembering our back-to-roots conversation. 'If anyone else calls me sensitive without really understanding the first thing about me . . .'

'Zoran didn't plan for you to pass out,' Grace advised as Ezra came back with a glass of water. 'Actually, he went to look for a medic to check you out.'

'I don't need one,' I said, taking sips from the glass and waiting for my head to stop spinning. 'I'll be fine.'

'Seriously, he was worried for you. He'd really been jazzed about meeting you – isn't that right, Ezra?'

'You were top of his list,' the dreamcatcher confirmed. 'People don't realize, a guy in Zoran's situation rarely makes a connection with the man in the street. It can be pretty lonely. So when he saw your name he grabbed the chance to have a conversation because he knew you two would have things in common.'

'He should talk to my dad,' I sighed. Then again, Dad wasn't into Zoran's music and I figured he would disapprove of the luxury lifestyle. My dad camps out and fishes in ice-cold creeks, remember. 'Actually, meeting him was an amazing experience,' I admitted.

To sum up, now that my head was clearing, Zoran the rock god was everything you would expect – vain, arrogant, in love with himself, all those things. But he had an unexpected side too – a willingness to share family experiences, plus the sheer, close-up charisma: the sculpted face with no sign of age lines, the tall, lithe body with the angel tattoo from shoulder to elbow, and above all the glittering sharpness of his gaze.

'Wasn't it though!' Grace was totally caught up in the whole experience and especially in Ezra. She hovered around him the way a bee is drawn to a flower. 'And the night isn't over yet. Zoran plans to sing again.'

'Cool.' I was standing unaided and definitely didn't need the doctor who showed up in Zoran's team colour of black from head to toe. Black T, black jeans, thick-soled black boots with zippers up the side. 'I can find a driver to take you home,' he offered, once he'd checked my pulse and shone a small flashlight into my pupils.

'No need, honestly. I want to see Zoran's second set.'

'Are you sure? It can get pretty wild.'

'Sure,' I insisted. Ezra spotted my intention to head out into the corridor and was there at the door before me. 'Thanks,' I murmured, resisting a strong urge to whisper Jude's name into Grace's ear as I passed by. Who was I to stand in her way? Plus, beneath the red and white streaks of war paint, Ezra was drop-dead gorgeous, there was no denying.

He led us to the main party room and soon we were back among the whirling lights and drumming, driving beat, shoulder to shoulder with costumed kids whose tunics were now creased and wrinkled, wings drooping and masks beginning to slip. It was hot – way above thirty degrees in the packed room, I guessed.

'Missed you!' Holly exclaimed, eyes wide under her tilted helmet. Before I knew it she'd rushed up to me and grabbed both my hands, dragged me along the corridors into the elevator then out of the building back into the huge amphitheatre. 'Where did you go? Never mind, don't tell me. You have a bad case of bed head and I don't want to know why. You gotta dance, Tania. Don't just stand there.'

'Where's Aaron?' He should stand out in his male version of the Mercury outfit – bare to the waist except for the straps criss-crossing his chest, and in his helmet standing head and shoulders taller than most of the guests.

'He already left.' Holly shrugged then dragged me into the middle of the crowd.

For which I read, We had another fight, he made an involuntary exit. Poor Aaron.

'Dance!' she ordered.

The band broke into a new number and a shout went up as Zoran strode back onstage, dressed once more in the black-plumed headdress and dark leather trousers, with silver cuffs around his wrists and this time wearing an unbelievable pair of glittering, gossamer wings more impressive and convincing than anything you ever saw as a special effect at the movies. These wings had a span of two metres or more and they reflected light from a million tiny silver discs. He came into the spotlight and dazzled us, standing there, waiting to open his mouth and sing.

'You spoke my name, I came.'

We all yelled and clapped. It was Zoran's first ever number one from way back.

'I stand by your side . . . your side . . . your side.'

He threw back his head to sing the words we'd had in our heads seemingly for ever.

'My love for you cannot be denied.'

'You spoke my name!' We joined in the chorus, our

voices loud enough to reach the stars. I was dancing with Holly, thinking about Orlando and remembering the moment by Turner Lake when we went swimming at midnight and I fell in love with him, missing him so much it almost felt like a knife plunged into my chest. I gazed at Zoran and for a moment he seemed to beat his iridescent wings and actually rise from the stage.

'On the ocean shore/ In the mountain shadow/ Search for me.' Once more that soaring voice, the speaking from the heart to you and only you. 'In the dark, dark valley/ You call my name.'

Someone came between me and Holly – Zoran's guy with the gold collar and feathered cloak, Lewis the loincloth-clad god of youth. He grasped her around the waist and slow-danced her out of sight. I danced on alone among the sweating bodies. Bare shoulders glistened around me, face paints melted and lip gloss smudged, dark eyes went blank.

The stage lights seemed to make Zoran float; a girl beside me covered her face with both hands, somewhere between agony and ecstasy, and when she dragged them clear, mascara smeared her cheeks. I glimpsed Grace again, still dancing with Ezra, arms wrapped around his neck, and now my own heavenly creature came and swept me off my feet, turned me slowly, dreamily, towards the edge of darkness.

I felt strong arms around me, looked into eyes shadowed by a dark beaked helmet, stumbled as the music faded and died.

'Daniel.' My partner formally introduced himself without loosening his hold.

'Tania,' I told him.

'I know – I remember. How was your talk with the boss?'

The bird headdress, the black wings – I was talking to Zoran's young sun god, stunned by his perfect features, limp in his grasp. 'Interesting,' I murmured. 'Except I made a fool of myself by fainting at his feet.'

'He has that effect,' Daniel grinned. 'And your girlfriend – is she doing OK?'

'Which one?'

'Aphrodite in the white robe.'

'Grace. She's more than OK, thanks.' I looked for her but didn't see her in the mass of bodies, only Holly near the stage, alone now and waiting impatiently for the next song.

It started low and slow but soon building and picking up tempo, driving a wave of people towards the stage where they danced mostly solo, limbs jerking and jumping, heads rolling on shoulders, eyes closed. My sun

70

god stayed on the fringe and kept hold of my hand.

Pretty wild, the medic had warned, and I got what he meant – some of the dancers were completely out of their heads, others grabbed water bottles from a table by the giant sound system, tipped their heads back and poured it over their faces. There was a lot of swaying and stumbling, falling into the person next to you, and some body-surfing as the wave of dancers pressed towards the stage. A girl in a cherub costume was lifted on to the platform, her wings broken. She sat huddled, with her head sunk on to her knees until a guy in black came out of the wings and carried her out of sight.

Zoran sang on: 'You don't know me, you have no clue/ Who I am, what I do to you.' He wailed the words above a racing whine of lead and bass guitar, gliding across the stage, twisting and turning, seeming to gloat as he mouthed the lyrics. 'You don't know me, you never will/ Shadows fall, voices kill . . .'

Another girl among the dancers passed and out and was lifted over people's heads, her body limp. She was carried offstage – Zoran's medic was having a busy night.

'And how about you, Tania – are you doing OK now?' Daniel murmured in my ear.

The top of my head felt as if it was lifting off, the drumbeat thudded through my whole body but I managed

71

to nod. I noticed that he'd lowered the visor on his headdress and that the bird mask looked eerily real.

'You don't want to dance?'

I shook my head. What was happening out there was less of a dance, more mass hysteria – a mess of gyrating bodies and flailing arms that looked scary enough from the outside so God only knew what it felt like when you were actually in the middle of it. My anxiety level rose as I looked for Holly and saw her at the front of the surge of bodies that pressed against the stage. But I shouldn't have worried – jammed against the platform, Holly simply put both hands on the stage and hoisted herself up like a swimmer slithering out of a pool. Next thing I knew, she was up there beside the lead guitarist, dancing on.

Bird man next to me slid his arm around my shoulder, his black wings fluttering against my skin. I didn't like that – the creepy feel of it or the fact that Daniel was in my space without being invited. I stepped away; saw his eagle eyes glitter behind the mask.

'I have to find Grace.' I gave a feeble excuse and plunged into the crowd, pushed my way forward until I reached the stage and waved wildly at Mercury girl to draw her attention. 'Where's Grace?' I mouthed.

Holly shrugged without breaking rhythm. By now there were half a dozen guests dancing onstage with the musicians and it felt to me like the whole thing was out of control. I was being pressed against the edge of the platform, struggling against the forward thrust and suddenly finding it hard to breathe. Holly must have seen me being crushed and about to go under because she crouched down and extended her hand. I grabbed it and she hauled me up beside her.

'You don't know me/ Though you see my face.' Zoran swept across the stage towards us, wheeling away at the last second so that I caught his features in blurred close-up – teeth bared and eyes flashing, driven on by some wild, untamed energy, seemingly fuelled by the control he'd gained over his audience. He swooped on smoothly. 'My name is lost in time and space.'

'Dance,' Holly gasped, dragging me to my feet.

I looked at her face. Her forehead glistened with sweat and her eyes were unfocused; wet strands of blonde hair stuck to her cheeks. 'Let's go!' I pleaded.

She looked at me like I was the crazy one. 'Go?'

'Leave! Let's find Grace and get out of here.' This was too much. I was feeling weird, crossing that line between what was real and unreal, falling into disorientation and chaos.

The music drove on, drums rolled, a cymbal clashed.

Holly pushed me back with both hands and carried

on dancing. She'd given up on party-pooper me.

I turned and saw two Zoran heavies standing guard in the wings. I spun back to find Daniel onstage next to me, arms and wings spread wide, seeming to hover as Zoran did, to levitate above the boards, his upper body captured in a vivid slash of green light.

*He is airborne, hovering over me, his cruel curved beak is real, his eyes have me in their sights. Man becomes beast, human features melt and transform, I'm living a nightmare.*

# 4

Next morning I was holed up in what I call my studio. Actually, it's part of the garage. My dad converted the space a couple of years back, when he saw how much I loved to paint. There's a clear panel in the roof to let in daylight, a sink with running water in one corner, shelves and a counter for materials and a professional easel that Mom picked up in a garage sale.

Here is where I do my artwork and where I go when the world closes in on me and I need time out.

Saturday was one of those days.

The inks were prepared, the silkscreen frame laid flat, the rollers ready. I was picking things up, fumbling, putting them back down, failing to make decisions.

'What's up?' Holly came in without knocking, dressed in sky-blue jogging pants and vest. 'You look lousy.'

'I *feel* lousy.' My head felt hollow, my eyes wouldn't

focus. No wonder I couldn't move forward with my printing.

'Wimp,' Holly grunted, though she herself didn't look great. 'Anyway, how much alcohol did you consume last night?'

'Not much.'

'What was it – wine or shots?'

'I don't remember.' Like I said, my head was empty of all facts relating to the night before, beyond the point when Daniel turned into a black eagle. 'This sounds crazy, Holly, but do you happen to know how I got home?'

'Jeez,' she sighed, leaning against the window sill and blocking my light. 'I didn't realize you were so totally out of it. You don't remember Aaron coming back to the party to drive us home?'

I shook my head. 'Cool. Remind me to say thanks next time I see him.'

'That's typical Aaron. We have a fight, he goes for a walk on the mountain, thinks it through, then comes back to check I'm OK.'

'Lucky you.' I meant it – from every way you look at it, it seemed like Holly had found herself an exceptional guy.

'He said he had to practically drag me away from the place, even though it was three a.m. and almost everyone else had left. Like you, I was totally out of it.'

'The girl admits to a weakness at last,' I sighed. 'Holly Randle is not superwoman!'

'I'm a bitch,' she frowned. 'Note to self – in future, be nicer to my man.'

We both managed a weak smile then another sigh.

'Aaron found you in a dark corner, all alone. And now I'm thinking – I'm wondering . . .' Holly faltered.

'Did someone spike our drinks?' I guessed what was on her mind.

'Yeah. I honestly don't believe I drank all that much.'

'Me neither. But I guess everyone says that on the morning after the night before. And, like I say, I don't remember what happened after the first song of Zoran's second set.' Man turns into bird, starts to fly . . . 'You say Aaron drove us home – cool, I have to believe it.'

'Scary, huh?' The frown was back on Holly's face as she tugged at the scrunchy that kept her hair in a high ponytail. 'We were up onstage dancing, remember? It was totally wild – people getting crushed against the platform, girls passing out. The security guys didn't have a handle on it.'

There was a long silence while I tried to block the image of Daniel hovering over me, eagle mask covering his face, feathers against my skin, drums beating loud, guitars whining. 'Suppose they did spike the drinks,' I muttered. 'What are we talking?'

Holly was reluctant to answer then came up with the word that had already crossed my under-functioning brain. 'Rohypnol?'

I blinked and looked out from under half-closed lids, through the blur of eyelashes. 'The date-rape drug?'

'Yeah.' Our conversation ground to a halt while we thought through what might have taken place in that lost interval when the drug held sway.

'Would we taste that in our drinks?' I asked with a big shudder.

She shook her head. 'I guess not.'

'*Who* are we talking?'

'I'm not sure. Maybe individual drinks were spiked, or maybe the water bottles on the table close to the stage—'

'Whoa!' I put up both hands, felt my stomach twist into a tight knot. 'Holly, this is serious!'

'So let's look it up,' she insisted, seeing my laptop perched on the counter next to the bottles of ink. Before I could stop her she'd googled *date rape drugs*.

'Alcohol, GHB, Rohypnol.' Over her shoulder I read out the alternatives thrown up on screen. Apparently alcohol was by far the most common date-rape drug, used in over ninety per cent of cases.

'But we reckon we didn't drink over the limit,' Holly reminded me. She clicked on to GHB – gamma hydroxy . . . something. Tastes salty, needs to be ingested in large quantities, so probably not a contender. Rohypnol – also known as roofies, takes effect in forty-five minutes, induces hypnotic, dissociative, amnesiac effect. We read the facts in silence.

When we finished, Holly looked up at me. 'Yes or no?'

I closed my eyes, took a deep breath. 'Maybe.' Hypnotic – yes. Plus the sensation of things not being real – Daniel melting into animal form, actually becoming the eagle. Plus forgetting everything that happened to me after the drug took effect. I thought of the glass of water that Ezra had brought for me after I passed out, before everything went weird.

'I'm thinking definitely yes,' Holly sighed. 'And I'm wondering, did Zoran know there was Rohypnol circulating at his party?'

This shocked me again – it seemed so nasty, so premeditated. 'And what happened to Grace?' I said suddenly. The knot in my stomach pulled tighter.

Holly sprang into action. 'I didn't hear from her. Let's go find out!' She was out of the door, grabbing my car keys from the hook on the way.

'What about lunch?' Dad asked through the kitchen window.

'Not hungry,' I told him hurriedly. I turned the ignition, slid into gear, rolled down the drive. I should write a manual: How to cause maximum stress to your parents when you're seventeen years old and don't get home from a party until dawn.

Grace lives right in the centre of Bitterroot. The big, detached house stands next to a bank on a corner opposite a fancy deli. The house is styled like an English country cottage with gables and shutters. When we arrived, there was only one car in the drive – Grace's white Toyota.

'OK, looks like she made it back home,' Holly muttered, ringing the front door bell.

For ages no one answered. 'Maybe she's out with Jude,' I suggested.

But then we heard footsteps and Grace opened the door.

'Wow!' As always, Holly didn't hold back. 'I thought Tania looked bad until I saw you.'

Grace used one hand to steady herself against the door, the other to shield her eyes against the light. It upset me to see that she was still dressed in the remains of her fancy dress costume – the white robe without the gold cords or the wings. The hem of the dress was ripped and I noticed bruising to her right foot and ankle. 'What time is it?'

'Midday,' I told her. 'Why is no one else home?'

'My folks are in Chicago on business, back Tuesday.'

'Can we come in?' Holly didn't wait for an answer. She slid past Grace, and I followed, heading straight across the big, polished hallway towards the kitchen where I took cold water from the fridge. I poured it into a glass, added ice then handed it to Grace.

She sipped slowly.

'Are you feeling nauseous?' Holly checked.

Grace nodded and put down the glass. I steered her towards a bar stool and sat her down, allowing her to prop her elbows on the counter and cover her face with her hands.

'What happened?' Holly asked.

'I don't want to talk about it.'

'Did you drive yourself home?'

'Don't ask me.'

'Have you seen Jude?' I asked more gently. 'Grace, take your hands away from your face – let us see you. Have you talked with him?'

Slowly she shook her head.

'And Ezra – did he come back with you?'

Grace closed her eyes and let her head sink forward. Then, with an effort, she jerked it back up. 'I said, don't ask, OK?'

'If it helps, we're all feeling pretty lousy,' Holly told her, pacing the room, fiddling with the slats of the venetian blind. 'And I'm feeling guilty that we didn't check up on you before we left Zoran's place. I just assumed that because I couldn't see you, you'd already left.'

'She was too drunk to drive,' I reminded them. 'So it must have been Ezra who did the driving. Did he?' I pressed anxiously.

'I have no idea,' she shot back. 'Is that good enough? I have no clue how I got from the party to here!'

'Ditto,' I breathed. 'How scary is that?'

'Not scary,' Grace argued. Her anger seemed to suddenly dissolve into weariness. 'Just stupid. We drank way too much. We messed up a million brain cells. So what's new?'

I nodded. Holly shook her head. 'Bullshit.'

There was another ring on the door bell and we jumped a mile. 'I'll get it,' I said.

I opened the door to Jude, freshly shaved and showered, dressed in pale-blue T-shirt and jeans. 'Hey, you must be feeling better,' I began.

He nodded awkwardly. 'Hey, Tania. How was the party? I came to see Grace.'

'The party was – well, it was interesting.'

'I heard it was pretty wild.' Jude almost had to stoop to get through the door he was so tall. He hovered beside the antique casement clock, unsure. 'To tell you the truth, I was kind of worried.'

'About Grace?'

'She didn't call me like she promised.'

I shrugged. 'We just got here ourselves. She's not feeling too good.' Better not mention the memory loss, our Rohypnol theory or Ezra. 'Otherwise, I'm sure she would have called.'

'Maybe I should come back later?'

'No.' I grabbed him by the arm and led him towards the kitchen. 'You two should talk.'

You follow your instinct and it's not always right. Maybe, on reflection, I should have let Jude go away, given Grace time to get her head together and take a shower.

'For Christ's sake, Jude!' she groaned when she saw him. 'I was about to text you, tell you not to come.'

She might as well have slapped his face. He winced and stepped back out of the room.

'No, sorry. Forget I said that,' Grace mumbled.

Tears welled up and trickled down her pale face; her bottom lip trembled. In fact her entire body was shaking, I noticed.

'I can leave if you want,' Jude murmured. The poor guy was shocked and confused by Grace's personality transplant.

'Stay!' she pleaded. 'I'm sorry. I'm sorry!' Sobs rose, her bare shoulders heaved up and down.

'We'll go,' I told Holly, picking up my keys and giving her a long stare, which she ignored.

'What did the hospital say, Jude? Do you have to go back for a check-up?' she asked instead.

'They gave me a new inhaler – increased strength. They say I'll be OK.'

'Now that the smoke is clearing.' How long would it take Superglue Holly to get the hint? I was giving her the look and she was still managing to blank me.

'Where did you get the bruises?' she asked Grace, crouching for a closer look. 'That'll swell up; you need an ice pack. You should get it looked at by a physio.'

'Let's go!' I jangled the keys, hovered in the hallway.

Grace held back the sobs. Jude went to her. He stood over her, let her wrap her arms around his waist and lean her head against his chest. Then he stroked her sticky, messed-up hair.

'Catch you guys later,' Holly said.

Finally! We were out of there, heading for the front door. The last I saw of Grace and Jude was over my shoulder – a parting glance. He was holding her tight; she was clinging to him.

'Maybe it'll be OK,' I said to Holly as we drove away.

It's the weirdest thing – suspecting something bad but not knowing how to prove it.

'Will you tell Aaron?' I asked Holly as we drove from Grace's house.

'Tell him what exactly? "You want to know something, boyfriend? Grace, Tania and me – we all got to meet the great Zoran one on one. Charming guy in spite of what you may have read in the press; really knows how to throw a party. Oh, and by the way, it's possible we were drugged and raped."'

'Not easy,' I admitted. And now that my brain cells seemed to be regenerating a little, I was pulling away from the whole Rohypnol theory anyway. 'So we let it drop?'

'Aaron *will* ask me stuff.' Holly sounded tired as she leaned her head back and closed her eyes. 'He'll want to know how come we were so out of it when he came to fetch us.'

I thought about this as I drove. 'It's been intense,' I pointed out. 'Making the costumes, getting to meet Zoran Brancusi, the whole build up.'

'Then Orlando pulling out, Jude getting sick.'

'You and Aaron having a fight every time one of you opens your mouth. Maybe it was the stress . . .'

'The heat . . .'

'The unbelievable underground house, meeting the ⬛at rock legend, watching the video of the fire . . .'

⬛nd I were singing from the same hymn sheet, ⬛g logic to the whole experience. And we were starting to feel better.

'So don't say anything to Aaron, OK?'

I nodded as we turned up Becker Hill. By the time we reached home, we'd made up our minds.

'There are some things in life that boyfriends don't need to know,' Holly sighed, sliding out of the car and heading up to her room to text Aaron and invite him over.

Whatever! I was almost twenty-four hours down the line, alone and retreating against my will from Holly's and my recently achieved logical position so that I ran and reran events of the night before until the topic wearied me. Were we drugged? Were we drunk?

Exactly what did happen there?

Eventually Dad must have read the last page about JFK and came to find me in the studio. 'So, baby, did you talk with legend?'

'A little.' The discipline of silkscreen printing had proved too much so I was back sketching new ideas for my portfolio – the one I would eventually take around the colleges to show my work.

'Zoran Brancusi – you like him?'

'Yeah, he's cool.' Best to be non-commital, I thought.

'His family – the Brancusis – many enemies in regime back home.'

'Yeah, he told me.' One enemy had been serious enough to assassinate his dad.

'Famous Romanian sculptor, Brancusi – way back, distant cousin, part of same family.'

'Hey, I didn't know that.' I did like Brancusi's work though – smooth, elongated stone heads, polished and stylized, now in a special museum in Paris and each one worth millions of dollars.

'Zoran Brancusi's father – he died in Prague, in Wenceslas Square.'

I stopped sketching and closed the pad. 'Yeah, how come?'

'Shot through head. Maybe political, maybe gang-related crime. Zoran, father, mother were on run. Afterwards, mother took son all through Europe.'

'I know – Zoran told me that too. He spoke a lot about his past, actually.'

Dad folded his arms and studied me through narrowed eyes. 'So don't let it make your head big,' he warned.

'What?'

'Rock legend talks about Romanian family. Seems nice guy. But maybe not.'

'Dad, will you stop talking in riddles. If you know stuff that you haven't told me, will you please let me in on the secret?'

'Maybe Zoran got money to live like king from black market in Romania.'

'He was only five when he left, for Christ's sake!'

'Through mother. She travelled to Mexico – I seen picture of house there. Palace by lake, Aztec temple in garden.'

So now I knew where he developed the taste for Mexican artefacts. 'Still not Zoran's fault,' I pointed out. 'What else do you know?'

'Plenty rumours.' Dad drew a deep breath, picked up my sketch book and leafed through. 'The usual stories – girls, drugs.'

'That's rock stars for you.' I managed to pass it off

casually, but inside I was churning with a mixture of curiosity and cold fear. 'Do you want to give me specifics?'

He enjoyed charging on down the Zoran route. 'He likes fast cars, bikes, owns two Ferraris. One story about accident in Porsche, before he quit music scene, became hermit.'

This was news to me. I guess I hadn't been interested enough to take in every last fact about Zoran at the height of his fame. 'Did someone get hurt?' I asked.

Dad shrugged. 'Rumour went around on Internet – Zoran dead, whole world ready to go in mourning. Lasts maybe three days then he comes out of hiding – video of him alive, no bones broken.'

'Crazy, huh?' I considered the macabre story and lined it up alongside other similar rumours. 'Don't some people believe Elvis is still alive?' Instead of dead in a bathroom with clogged-up arteries and a whole pharmacy of uppers and downers running through his veins.

'Marilyn too. That wasn't real body they found on bed, only look like her.'

'Really? I never knew that. Anyhow, a thousand people at last night's party can't be wrong – Zoran Brancusi is totally alive.'

'And maybe you still can't trust him,' Dad said again.

'Rich guys, they think money buys everything, and I guess in America it's true.'

'Cynic.' Right here was where I could have shared my date-rape suspicions, but this was my dad I was talking to and I wasn't ready, so instead I chose to tell him how intelligent and sophisticated Zoran was, and generous. 'He plans to make a donation to the Forest Service, in memory of Tony West.'

'Ah yes, dead firefighter.' Dad closed my book, went to the window and looked up at the smoke still hanging over Black Rock, then sighed. 'Life moves on; we forget too quick.'

If I admit it was the loss of control during the party that scared the crap out of me, what exactly does that say about me?

It's not that I'm a control freak in my day-to-day life – in fact, the opposite. I tend to drift and dream, let things slide like making sure my car has gas, knowing where I left my phone – stuff like that. It drives my mom crazy. Tania, you'll be late for school! Tania, did you put your dirty laundry in the basket?

But having a black hole in my memory, knowing there are whole hours when I probably had zero control over my own actions, is really scary.

I stayed all of Saturday evening holed up in my room, trying and failing to remember, picturing synapses missing their targets, imagining them as day-glo orange and green squiggles fizzling out on a monitor.

Hey, Tania, less than 24 hrs 2 go! Orlando texted, plus smiley face.

Yeah. C u at airport xox, I texted back. Oops, I forgot the smile.

When it grew dark I turned on my bedside lamp and tried to focus on tomorrow. Orlando would step off the plane from Dallas, I would be at the Delta arrivals gate next to cab drivers holding up notices for incoming travellers. Orlando would grab his bag from the overhead locker and rush through the gate ahead of his mom and dad . . .

My phone buzzed. I picked it up to read the new message: Tania – Daniel here. Meet me 4 coffee?

'How the hell did Daniel get my number?' I demanded on Holly's front porch. I'd waited until I knew she'd be up and having breakfast, slipped next door without bothering to text first.

Holly was back to normal, looking like she'd stepped right out of an exercise video, toned and glossy. 'Don't stress,' she told me. 'The guy sends you a text and invites you for coffee. End of.'

'You don't think it's weird?'

'No. I think he likes you enough to do a little detective work and track down your number. He's a hunk – you should be flattered.'

Confused, I took a step back out of the porch. 'So what changed?'

'What do you mean, what changed? Ah – are you saying, how come I got over my hangover and moved on?'

'Hangover?' I repeated. Last time I saw Holly, hadn't we been considering something a little more serious?

'Duh – yes! Listen, Tania, I'm out of here in five. Aaron and I have hired a tennis court at the country club.'

'Sorry. Only, I thought—'

'That's your problem, girl – you always *think*! Bad habit – try a little action for a change.'

'Yeah, remind me to take up beach volleyball,' I muttered, turned and started walking down the drive.

'Hey!' she called. She softened her tone and came after me, spoke in a low voice with a couple of backward glances at the house. 'I *was* stressed, I admit it. So yesterday, after I dropped by Aaron's place, I did something about it. I went to the hospital for a urine test.'

My jaw dropped and I stared. 'And?'

'I explained to the nurse in the ER that I wanted to be tested for Rohypnol. You have to do it within twenty-four hours, so she went ahead without asking too many questions. If it turns out positive, they offer you counselling and everything.'

'*And?*'

'Negative!' she announced. 'No trace of that particular drug or any other in my body. That's it – we imagined the whole thing. Nothing bad went on out at Black Eagle Lodge after all.'

So we were back to normal and smash volleys from Holly but not Grace, who called me as I was about to set off for the airport.

'You're never going to believe this,' she began in a wobbly voice.

'Ezra asked you out on a date,' I interrupted.

'Hey, how did you—?'

'I got a text from Daniel. Same garbage. So what are you going to do – ignore it?'

'No way!' Grace gushed. 'Anyhow, it's not a date – it's coffee.'

'It's a date. What does Jude say?'

'That's the reason I'm calling. Jude's here. We're having a fight. I want you to talk with him, tell him it's only coffee, but if you plan to take his side, forget it.'

'Are you at home?'

'Yeah. Why?'

'Wait right there. I'm on my way.'

I made my way to Grace's house with a time slot of about fifteen minutes before I had to drive to meet Orlando. This felt important enough to make the diversion through town. By the time I arrived, Jude had reached boiling point and was on his way out of there. He looked shaken and angry – not words I normally associate with loved-up, lovely Jude.

'Stop!' I told him, blocking the drive with my car. I got out and ran into the house to fetch Grace. 'OK, everyone take it easy. Jude, I can understand why you're not comfortable with this. Grace, we need to talk!'

'What's to talk about?' Jude protested after I'd dragged him back on to the porch. 'I've already heard everything I want to hear.'

'Jude is being dumb,' Grace argued. 'How can he even think that I'm interested in Ezra? How come he doesn't trust me?'

'OK, let's go in the house,' I said, leading them inside. There was a carved wooden bench in the hallway and I sat them both down. 'You first,' I told Grace.

'He's acting dumb,' she insisted. 'I told him – Ezra is an OK guy, he's new in town and this is his way of getting to know people.'

'By inviting my girlfriend on a date,' Jude cut in. 'A really OK guy!'

'He's way too old for me,' Grace protested. 'Tell him, Tania. He has to be, what – twenty-one, twenty-two?'

Jude wasn't listening. 'He thinks because you went to the party alone, you're a free agent.'

'I told him I had a boyfriend. He knows about you.'

'And still he makes his move.'

'What move? He invites me for coffee!'

'And what else?'

'Nothing else. What are you saying – that I can't have guy friends?'

'Switch it around. How would you feel if I suddenly wanted to meet up with a drop-dead-gorgeous girl?' Jude turned his attention to me. 'This guy is attractive, huh? How did it look to you, Tania? Am I right or am I wrong?'

'I see it from both angles,' I said awkwardly. Grace has been my friend since we were eight years old, so I did want to support her through this. At the same time, I really, really like Jude and I hated to see him hurting. 'I can see the way it might look,' I told him, 'but maybe this

95

is as much connected with your insecurity as with Grace's plan to meet up with this guy. If that is what you're going to do?' I turned to her.

She blushed and avoided eye contact. 'I don't know – I haven't even sent a reply yet. Jude is just blowing this way out of proportion. And he can't lock me up in a closet and expect me not to have a life!'

Jude winced and got up from the bench. 'That's not what I want. I never stopped you having guy friends before now. There's just something about this that I don't like – the way you were after the party for a start. I was just home from the hospital and you didn't even phone me.'

'Yeah, I was hung over – major crime,' Grace muttered.

'Plus, the bruising on your leg – how did that happen? And the fact that somehow this guy gets a hold of your phone number.'

'Yeah, that is weird,' I agreed quickly. 'I told you, Grace – Daniel did the exact same thing to me. I don't remember giving him my number, but I still get a text.'

'You did?' Jude said. My news made him step outside his own bubble for a second. 'And?'

'I deleted the message,' I said with a shrug. 'Sorry, Grace, but I want to keep the channels clear between me and Orlando.'

* * *

'Keep talking' was my advice as I left Grace's house. I wasn't inside their situation so I couldn't judge how serious it was. I only knew that Jude wasn't normally the jealous type and that as a rule he was pretty mature. It seemed to me that Grace was doing her over-literal, slightly naive thing again with the text from Ezra, but that she would soon begin to see Jude's point of view. By tomorrow it would probably all be OK.

I hope, I thought as I drove to the airport. I passed the exit for Turner Lake, caught sight of Black Rock in my rear-view mirror and for a split second saw the whole mountain alight, flames tearing through the trees, roaring down canyons, gobbling up houses.

I gripped the steering wheel, blinked and cut out the vision.

'Grace will say yes to Ezra,' I said out loud as if a thunderbolt had struck. 'She'll meet him for coffee; the situation will spiral out of control.'

I was in the airport ten minutes early, standing by the arrival gate, still uneasy about Jude and Grace. OK, so Holly's hospital test had extinguished my worst suspicion, but something was going on here that didn't feel right and certain random images from Friday night were still vivid – the primitive masks on the wall inside the house, for instance, Daniel's eagle headdress that seemed to morph into the real thing and Zoran's manic energy as the band played and he swept over the stage in his glittering wings, swooping, whirling, mesmerizing us all.

'This is the final call for passengers on flight number AA652 for Philadelphia.' The announcement, only half heard over the buzz of conversation, pulled me back into real time. I checked the monitor – Orlando's flight was on schedule. I was expecting him through the gate any moment now.

The time came and the first passengers from his flight were through. Why wasn't he there at the front as I'd envisaged? Did he have check-in bags to collect? Had I missed something – a switch of gate, an unexpected delay?

'Hey, Tania.' It was Orlando's mom, spying me as she came through the sliding doors with his father. They looked relaxed, pleased to see me. 'Orlando had to check in his design folder. They wouldn't accept it as hand luggage.'

'Cool,' I said, the knot in my stomach unwinding.

Carly Nolan gave me a hug. 'Have you been waiting long?'

I shook my head, smiled at Orlando's dad. 'Did you have a good trip?'

'The college visit was awesome,' Carly informed me. 'Orlando loved the place – the course and the professors.'

'It looks like he made his choice,' Scott Nolan said. 'Dallas over Chicago. Then we spent a couple of days journeying down memory lane.'

'With my cousin.' Orlando's mom cut the conversation short. 'Come along, Scott. Tania will drive Orlando home. Let's find our car and leave the young lovers to their reunion.'

Mr Nolan did as he was told. 'He'll be through in a couple of minutes, still on a high and waiting to share every last detail,' he assured me as they walked away.

More passengers came through. They wheeled large bags, dragged along small kids, looked out for their rides home.

Then at last I saw Orlando. He was walking towards me carrying his portfolio, smiling as he spotted me, bending to rest the folder against his leg, holding out his arms.

# 5

In that moment, with Orlando's arms around me, everything was perfect. My heart soared, I was smiling and kissing him, his lips were on mine and I felt total love for this amazing, beautiful, gifted guy.

Sure, I'm prejudiced. I love Orlando and love distorts. But get the facts: he's six-two with a six-pack; dark-haired with grey eyes (killer combination in my opinion); he has a laid-back-to-the-point-of-falling-over style; wears dark T-shirts and jeans; has just enough stubble; and gorgeous, soft, kissable lips. OK, so that last bit isn't a fact exactly, but I just can't get close to those lips without wanting to lock mine on to them. Enough!

We went for coffee in the airport café – bad coffee, excellent conversation. At least in the beginning.

'Tania, it was so cool!' Orlando told me, holding my hand across the table. He was breathless, shining with excitement. 'The college has a studio with all the latest design technology – incredible stuff. They offer specialist options you wouldn't believe. And you should see the list of visiting lecturers, all A-listers in the international fashion world!'

I smiled and nodded, felt totally happy for him. 'Did they like your work?' I asked.

'Actually they didn't ask to see it. We were a large group – maybe fifty potential students. If we're serious about the course, now is the time to send in an application.'

'Then they invite you for formal interview?'

'Yeah. That's when they need to see your portfolio.'

'They'll love it,' I insisted, thinking of his flair with colour and texture. He knows at a glance how fabric sits on the human figure, how to cut it, where to insert darts for a perfect fit. 'Then when they get to meet you one on one they'll love you too!'

Orlando laughed and squeezed my hand. 'You're my number-one fan, you know that?'

'No contest.' He knows I adore him – his sudden movements, the way his smile flits across his normally serious face and his grey eyes light up, his Irish eyes, his wide Irish smile.

'Will you help me with my résumé? You're good

with stuff like that.'

'We'll work on it tonight.'

'Tomorrow's better. Tonight I need some sleep.'

'Too much partying with your mom's family,' I teased, not meaning any criticism but just for something to fill a gap.

Orlando sucked his teeth, said nothing.

From which I knew I was right about the partying but probably wrong about the family. So whose party? Who with? I body-swerved away from the dangerous topic. 'Tell me about the college campus.'

'Really grand old buildings, classical architecture with columns and wide stone steps, but with modern blocks mixed in, so it's not a museum. There are lawns and a lake, sports facilities, a big library.'

'It sounds fabulous.'

'It is.' Letting go of my hand to check his watch, Orlando stood up. 'Do we need to take a bus to pick up the car?'

I nodded. 'We're in Zone C.'

'I'm hungry. Mom's cooking pasta. Let's go.'

I stayed at the Nolans' place for pasta. Orlando didn't ask me about my weekend and he seemed to have totally forgotten about me driving out to the fancy dress party at Zoran's place.

'How are your college applications shaping up, Tania?' Scott Nolan asked me over dessert. He's a dad who always takes an interest in his son's friends. His manners are old school and it's hard to break down the formal barriers.

'They're not,' I told him. 'I plan to take a year out, maybe travel to Europe.'

'Oh, Italy, France, England – you'll visit the big galleries, see the Old Masters.' Carly sounded jealous. 'You don't know how many years I've been begging Scott to take me to Europe. So far, no luck.'

'Somebody tell me where I find the money,' Orlando's dad grumbled. 'And now we have college fees to pay in addition to normal everyday expenses.'

'You're lucky, Tania.' Carly began to clear dishes and pull down the blinds. 'You belong to a family who gets to travel a lot – your mom, at least.'

'Yeah. Right now she's in Russia,' I told her. It was ten whole minutes since Orlando had spoken to me. Since before dessert arrived, he'd been constantly checking his text messages, running a hand through his thick dark hair, yawning and tapping his fingers on the edge of the table.

When I got up to leave, he came to the door and kissed

me on the cheek. On the cheek!

'See you tomorrow,' I said, letting my anxiety peep through.

That's the problem with the being-in-love thing – one minute you're soaring among the clouds, next minute it's like you've thrown yourself off a cliff and are plunging into the cold, grey ocean. I mean, didn't Orlando care about where I fitted into his bright college future? Did he even see us lasting until the fall here in Bitterroot?

Monday we worked on Orlando's résumé, Tuesday we met up in town with Jude and Grace, Holly and Aaron. Our plan was to catch a movie, but Grace was late so the guys went ahead while Holly and I hung out in the foyer to wait for her.

'She missed school today,' I reminded Holly. 'Maybe she's sick.'

'Jude just spoke to her. She's good.' Flicking through a magazine, Holly came out with one of her shock statements. 'Me and Aaron – we're thinking of taking a break.'

'No!' I gasped. 'Since when? I mean, why?'

'Not a permanent break,' she explained. 'Just a cooling-off period for us to get our heads together. And we're still buddies, which is why I'm here tonight.'

'You still haven't told me why.' I was ready to jump into 'Poor Aaron' mode until she stopped me dead with her next statement.

'We had a major fight and he said that was it – he didn't love me any more. The very next day he met someone else.' Holly's hand shook over the page of the magazine but she held her voice steady. 'Actually yesterday – at the country club. He didn't tell me her name.'

Wednesday I stayed home. Thursday evening Orlando came up to my place. He stayed through till Friday. If you'd asked me during that twenty-four-hour period how happy I was, I'd have given you a perfect ten.

'The house feels empty,' he said when he arrived, backlit by the setting sun, hovering in the doorway and looking beautiful even in silhouette.

I had the studio door and window open to disperse the smell of oil paints and he found me there, hard at work on a landscape. The picture was turning out pretty well. It featured Black Rock overlaid with a shadowy outline of an eagle, the two images merging in a dreamlike way.

'Mom's still in Moscow,' I reminded him. 'Dad took off into the mountains for a couple of days.'

'Cool.' He broke me off from my painting with a shower of small kisses on the back of my neck and shoulders and five minutes later we were lying in bed.

'Mom emailed to say Moscow is a great city,' I told him, safe in his arms and happily breathing him in. 'She thinks I should visit.'

He stared at the ceiling for a while. 'How long will this Europe thing be? Will you be gone the whole year?'

'A few months maybe. Who knows how long the money will last?'

'You'll travel to new places and forget about me.'

'No way.' I leaned up on my elbow and studied his face. 'What's this? Don't you want me to go?'

'I do,' he argued. 'And I don't.'

'Suddenly you'll miss me?' I teased, running my forefinger down his nose and across his lips.

He didn't answer but he made love to me in a way that said, don't ever forget how good this feels. Which meant that, yes, he would miss me and he was giving me every reason in the world to come back to Dallas to be with him.

So when Daniel sent me a second text at midday on Friday – Hey, Tania. Daniel here. What happened to our coffee date? – I wasn't remotely tempted to reply.

'Who's this Daniel guy?' Orlando asked, reading over my shoulder.

'No snooping!' I held the phone out of reach.

'So who is he?'

I'd convinced myself I had nothing to hide so I told him. 'He works for Zoran Brancusi out at Black Eagle Lodge. I met him at the party. No, I don't know how he got my number, and no, I don't want to go for coffee with him.'

There was a too-long pause before Orlando grunted. 'Hey, don't let me stand in your way.'

'You're not. I don't want to go.'

'I mean, I'm not your keeper. Feel free.'

'Orlando, watch my lips – I do *not* want to go!'

This was it – flinging yourself off a cliff, lemming time again, but now it was Orlando's turn. 'Soon I'll be in Dallas, you'll be in Paris, oh-la-la! There'll be a hundred people to have *coffee* with.'

I sighed and turned away. 'I don't need this,' I said. Mom was due home any time. Dad was probably rolling up his tent to walk down Black Rock as we spoke.

'We never said this was an exclusive relationship,' Orlando reminded me, his voice harsh and precise. 'Say I meet a girl at a campus open day, we spend some time together – what's the problem?'

My stomach lurched, my heart thumped. I had all the usual physiological symptoms. 'Whatever,' I whispered.

'I'm not saying it actually happened in Dallas,' he

backtracked. 'I'm saying it could have.'

I walked away from him into the studio. 'Grow up, Orlando, for Christ's sake.'

He didn't seem willing to take my advice. Instead, I heard the front door slam and the sound of tyres squealing on tarmac as he drove away.

He says it's his Irish temperament – the Celtic quick temper. I say his mom spoiled him when he was a small kid. There was a baby boy who died before she gave birth to Orlando. After a cot death, as a mother how can you ever relax?

I didn't hear from Orlando after he stormed out of the house. I spent Friday evening with my parents, and early Saturday I set out on a hike of my own up Black Rock.

'Take my GPS,' Dad offered. 'Everything looks different after wildfire has run through. And watch out for new sink holes.'

I guess they would both have preferred for me not to set out, but neither had got in the way of me making my own decisions, not since I was around twelve years old, and so they weren't about to start now.

'I need some me-time,' I told them, putting a camera into my pocket alongside Dad's GPS. 'Plus, I've begun a new project. I want to make more landscapes – part photography, part painting – a kind of montage. I need to take pictures.'

So I drove the highway then took the track leading up the mountain, parking my car under a stand of aspens near to a Forest Service notice board showing a red flag alert and a warning list of all the fire hazards in the area. For those who couldn't read English there were drawings of cigarettes, matches, bottles of flammable liquids and campfires with bright red crosses through.

I left the car and struck out on foot, enjoying the silence and the wide-open space ahead of me. My boots crunched over pinkish-grey gravel, a surface created by the weathering of the granite boulders that lay scattered on the steep slopes. Spiky yucca plants thrived here at ground level, plus thorn bushes and the coarse, fleshy Indian tobacco plant with its poker-shaped, yellowing flower spike. I shot close-ups, thinking I could use the intricate plant formations in my paintings.

Walking on, I made for an area of felled redwoods that the Forest Service had cut down ready for chainsawing into sections and trucking off the mountain. This must have been some time back, because there was no smell of resin, and long, feathery grass had grown up around the fallen trunks. I sat down on one and flicked back through the morning's pictures.

'Tania?' a familiar voice queried.

I looked behind me and saw a tall figure approaching. He was dressed in a dark jacket zippered to the chin and a black knitted hat that fitted his head as closely as a skull cap, coming down over his forehead but not hiding the sculpted lines of his lean cheeks and jaw – Zoran.

He came within twenty feet then stopped to wait for a couple of dogs, sleek and grey like oversized greyhounds, which sprang out from behind a tall boulder. 'I thought I recognized you. Hey, good to see you.'

My first thought was that he'd spoiled my solitary morning, my me-time. My second was that for some reason it didn't feel like a total accident, and my third was that our rock star looked remarkably like any other hiker on Black Rock. 'Hey,' I replied, slipping my camera back into my pocket and fending off the panting dogs.

'How are you doing? It's a great morning to be out on the mountain, isn't it?'

'Yeah. I'm doing good, thanks.'

'No sign of the fire up here, huh? That was the miraculous escape when the wind took it in the opposite direction, towards the lake. Still, I thought I'd take a walk up this way to check there are no rogue embers lying around.'

'How far are we from Black Eagle Lodge?' I asked.

Holding out a hand to help me scale the nearest rock, Zoran invited me to take a look. 'Put your foot on this ledge, now this one. It's OK, I won't let you fall.'

My hand was in his; he was hauling me up to the top of the rock then pointing to a canyon half a mile away where his house nestled. Tails up and tongues lolling, the dogs had already headed home. 'See it?'

I nodded. 'I thought I'd walked further than that.'

'Distances can be deceptive on the mountain. This is actually my land, though I don't fence it off. Hikers are free to walk where they want, within reason.'

I got it! Zoran must have high-level security around his actual ranch house. There would be cameras covering every angle – someone had caught me on camera, told the boss and he'd come out to investigate. No, not quite correct – Zoran had been higher up the mountain, walking down to my level. OK, so a security guy whose job it was to check the monitors had used a two-way radio to communicate my presence. This was how Zoran had known I was here.

'Actually, Tania, you're not our first visitor of the day,' he continued. 'And I think maybe you know the guy I'm talking about.'

I was feeling uneasy, getting ready to walk on, but now I hesitated. 'Really?'

'A guy named Aaron.'

'Really?' Not Holly's Aaron, surely? He was the last name I expected to hear.

'Yeah, that one,' Zoran grinned, apparently interpreting my internalized reaction. 'He goes to your high school. You do know him, right?'

'He's . . . he *was* my neighbour's boyfriend.' Until he suddenly broke it off.

'Was?' The past tense seemed to throw the great man momentarily off balance.

'Until a few days back. Then they had one of their fights and fell out of love – again!' Even as I delivered the information, I knew it was none of Zoran's business and I regretted sharing with him.

'Out of love?' he repeated, jumping down from the rock with unexpected ease and waiting for me to follow. 'That's news to me.'

'Holly told me he'd started dating another girl.'

Zoran nodded. He strode a few steps down the mountain, waited again. 'She'll be interested to hear that Holly is out of the picture.'

'She will?' I was totally confused. Why did he keep on saying things that kept me intrigued? Why didn't I feel free to walk away?

'Cristal is the name of the girl who just got together

with Aaron,' he explained. 'She works for me. Why not come down and join us for coffee?'

Which is why, against my better judgement, I visited Black Eagle Lodge a second time – out of sheer, unadulterated curiosity about Aaron's new girl.

I walked down the mountain with Zoran, watching the sun glint on the glass frontage of the house, noting that my memory of a vast main entrance with an elevator and an underground corridor leading deep into the rock was correct.

'You like the concept?' Zoran was clearly proud of his architect-designed home. 'We faced some tough engineering challenges, but I came out with a totally unique building, don't you think?'

'I do.'

'Electronically it's extremely sophisticated. The doors don't have conventional locks or handles – they're all operated remotely. Every room has a sound system and a plasma TV screen built into the walls. And you see the block that lies next to the main house? That's my recording studio.'

'Cool,' I said. To me all the electronic wizardry seemed too much like big boys' toys. Personally I'm more interested in the artwork people hang on their walls than the circuits they put behind them.

'Behind that is the chapel,' he continued.

Chapel! Now, I hadn't been expecting that. I mean, in this day and age, whose faith is strong enough to include a chapel in their architect's plans? 'You have your own place of worship?'

Zoran looked closely at me and smiled. 'It's very important to me, especially since my accident.' He waited for my response and when I didn't give one he went on. 'You read about my car crash?'

'Actually, my dad told me about it.'

'I drove my Porsche over the brow of a hill at ninety miles per hour, the wheels lost contact with the ground and I hit a wall. I had a few slow-motion seconds to think, OK this is it – the end. But, what do you know, I came out alive, which was another of those miracles, I guess. After that, why would a person not believe in a higher power?'

'Sure, I see that,' I agreed, distracted by the transformation of the outdoor amphitheatre where the concert had taken place. Instead of a stage with its sound and lighting systems, I saw a fenced area containing the two grey dogs I'd seen earlier, plus around twenty horses standing beside what looked like a brand-new prefabricated barn.

'You like horses?' Zoran asked, changing direction so that we headed away from the chapel towards the arena. 'These are wild mustangs. It's part of the reason I built this place – I intend to buy a couple of dozen each year from the government as part of a planned adoption scheme.'

'That's neat.' After our talk about the chapel, I was beyond being surprised by anything Zoran said. He could have told me that he was importing Buckingham Palace brick by brick from London to rebuild it here on Black Rock and I would have believed him.

Was I impressed? Sure I was.

Those mustangs were so beautiful. The dogs ran towards us and the horses raised their heads as we approached. They flattened their ears and flared their nostrils before the whole bunch set off at a lope around the arena. Their hooves thudded on the dirt surface, raising dust. One stopped close to the barn door and reared up, another rocked forward to kick out with its back legs. Then Daniel walked out of the barn.

My sun god was now dressed in jeans and a dark green and blue plaid shirt over a white T and he carried a coil of rope, kicking up dust with his cowboy boots as he walked towards Zoran and me. He was lean and mean and could have walked straight out of a western movie – I'm serious.

'Hey, Tania.' He greeted me casually before launching into a discussion with Zoran about documentation for the mustangs. 'It's more complicated than adopting a kid,' he grumbled. 'I can work with horses no problem, but I'm the first to admit I'm not good with paperwork.'

'Hand it over to Cristal,' Zoran suggested. 'Did you pick out a horse for me to ride?'

'They just trailered them up here,' Daniel explained. 'But straight away I like the big sorrel with the white flash.' Pointing to the horse he'd chosen, he waited for Zoran's approval.

'Good choice,' his boss agreed, accepting Daniel's obvious expertise and already walking away, expecting me to follow. 'You can start work with her later today. Right now you can put them all in the feed stalls and give them grain.'

I almost had to run to keep up, so I had no time to stop and talk with Daniel, even when I heard him call my name.

'Tania, you never texted me back about meeting for coffee!'

'Sorry, I didn't get the chance,' I yelled. A glance over my shoulder told me that my once-upon-a-time sun god Daniel was leaning on the fence rail in the full sunlight, sleeves rolled back and looking like a young Brad Pitt. My shallow heart skipped a beat.

'Feed the horses then join Tania and me,' Zoran called. 'We're in the studio.'

If Aaron wasn't expecting to see me among the banks of switches and screens in Zoran's recording studio, he didn't show it. Who knows, maybe he was too fixated on Cristal to even notice my arrival.

Surprise – Cristal was out-of-this-world gorgeous! I mean really, *no* surprise. Her smooth skin was so pale against her wild, flame-coloured curls that it seemed actually to give off light. Her green eyes were set wide apart and the permanent position of her full, cupid-bow lips was slightly open. I stored the details of my first impression for when Holly dragged them out of me next time I saw her. 'Nothing like you,' I would report. 'Cristal doesn't look as if she ever went near a gym.'

Zoran introduced us. 'I found Tania on the mountain. She was taking photographs for her new art project.'

'Hey, Tania. Daniel told me all about you.' Cristal's voice was clear and deep, not breathy and girly. She looked me in the eye when she spoke, probably wondering why I was frowning. She wouldn't know that what worried me was that I didn't recall mentioning to Zoran

117

the exact reason for my hike up Black Rock. 'He was wowed by your bird of paradise costume at the party, said he picked you out from all the other boring angels.'

I smiled briefly, turned and said hi to Aaron. He nodded back and I thought he looked more than a little sheepish.

'Cristal sure knows her way around this sound board,' he mumbled.

'I'm so sad I missed the party,' Cristal went on eagerly. 'I only flew in on Monday. I took a bus from the airport then Daniel came down to the country club to drive me up here, which is where I met Aaron.'

'Zoran says you work out here,' I said lamely.

She nodded. 'I'm a sound recordist. We're remixing tracks for a Zoran Classics album.'

'Cristal's hoping that I'll lay down some new tracks too,' Zoran interrupted. 'But I tell her I'm sorry to disappoint her – she'll have to be satisfied with old songs.'

Cristal arched the most delicate pair of eyebrows I'd ever seen. Subtle green shadow on her upper lids enhanced the colour of her emerald irises. 'We live in hope,' she sighed.

'Coffee!' Daniel entered through the sliding glass door. He offered us a tray loaded with steaming paper cups decorated with stencilled silver angels, presumably left over from the Heavenly Bodies party.

'Aaron!' I hissed while Cristal, Daniel and Zoran took their drinks then put on headphones and gathered over a sound board. There was an issue with balance, volume, whatever, on one of the old recordings. 'What are you doing here?'

Aaron blushed then shrugged. 'Cristal invited me – it just kind of happened.'

'And you don't say no. I mean, you really lucked out!'

'You don't get to be sarcastic,' he warned me sharply, nodding towards Daniel. 'As far as I know, you and Orlando aren't even on a break.'

And that was enough hissing and whispering because Zoran had settled the sound problem and Daniel was beckoning us across.

As we drew near, I half heard the tail end of a conversation between Zoran and Cristal.

'They fell *out* of love?' Cristal queried in a low voice, obviously surprised and repeating what Zoran had told her. She shot a quick glance in Aaron's direction.

'. . . Not a good fit,' he muttered back. 'Oliver is a better candidate.'

Like I say, I didn't hear most of what they said and I didn't know who Oliver might be, but I did notice Cristal stayed at the sound board while Daniel, Aaron, Zoran and I left the studio and headed for the house.

'Cristal has work to do,' Zoran explained to a puzzled and disappointed Aaron. 'Daniel, maybe you can take Aaron outside and show him our new arrivals.'

With a quick nod Daniel took Aaron towards the arena where the mustangs stood sniffing the air and tossing their tangled manes. I watched Daniel's rear view – long legs, tight butt, broad shoulders – maybe looking for a single imperfection that would steady my rapid pulse. Nope, nothing. And now the guy could train horses too.

'I'll let you into a secret – Daniel is really into you,' Zoran confided without a shade of embarrassment.

What can I say? I didn't know what to do with the information but I was deeply flattered and my pulse continued to race. 'So I guess I should carry on with my hike,' I sighed.

'Let me show you something first,' he offered with a smile. 'With your background, I just know you'll find this interesting.'

He led the way through the main door into the white marble hallway, down two storeys in the elevator and along the silent corridor beyond. 'You like ethnic art?' he checked. 'I have an extremely rare object to show you.'

I nodded, expecting him to stop and deliver a short lecture as we reached the row of Aztec masks – origins, spiritual significance, that sort of thing. He would pick one out – maybe Tepeyo-thingy, god of the underworld. But no, he was in so much of a hurry to show me his latest precious object that he brushed carelessly against the last mask in the row. I held my breath and watched as the mask – a ceramic representation of a primitive elongated face decorated in a red and black – slipped from its hook and fell to the floor.

I heard the impact, saw the mask smash and fragment, immediately crouched to help Zoran pick it up. But the shards seemed to shift under my fingers, sliding together again as if drawn by a magnet and fitting right back into place. I found myself staring down at the black circles painted around two bulging eyes and the piece of bone piercing a broad nose. The mask was back to its original condition as if the accident had never happened.

'Not a problem,' Zoran said with a strange knot of concentration between his brows. He put the mask back on its hook.

'But how—'

'Don't ask,' he cut in. 'Just follow.'

First I wanted to yelp then I wanted to groan. That

was so weird, like stepping out of reality into a dream for five brief seconds – so short that now I couldn't believe that it had happened. Shaking my head, I almost felt my brain rattle inside my skull.

'Come with me,' Zoran insisted. He led me into a storage room next to the small cinema where we'd watched the recording of last week's wildfire and went to a white cabinet built into an alcove in the wall. Sliding out a drawer, he beckoned me across.

So now I was looking down at a small, solid gold figurine – a snake's head with pointed teeth in its jaws and a long, forked tongue hanging down. The body curved in an S-shape and ended in a plate decorated with bright-green stones. The whole thing was perhaps three centimetres long. 'What is it?' I asked, still queasy after the mask episode.

'A labret,' he told me. 'Hold it. Feel how heavy it is.'

I saw what he meant – the ornament was solid, smooth and heavy, cold in my palm.

'An Aztec ruler would wear it through his lower lip. This one belonged to Mochtezuma in the year 1519, the year of disaster when the Spanish came to Mexico.'

'This is almost five centuries old!' I whispered. The thing was ugly but held some kind of fascination – maybe in the fact that those people would voluntarily mutilate their faces to wear them. Face piercings go way back, it seems.

'They believed in omens – a comet blazing across the sky at noon, a temple destroyed by lightning and flames.' Zoran paused and studied my reaction. 'What's your take on omens, Tania? I know your opinion of miracles, but do you believe in supernatural warnings?'

'I never thought about it,' I murmured, wondering why Zoran's attention was once more focused on deep subjects. The snake's eyes were made of the same sparkling stones – probably emeralds. They seemed alive in the gold head, following you as you moved.

'The year 1519 was the year Mochtezuma saw a huge tongue of flame burning in the night sky above Tenochtitlan, the Aztec capital. That's when he knew that his empire was at an end. Look here.' Opening another drawer, Zoran lifted out a rolled parchment. 'Not the original, of course,' he told me. 'It's a facsimile. Actually, this is a translation from the Spanish describing what the invaders found when they seized the city: "A land rich in gold, pearls and other things . . . There are in the city many large and beautiful houses . . . along one of the causeways run two aqueducts made of mortar . . . the citizens are dressed with elegance.

123

Considering that these people are barbarous, lacking knowledge of God, it is remarkable to see all that they have." What do you think of that?'

'Amazing, totally. Is it OK if I take a picture of the snake?'

'I'd prefer it if you didn't,' Zoran objected, seeing me slide my hand into my pocket for my camera.

And here was something else weird – suddenly I couldn't move my fingers. They stiffened up and started to tingle, like a bad case of pins and needles.

Zoran took the parchment and the gold snake and put them back into their shallow drawers. 'My insurers are pretty strict over how this stuff is stored,' he explained, staring hard at the pocket where I kept my camera. 'One of the clauses states absolutely no photographic imagery.'

'Sure.' I felt a shiver of fear then my hand stopped hurting and my normal movement returned. 'Now I really have to leave.'

This time Zoran didn't stop me. 'Cristal will show you out,' he said abruptly.

His beautiful sound recordist showed up right on cue. She arrived silently, smiled at me and beckoned for me to follow.

I left feeling that I'd just undergone some kind of test

and wondering if I'd passed. I don't know how I got that impression – maybe in the way Zoran seemed to have stage-managed everything; the meeting on Black Rock, the presence of Aaron at the house, the presentation of horse-whisperer Daniel in the best possible light. And now his sudden and total fading of interest in me as Cristal led me from the house.

'I'll find Aaron, check if he wants a ride back to town,' I told her as we said goodbye.

'Sure. Try the arena,' she said, turning back through the sliding doors without showing the slightest reaction. Had she really been dating him, or had Aaron made the whole thing up just to make Holly jealous?

I made my way across to the round pen to find Daniel alone with the mustangs.

'Aaron left,' he said, flashing me a warm smile. 'He had things to do.'

'Me too.' Straight away forgetting the topic of Aaron, I felt my heart rate speed out of control. The dust-covered horses milled around Daniel, who stood calm and confident amongst them.

'Before you go,' he said, stepping on to the lower fence rail then vaulting clean over, 'I do really want to spend time with you, Tania. No strings; just getting to know you.'

Oh God, my heart bumped and raced along! 'It's difficult,' I murmured.

'Really – no strings.' He looked at me long and hard then turned with me to walk up the mountain, hands in pockets, staring at the ground.

I felt the impact of that golden gaze, found that I couldn't talk and didn't have the power to tell Daniel no.

'You're special. You don't know it but you are,' he said. Then we walked a while in silence before he elaborated. 'I think you're exotic, like the bird of paradise – like you don't belong round here.'

I listened, looked up at the peak of Black Rock shimmering in the midday heat, glanced at Daniel's amazing face. 'Same here,' I breathed. 'You guys are totally different.'

'A breath of fresh air?' he grinned. He stopped suddenly in the shade of a gnarled pinon pine, bowed his head and looked up at me from under half-closed lids. 'Don't let Zoran intimidate you.'

'He doesn't,' I lied.

'He's in control around here and that's the way he likes it. But we don't have to meet at Black Eagle Ranch. It could be someplace else.'

'I don't know,' I pleaded. 'I need to think.' Shaded

pale-blue eyes were staring at me, heavy lashes casting deeper shadows.

'I'll call you,' Daniel promised, quickly turning and walking away.

# 6

My shallow, shallow heart.

I was so caught up in my latest meeting with Daniel, endlessly replaying our short conversation and the precious glances that passed between us that I wiped the morning's images from my digital camera – maybe when my hands cramped and I got pins and needles. I guess I pressed 'delete' by mistake.

'Play!' Holly commanded that same afternoon. She'd thrust a tennis racket into my hand, shoved me on court to partner Orlando then gone to join Aaron on the other side of the net. Let me add right here that Orlando and I had not yet talked through his latest high-drama, door-slamming exit from my place, and hostile rays were currently zapping me from his side of the court.

The game began and I struck the ball without giving it my full attention. It landed in the net.

'Fifteen love,' Holly announced, crouching low at the net for Aaron to deliver his next serve.

I'd accidentally deleted my photographs but not the memories of Daniel working with the mustangs – long and lean, surrounded by dusty, sweating horse flesh. *Whack!* – I hit a forehand straight at Holly. She volleyed back, found the gap between me and Orlando.

'Thirty love!'

Daniel had told me I was special and exotic. I returned the third serve down the line; Aaron hit it into the net. Thirty fifteen. 'Did you get home OK?' I muttered as he stooped to pick up the ball.

He nodded uncomfortably. 'Don't tell Holl I was at the lodge, OK?'

'Are you two still on a break?'

'Yeah, but . . .'

'OK, I won't say a word.'

He served again – a double fault. Holly looked disgusted with her partner's poor performance.

Daniel had promised a no-strings, getting-to-know-me deal. How would that work? Ouch! A ball from Holly hit me in the gut. Forty fifteen.

'You played like an idiot,' she told me after the game had ended.

* * *

Later, in the clubhouse, Jude showed up without Grace. If you knew how joined at the hip those two used to be, you'd realize how odd that was.

He came in looking lost and worried.

'No Grace?' Holly asked, making space for him on the sofa.

Jude shook his head and accepted a Coke from Orlando.

'How are things?' I muttered. 'Are you two getting along any better?'

'Worse,' he sighed. 'I just came from her house. She won't even see me.'

Holly soon muscled in, leaning across and tackling the topic head on. 'You want my advice? Things between you two have gotten too intense; you should take some time out.'

'Like you and Aaron?' Jude shrugged. 'The problem with that is – I care about Grace.'

'So?' she bristled. 'Aaron knows I care about him, don't you, Aaron? It doesn't mean we can't give each other some space.'

Aaron gave me a meaningful stare.

OK, OK! I stared back.

'But I'm worried about her.' Jude's not normally a guy who shares his feelings, but right now he obviously needed to vent. 'She's changed so much I hardly know her.'

'In what way?' Holly pressed.

'She's different. I haven't seen her smile in a week.'

'Yeah, that's not normal,' Orlando agreed. 'Grace is always so chilled about things.'

'Now she stresses all the time. It's making her sick. Plus, she won't eat.'

'You guys didn't make up properly after the party?' I checked. I was thinking a million things that I wasn't free to mention, not only about Aaron and Cristal but about Grace and Ezra at the party, and I felt certain that Jude and Grace's current problem would link straight back to Black Eagle Lodge.

He sighed then picked at his fingernails. 'Grace went ahead and met the Ezra guy. You saw him at the party, right?'

I nodded, still said nothing.

'I spoke to her on the phone. She denied it, but Leo saw them together by Turner Lake. He was out there fishing until he was rained off by a freak storm. They didn't see him. He said there was something going on between them for sure.'

'That's bad,' I acknowledged.

'It's not just that she's lying to me,' Jude went on.

'She's started to totally make things up – weird things.'

'Such as?' I asked queasily, casting a worried glance in Holly's direction.

'She told me more about the party, admitted it was pretty wild. She said there were shooting stars in the sky, brighter than you've ever seen, and some of the guys dressed as gods and angels – they actually flew into the air.'

I kept on looking at Holly to see if she'd taken this in and saw her suddenly catch her breath, though she soon covered up her surprise. 'Weird shit happened,' she muttered. 'We all drank way too much.'

We agreed we didn't, I thought. My old anxieties flared up. I still really believed this wasn't just alcohol we were talking about. 'What else?' I asked Jude.

'I'm not making this up – Grace was convinced she could fly too. She recalls looking down on you guys dancing, like, levitating high above your heads.'

Now everyone was giving Jude their full attention and even Holly was silent for once. He let out a long sigh. 'That's how come she bruised her ankle. She says she didn't know how to end it so she kind of crash-landed.'

'She needs to see a doctor,' was Orlando's snap judgement before Jude had even finished. 'You know what I'm saying – a shrink.'

132

Jude shrugged. 'Her mom made an appointment with a counsellor. Grace refused to go.'

'I'll go see her, try to talk her into it,' I promised, getting up straight away. This latest news had hit me hard.

'I'll come with you,' Orlando offered, apparently wanting to make up at last.

'No, thanks. It's better if I go alone.' Eager to get to Grace, I half ran from the clubhouse.

'Whoa!' Radiant Cristal was walking across the car park with a young, fair-haired guy and Daniel. Dressed in five-inch heels and a floaty emerald-green dress with a plunging neckline, she stepped across my path. 'Where's the fire?'

'Hi. Sorry, I have to go.' I glanced at Daniel, smiled my apology and hurried on.

'Daniel, since when did you have such a God-awful effect on a girl?' Cristal wisecracked, making sure she drew the new guy into the joke. 'All he did was invite her for coffee and see how she reacts!'

The besotted blond boy giggled more than the joke deserved.

'It's not that,' I stammered then blundered on. 'By the way, Cristal, Aaron's in there with Holly and a group of buddies. I have to hurry – sorry!' I reached my car, jumped in and turned the ignition. When I looked in my rearview mirror I saw the three of them laughing and joking in the clubhouse porch. What was so funny? Was it dumb-ass me they were laughing at? And wow, the glorious Cristal moved fast, dropping Aaron and moving on to her new guy in the space of a single day.

I stopped at the car park exit to wait for a gap in the traffic, looked in my mirror again and saw that Daniel had stepped down from the porch and was heading in my direction.

An unexpected tsunami of indecision crashed over me and I stalled the engine. Should I wait for Daniel? What did he plan to say to me? Would he ask me out on a date and would I drown in those blue eyes?

He drew closer. Hurriedly I turned the ignition, stepped on the gas and sped away.

Keeping my promise to Jude, I drove straight to Grace's house and found the front door open and music drifting out. I recognized Zoran's soaring voice, and his song 'Come with Me'. There was only one car in the drive – Grace's white Toyota.

I knocked and said hi, ventured inside, waited a full minute without a reply.

'Grace?' I called, crossing the hallway.

She appeared at last at the head of the stairs, gave a delighted gasp and ran down to greet me with a warm hug. 'Cool, Tania, I'm so glad you're here! Come upstairs. I'm in my room listening to music.' She half sang, half hummed the words as I followed her – 'Fly with me/ You're stardust, you're heavenly.'

'So you're OK?' I checked, following her into her room, which was its usual mess – CD cases scattered across her pillow, school psychology books and laundry booby-trapping my progress across the floor.

'Totally,' she breezed. She fixed her hair in front of the vanity mirror in her bathroom. 'Don't you love this song?'

'You missed school,' I reminded her. Though she seemed more like her old self, I didn't quite trust it.

'Only a couple of days, no big deal. And before you say anything, I know what this is about – you've been talking with Jude.'

I paused. Grace was cheery and bright, like a little bird puffing out its chest and warbling its song, which should have been reassuring but somehow wasn't.

'You have!' she trilled. 'He's so down about life in general, isn't he?'

'Who can blame him? He's worried about you, says you won't see him.'

She danced a couple of steps across the carpet then flopped down on the bed. 'Jude makes everything such a big deal. You know how he is.'

I sat beside Grace and chose my words carefully. 'I don't actually see it that way. What I do know is that Jude is a really sweet, laid-back and positive guy and right now he's hurting because of you.'

Up she sprang, dancing away. 'He'll be OK. He'll move on.'

'Does *he* know this?' I asked sharply. 'I just saw him at the tennis club and my impression was that he's not OK and he's desperately holding his breath, waiting for you to be normal with him again.'

'OK, so I'll spell it out next time I see him,' she assured me, back to fixing her hair in the mirror. 'I'll tell him we're through.'

'So that's it – no explanations, no thinking it over – you two are history?' This was unreal. Grace humming and preening while she talked about the end of a two-year relationship.

'Stuff happens,' she shrugged. 'Look at Holly and Aaron. No one turns a hair when they split.'

'Because it happens all the time,' I pointed out. 'They fight, they split, they get back together. They fight again. Whereas you and Jude were so close. You're even applying to the same college so you can be together next year.'

For a moment the reality of what I was saying got through to her and she fumbled with the hairbrush on her dressing table. Then she gave a final tap and put it down. 'Plans change. I may not even go to college – who knows?'

'OK . . . OK!' I stood up and flexed the fingers of both hands then curled them into two fists. 'So change the subject, talk to me about Zoran's party. You told Jude you saw shooting stars.'

She smiled and turned towards me. 'Really bright. They glowed green like the Northern Lights. It was beautiful.'

'Which I didn't see, and I was there,' I contradicted coolly. 'And what about the levitating thing? You're not saying in the cold light of day that really happened?'

Grace took my hands and her eyes shone with excitement. There were spots of high colour in her pale cheeks. 'Tania, you know it did and it was so cool! Ezra showed me and told me I could do it too and he was right.'

'Ezra.' I repeated the name softly. 'Grace, this is scaring me. I already know there was something weird about the party – Holly and I talked about it a lot. For starters, there's an eight-hour gap in my memory of that night, the same with Holly. And I think we all went a little crazy—'

'I'm not crazy!' She pushed me away so hard that I staggered backwards and overbalanced on to the bed. 'Yes, the party was a big deal for me. It opened the door to choices I never dreamed of. I know now the human mind is capable of amazing things if only you open up to the possibilities.'

I shook my head. 'Stop. Think what you're saying.'

'Whereas you and Holly, Jude, Aaron – you don't even want to look at the fantastic opportunities. Well, that's your choice; it's down to you. But it's no reason to stop others from moving on up to another level.'

'That's not what I'm doing. Stop, please.' Grace's manic energy took her to the open window. For a moment I thought she was going to step right out into thin air. 'Come back. I'll listen to what you're saying.'

She turned away from the window, eyes still shining. 'You should hear Ezra talk. He tells me stuff about the planets, how you can move them around with the power of sheer thought. And this brings about changes in the weather. If your head is clear of all its old negativities, you can control the wind, the rain, everything!'

'Ezra believes this?'

She nodded. 'And so do I. Tania, I saw him do it – out at Turner Lake. He made the clouds roll down from Black Rock and rain over the water. It was the best rain, so clean and pure. And then he sent it away again, down the valley, and the sun was shining and there was a perfect rainbow!'

'I remember Ezra at the party,' I said, keeping my voice under control while I desperately wondered how I should deal with this. 'His shaman costume, the dreamcatcher thing was stunning. I see the attraction.'

'I'm not talking about appearances and surface stuff – this is spiritual.' Once more Grace drifted around the room, humming Zoran's music. Her eyes shone with the wonder of it all. 'That's what I mean by clearing your mind and opening yourself to new possibilities. You wouldn't know about that, Tania, unless you were actually prepared to do it. The same with poor Jude.'

'You have to talk to him.' I needed help here so I took my phone from my pocket. 'Let me call him for you.'

'No!' Her mood changed quickly to irritation. She snatched my phone and threw it to the floor. 'Listen to me. You people don't realize what they're offering you – all this knowledge and power. I can't really blame Jude for that because he wasn't there, but you and Holly were, yet you still choose not to see it.'

'Who are we talking about? Who's "they"?'

'*Them!* Ezra, Daniel, Cristal. And there are others who you didn't see, living at the lodge. They're all so beautiful on the outside because their spirits are pure – pure on the inside and incredibly beautiful on the outside, every one of them.'

'How many?'

'Twenty-five, thirty, including the musicians from Zoran's band, plus Lewis and the medic who checked you were OK after you passed out. They're all young, like us. And they believe in a wonderful life, living in harmony, worshipping in chapel and turning their backs on stuff that isn't important – money, jobs, all the boring things.'

'It's a cult,' I murmured, suddenly finding the word that fitted. 'Zoran is the head of a weird sect.'

Grace threw me a patient, pitying glance. 'It's more than that, honestly. This is totally different.'

'And how many times have you been there?' I was shaking my head, not wanting to fall for what I was hearing, yet not totally closing the door on what Grace was describing. A tiny part of me – the part connected with my feelings for Daniel – even wished it was true.

'Three times,' she told me. 'Each visit is more perfect than the last. I promise you, Tania, it's heaven up there on Black Rock. You have to believe me.'

* * *

I didn't, of course. But what I read next day in school made Grace seem either less crazy or more – I couldn't decide.

It was Shakespeare, *A Midsummer Night's Dream*, and Leo Douglas was acting the part of Puck, coming to the place in the text where he drops flower juice on to Titania's eyelids to make her fall in love with the next thing he sees. The small purple flower is called love-in-idleness.

> 'The juice of it on sleeping eyelids laid
> Will make or man or woman madly dote
> Upon the next live creature that it sees.'

Leo paused while the teacher explained the word 'dote'. To dote = to love beyond reason. I looked at Jude, sitting beside me and he understood what my covert glance was saying. That's it – that's Grace we're talking about. She madly dotes on Ezra.

According to Shakespeare, the fairy queen might fall in love with a lion, a bear, wolf . . . you name it.

> 'And with the juice of this I'll streak her eyes,
> And make her full of hateful fantasies.'

141

A drug can do that in Shakespeare's world, and maybe in modern-day America too.

The drama is about love and confusion. People elope by moonlight, they grow jealous. All you need to throw into the mix is a flower called love-in-idleness, smear it on the wrong person's eyes and you get a whole lot of heartache. So I sat in class wondering was it a mind-altering drug after all? And was Grace being given a fresh dose every time she visited Black Eagle Lodge?

Grace missed school on Monday and again Tuesday, and you just had to look at Jude to see how much he was struggling.

'She still won't talk to you?' I asked as a gang of us took the elevator from the car park into the mall after class. Orlando was there, along with Holly and Aaron holding hands (Cristal, please note), plus Leo and his girl, Tarsha.

'I spoke with her mom after your visit on Sunday. They really want to take Grace to the Bitterroot Clinic to see James Morel. He's a guy who specializes in bipolar disorder.'

'But she won't go?'

'They think she's manic. It's the way she won't sleep or eat or even sit still for more than thirty seconds, and she plays her music twenty-four seven. Then she dips right down, won't even get out of bed. Mrs Montrose read up on the symptoms.'

'Can that happen out of nowhere?' I wanted to know. 'Wouldn't there be warning signs before the full-blown bipolar thing hits?'

'I'm no expert,' Jude confessed, lagging behind the others as Holly headed into a Starbucks. 'Hey, Tania, if you don't mind, I'm going to call a rain check.'

'You don't want a coffee?'

He shook his head. 'I'm just not in the mood.'

'But you're cool?' I checked, thinking that his breathing seemed fast and shallow. 'You've got your inhaler?'

'Yeah, I'm good. Tell the others I said bye.' He smiled lifelessly and peeled off towards the exit.

'Bye,' I told him. I felt so sad for him as he walked off alone, head down and hands in pockets, that I almost had tears in my eyes.

'Hey,' Orlando whispered when I went into the coffee shop and he saw how down I looked. Finally forgetting to be jealous of my Europe trip, he said, 'Come and sit here, Tania. Did I tell you lately how much I love you?'

Early summer and the mountain meadows are a riot of hot-red, rich-purple and golden flowers. The wind runs through the feathery grass, wave after green wave.

Orlando and I stayed until after dark and made love under a starry sky.

'Come to Dallas with me,' he murmured, his lips against my cheek, the full weight of his body on mine.

I heard aspen leaves rustle. The lake water lapped against the pebble shore.

'How would that work?' I whispered. I would have been happy never to have moved from that special place, with Orlando's smooth, warm skin against mine and the moon looking down.

'Forget Europe,' he urged. 'We'll find an apartment close to the campus. You can paint, I can study.'

'And we pay the bills how?'

'We take jobs in a bar, in Walmart. You sell some paintings.'

'Keep talking,' I pleaded. I closed my eyes, held him and dreamed. He only had to whisper promises to rouse me to make love again – his husky voice, those honeyed words. Our bodies entwined.

But I didn't give up on Europe. I never made that promise.

'Art is more important to you than I am,' Orlando complained. The school week was finished and we were sitting in my room with the TV playing an old romantic comedy in the background. 'Rome and Leonardo da Vinci, Florence and Michelangelo.'

'Why does it have to be one or the other?'

With an impatient flick of his hand he stopped me from stroking the back of his neck.

That flick felt like a major slap. 'Honestly, Orlando – why are you making me choose?'

'Because that's life. Every step of the way we make choices.'

'So you get to study in Dallas but I don't get to travel. How is that fair?'

'You think getting on to the course will be a breeze for me? It won't.' He thought for a while, and when he spoke again his voice was soft, almost pleading. 'This is a competitive field, Tania. Kids from all over the country have applied. I have to focus on getting together my portfolio, not fight with you over our future together.'

I shook my head. 'How did you suddenly turn that around and make it my fault? Who brought up this topic in the first place?'

I was surprised when Orlando lost the will to argue, dropped his head and covered his face with his hand. 'Forget it.'

'No. This is serious. I want to understand. I want us to agree.'

'Forget it,' he sighed, standing up and grabbing his jacket from the back of the couch. 'We just hit a wall every time we talk.'

He looked so beaten by it, so sad that I had to put my arms around him and hold him tight. The only sound that broke the silence was the theme tune on TV as the credits rolled.


I woke early next morning to an unread message from Grace. It had been sent at midnight and said Did u ever dare 2 believe?

Where r u? I texted back but didn't get a reply. What did she mean, did I ever dare to believe? I thought she must be somewhere on planet Ezra and I was immediately scared for her so I called her house.

'Grace isn't here,' Mike Montrose confirmed. 'She slept over at Tarsha's house.'

I told him thanks and simultaneously thought this was odd. Since when had Tarsha and Grace been close buddies? Also, the last I heard from Jude was that Grace hadn't left her house for days. I got this indirectly through Jude's sister, Mia, who also told me that Jude's asthma was bad again and that their parents blamed Grace.

'Grace finally ditched my brother by text message,' Mia had said when I ran into her on the Thursday. 'Can you believe that?'

'He took it badly?' Of course he had – stupid question.

Mia was thirteen, sometimes wore her hair in corn rows and hero-worshipped her big brother. 'We never thought Grace was the right girl for him,' she'd said, aping her parents' opinion. 'We tried to tell him she was a total egotist but he wouldn't listen.'

'No way,' I'd protested then stopped. Right now that was exactly how Grace came across, I realized.

So all week Jude had been on his high-dosage inhaler and Grace had been pleading sickness to stay off school.

'It's because she can't face Jude after the way she treated him,' Mia had declared.

I'd nodded but I knew it was way more than that. Now I went next door to Holly and showed her the dare-to-believe text.

'Oh my God!' Holly groaned. 'When did she send this? What planet was she on?'

'Exactly.' And I told her about the so-called sleepover at Tarsha's.

'No way. Call her right now. Do it.'

'I texted. Grace didn't reply.'

'Don't text – call! And if her phone is switched off, call Tarsha.'

'Wait.' I sighed and sat down at Holly's kitchen table. 'I want to try and figure this out. Grace doesn't come to school and she officially breaks off with Jude. She's fixated on this guy Ezra.'

'So far, so normal.' Holly sat down opposite me. 'It happens all the time. Let's keep this in proportion.'

'Except that it's Grace we're talking about, and Grace is the sweetest, kindest girl we know, right?'

'Occasionally wacky,' Holly pointed out. 'Her head can be a little vague sometimes.'

'But still sweet and kind,' I insisted. 'So where did this monster version of Grace suddenly come from? Why the lies, the delusions about flying and daring to believe?'

'And ditching Jude by text message.' Holly tapped the table, got up, walked away and came back again. 'Even I don't treat Aaron that bad.'

'Ezra!' we both agreed.

I waited a while before I shared the theory that had been lurking in my head ever since the party. 'It's like they set a trap for her.'

'They?' Holly narrowed her eyes and got ready to argue against one of my overimaginative interpretations.

'Ezra and Zoran – everybody out there at the lodge.

The whole thing – the heavenly bodies theme, the invite to the special gathering inside the house, the way we later forgot everything that happened; it was a trap.'

'A conspiracy.' Irony is what Holly turns to when she disagrees. She used it now.

'Yes. Somehow they're drawing Grace into their world. You know they have a commune up there – did Grace tell you?'

'Wait. Rock legend builds house on Black Rock, sets up happy hippy commune, invites people from neighbourhood to join them. Am I getting this right?'

'The way you say it you make it sound less sinister. But it's bad, I'm telling you.'

'Because it's a cult and they laid some kind of trap?' Holly considered the last word forensically.

'Listen.' I persisted like a little terrier gnawing at Holly's ankle. 'One day Grace is normal. She's happy, she's looking out for other people, noticing that I'm down and persuading me to go to Zoran's party without Orlando, the whole deal. Then she meets Ezra and is sucked into something she can't control. Next day, her whole life starts to fall apart.'

'And you're saying Ezra deliberately did something to her. We don't know what, but it wasn't legal and it triggered off this weird behaviour?'

149

I nodded and murmured a line that came whizzing into my head. '"So quick bright things come to confusion."'

Holly recognized the quote. 'Whoa! Now Ezra is some kind of woodland spirit dropping poison on Grace's eyelids and Zoran is the Oberon figure orchestrating it all?'

'Kind of. Only there are no laughs in this. I think it's more serious.'

Holly had heard enough. She got up from the table with an 'Oh jeez!' groan.

'I do!' I insisted. 'And I think they targeted Grace *because* of her and Jude. They chose her because the two of them were crazy for each other.'

It turned out that Grace didn't sleep over at Tarsha's house, had never planned to, had never even been in touch.

'She can't just vanish,' Orlando said over the phone when I told him the latest.

'I spoke with Tarsha. Grace lied to her parents,' I pointed out.

'Yeah, we all do that.'

True – the useful little white lie to stop them stressing. But it wasn't just this. 'She missed a week of school,' I reminded him.

'Still not a major crime.'

'I know. Holly already told me I was overreacting. I just came away from her place.'

'She's right. Where are you now?'

'I'm in the car park at the mall. Where are you?'

'At my computer. I got an email from Mimi Rossi at the college. She invited me to make a full application.'

'Cool.' I absorbed the fact and its implications, hoped my voice sounded sincere when I said, 'Excellent! You need to work on that.'

'You're sure you don't want me to come to town?'

'No, I'm fine. Write your application. That's such great news, Orlando. I'm so happy for you.'

'I love you,' he told me.

Oh, my heart sang out! Tell me again, say it louder. But I didn't have chance to reply. Either he clicked off his phone or the signal cut out, I don't know which.

I got out of my car and walked between the rows of parked vehicles, stepped over a big black oil stain in the shape of a giant moth.

*I see the stain ignite, flare up orange out of the shadows. The curious flames lick at me then a wind fans them and makes a fireball that blasts all the way to the far end of car park level B.*

*'Aimee!' a woman's voice whispers, as if she's sighing over the cradle of an adored child.*

There's a western equipment store in Bitterroot, the Black Horse Country Store, geared mainly toward tourists and visitors. You can see it as you exit the mall and make a left turn on to Main Street, which I did because, after the illusory fireball experience in the multi-storey, I needed to walk and clear my head.

There was no fire, I told myself. There was no voice, no Aimee. But what happens inside my head often feels more real than what I can actually see, touch and smell all around. It always has and most likely always will.

'That's the way creative people experience life. It's why you paint,' Mom tells me whenever I try to explain.

Anyhow, I've never in my life walked through the door of the Black Horse store, but today for some reason I did. I walked slowly down the rows of pointy-toed, Cuban-heeled, tooled leather boots towards the Stetsons.

'I'm looking for silver spurs,' a familiar voice told a sales person and when I rounded the corner I came face to face with Daniel.

'How much do you want to spend?' the sales guy asked him, reaching for the fanciest pair.

'Later,' Daniel told him. He smiled at me without surprise, took my arm and walked me back down the boots aisle. 'Hey, Tania, you look like someone who needs a coffee.'

'I'm good,' I protested feebly. Daniel's hold on my arm was firm but not too forceful. I let him steer me out of the store on to the sidewalk.

'Zoran wants me to buy all the equipment we need to train and ride the mustangs,' he explained. 'Everything has to be high quality, as usual; to hell with the cost.'

'Lucky Zoran,' I murmured. I'd felt my day slip further out of control the second I set eyes on Daniel and now my mouth disconnected itself from my brain to run in random directions. 'You looked like you'd always worked with horses when I saw you in the arena.'

'My uncle runs a spread in Montana. We vacationed there when I was a kid.'

'Lucky *you*.'

'I guess.' He was still smiling, still steering me back towards the mall. Before I knew it, we were sitting in Starbucks. 'Training these mustangs is a big ask. They've been out on the Californian desert all their lives. This is the first time they ever saw the inside of an arena.'

'That makes me feel sad for them,' I admitted. 'Won't they miss their freedom?'

Daniel shrugged. 'It's government policy to take a percentage of wild mustangs off the open range each summer to stop overbreeding. The Bureau of Land Management offers them up for adoption at a hundred and fifty dollars a head.'

'That's nothing.'

'Right. The government sells them cheap because they want to avoid culling. You know, where they send surplus animals for slaughter.'

'Yeah, I understand culling,' I said quickly. 'It makes living in captivity on Black Rock seem like a good deal.'

'Exactly.' There was a pause before Daniel switched topics. 'I hope it doesn't feel like I'm stalking you,' he said with an embarrassed grin.

'No. You haven't called me since I saw you at the lodge,' I reminded him. 'And it was me who ran into you back there in the store.'

'Yeah, I lucked out.' Daniel's hands around his coffee cup were tanned, his fingers were long, with broad, well-trimmed nails. 'The same way Ezra lucked out with Grace.'

'She really likes him,' I sighed. 'Which is tough on Jude, I guess.'

'These things happen,' Daniel shrugged. Those sinewy hands were connected to muscular arms and broad shoulders that he didn't parade in a macho posture like bodybuilders do. Instead he seemed to accept and underplay his physicality – something which I generally like in a guy. 'If you want my opinion, Grace and Ezra are made for each other.'

'In what way?'

'They share interests for a start. Ezra knows the names of the planets and the star systems. It turns out Grace is a stargazer too.'

'I never knew that.' My short replies were a result of Daniel's clear blue eyes staring deep into mine. It had the effect of further scrambling my brain.

'And Ezra studied psychology. It was his college major.'

'Hey – coincidence! That's going to be Grace's major too.'

'That's what I'm saying. I look at them and think those two are a natural fit. She seems so happy to be with him.'

His use of the present tense unexpectedly got through to me and I frowned. 'Actually, I've been trying to contact Grace. I need to speak with her. You don't happen to know where she is?'

Daniel nodded. 'Sure. She's with Ezra at Black Eagle Lodge. Why don't I drive you up there now?'

# 7

At the time I convinced myself that I accepted the invitation because it was important for me to see Grace, but looking back I can see how much my rabbit-in-the-headlights attraction to Daniel had to do with it.

I said yes and we didn't hurry. We finished our coffees and ran back to the Black Horse store for Daniel to choose Zoran's spurs. We bought a pair and stored them in the trunk of his SUV. By the time we were driving the dirt track up to the lodge it was past midday.

'Are you hungry?' Daniel asked.

'No, really.' I was paying attention to the landscape, trying to concentrate on picking out angles for my next trip up here with my camera to replace the shots I'd accidentally deleted – especially where a creek snaked through a valley between rocks and aspens, and again when I spotted an area of burnout on a distant slope; an empty grey patch the shape of a tear drop.

'There'll be food later,' Daniel assured me. 'Zoran is planning a pool party with barbecued ribs. Does that sound good?'

I bit my lip and gave a shrug. No commitment.

'Grace will be there,' he promised.

'I didn't bring a swimsuit,' I told him and subsided into awkward silence for most of the journey.

When we arrived at the lodge, Zoran's grey dogs heard our car and loped out of the barn to meet us. They wove between Daniel's legs then stayed to heel as we lifted boxes from the trunk and carried them across the empty arena.

'What breed of dog are they?' I wanted to know.

'Lurchers – a type of hunting dog they use in Eastern Europe. You can put the stuff on the table through here.'

'What are their names?'

Daniel shrugged. 'They're not pets. They don't come with names.' Then he led the way into a neat new tack room complete with saddles and bridles. My arm brushed his as we deposited the boxes. My skin tingled. Before I knew it he'd leaned forward and landed the lightest kiss on my lips, smiling slightly as if he'd scored a victory, then walked back through the barn.

My face burning with embarrassment, I followed him and saw that a boy around my age was standing in the cool shadow by the wide doorway. It took me a while to place him – he was the golden-haired guy who had been laughing too loud at Cristal's joke outside the clubhouse.

'Hey, Oliver. I guess you're looking for Cristal?' Daniel asked in passing.

The kid was shorter and slighter than him, preppy looking in white button-down shirt and loafers and seeming kind of lost and out of place here on the ranch. He didn't answer, as if his mind were on other things.

'She's in the studio,' Daniel told him and walked on with the dogs.

'So where's Grace?' I asked, hurrying to keep pace. The kiss had stayed on my lips, stolen my breath, made me shake all over. My question about my friend was meant to steady me so that I could focus on something else.

'In the house. I'll take you.'

Considering he was the one who'd just landed the kiss, Daniel had suddenly turned a whole lot cooler. But then we were entering between the sliding doors of the main block and Zoran was in the hallway, stooping to greet the nameless dogs, their images multiplied in the angled, floor-to-ceiling mirrors. I guessed this meant that Daniel was back on duty.

'Tania, good to see you!' Zoran made up for the change in Daniel with the broadest of smiles, the warmest of greetings. He was dressed down in a black T-shirt and jeans, with the lower half of the angel tattoo on display. 'I was hoping you could be persuaded to visit us again.'

'Hi.' Here he was, the iconic figure from over two decades of rock music, the face from album covers, posters and magazines, meeting me for the third time and treating me like an old friend.

'Don't worry, I'm not giving any Aztec lectures today,' he grinned as he handed the dogs over to Daniel and we walked into the elevator. 'You don't have to fake an interest.'

'Oh, I wasn't faking,' I protested, pulling myself together. 'I mean, how many people do I know who own priceless pieces of ethnic art?'

'Ha!' He seemed pleased. 'You came on a good day. We're having another party – a celebration.'

'I know. Daniel told me.'

'This time I only invited my staff and their close friends.' Zoran paused to study the two gold charms hanging from a slim chain around my neck. One was in the shape of a heart (a birthday gift from Orlando), the other a crucifix studded with blood-red garnets which had belonged to my dad's grandmother back in Romania. 'Pretty,' he said dismissively as we exited the lift and walked along the familiar main corridor. 'Are you wearing a swimsuit? No, of course not – how would you know to bring one when you left the house this morning?'

He'd no sooner thought of it than Cristal was emerging from a side room and Zoran was ordering her to find me a costume before he went on towards his private cinema.

'Actually, I'm looking for Grace,' I hurriedly got in before Cristal put her arm around my waist and waltzed me off through another side door.

'Swimsuit first,' she insisted. She was wearing a short azure chiffon robe over her own two-piece. The neckline was studded with square turquoise stones set in silver that looked expensive. When she caught me looking at them, she smiled modestly and said, 'Not genuine.'

'I didn't think they were,' I said, again too quickly to sound natural. I told myself that those stones were one hundred per cent the real deal.

The small room we'd entered was lined with closets and full-length mirrors.

Opening one of the doors, Cristal invited me to take my pick among a rack of swimsuits and poolside robes.

'White could be your colour,' she suggested.

'Or silver. You have wonderful dark hair and dark skin tones. You're like a glossy, elegant bird – did anyone tell you? Anyway, take a good look. I'll come back in ten minutes, OK?'

In spite of the feeling that events were sweeping me along in a direction I hadn't expected, I found myself acting like a child in a candy store, wide-eyed and greedy. I mean, these outfits were to die for, especially the shoes that I found lined up on a rack inside the closet – Grecian-style sandals in white, gold and silver, soft kid-skin ballet pumps in aquamarine, crimson and yellow. I chose the shoes first – silver Grecian ones that laced high up my calves – then a sea-green bikini held together at the hip and neck with metal clasps in the shape of intertwined dolphins, and last of all a shimmering silver robe, also with a Grecian styling. I was wearing them all and experimenting with twisting my hair on to the top of my head when Cristal glided silently back into the room, together with Grace.

I saw Grace's reflection in the mirror and swung quickly round. 'Finally!' I cried. 'I've been calling you all day. Where were you?'

'Here,' she said, the smallest of frowns creasing her brow. 'What are you doing, Tania? Why are you here?'

161

'I came to see you. Daniel brought me.'

'Oh, Daniel – cool.' The frown stayed, the kind that suggested she'd lost something and wasn't sure where to search. It seemed she was ready for the party, dressed in a short robe patterned with big white daisies on a green and yellow background over a plain white one-piece costume. Her feet were bare, her toenails painted shell pink. 'Actually, I was looking for Ezra,' she said.

Cristal the fixer stepped forward to soothe her. 'Why, honey, he's working – remember?'

'Working,' Grace echoed. 'I want him to be with me for my big celebration.'

'He'll be here soon,' Cristal promised before leaving Grace and me to chat.

The door slid smoothly behind her and we were alone.

Straight away I took both of Grace's trembling hands in mine. 'Grace, I've been out of my mind worrying about you. How long have you been here? Did you stay the night?'

'Take it easy, Tania.' Twisting her hands free, she began to pace petulantly around the windowless room. 'I need to see Ezra.'

'Sure, I know you do. Grace, listen to me. What about your parents? You can't just tell them a big fat lie about Tarsha's place and come up here instead, not after the kind of week you just put them through.'

'Leave me alone. I know what I'm doing,' she mumbled, shaking her head as she tried to find a catch or a handle that would open the door.

'That's the point – it's not safe to leave you alone!' I cried. 'That's why I'm here. I came to tell you, you should come home with me, try to sort out this mess.'

Grace took no notice whatsoever. 'What did Cristal mean Ezra's working?'

'He has a job, I guess. They all work for Zoran, don't they?'

'He never mentioned a job.' Finally discovering that there was no catch or door handle, Grace made a fist and thumped the glass. 'What am I supposed to do while he's working?'

'What are any of us supposed to do when we visit here?' I asked. I began to feel it was like trying to catch the attention of a very small, tired child. 'We sit around and wait for the entertainment – the party, the gig or whatever – to begin. Anyway, what's this about a celebration?'

'It's a big day for me,' she said vaguely, hovering by the door as if she still expected Ezra to walk in.

'Grace, we need to talk. Do you hear me? Am I getting through?'

She swung away from the door and drifted over to the closet, where she ran her fingers along the hangers which clicked together and swayed. When she turned back it was with a new, unexpected expression – one of high, childish enjoyment that lit up those grey eyes and brought a flush to her cheeks. 'Oh, Tania, isn't it just so cool here? There's an infinity pool and a cinema room—'

'I know – I saw that, remember.'

'Last night Ezra took me up to a telescope on the roof of the studio. We sat for hours and looked at the sky.'

'Cool. Did the shooting stars put on another display especially for you?'

Obviously Grace missed my sarcasm. 'He helped me understand the movement of the planets.'

'Will you stop talking to me about planets! Focus on what's actually happening here. Grace, I don't even recognize you any more – it's like suddenly you're a different person.'

'Ezra taught me about Mars and Neptune. And afterwards, we swam naked in the pool, just the two of us. It was so dark and silent under the stars. Then we walked up the mountain and Ezra made love to me – the most perfect, magical love-making . . .'

I put my hands to my ears. 'Grace, don't tell me. I don't want to hear.'

'Why not? You're my friend. Why shouldn't I share with you the most wonderful thing that ever happened to me?'

'Because . . . Jude!' I reminded her helplessly.

As I said his name the door slid open and Ezra came in. His dark hair fell forward across one eye, he wore a couple of days' beard, a crumpled T-shirt, frayed jeans and bare feet, yet still he managed to look totally hot. Grace ran to him and flung her arms around his neck.

He kissed her then extricated himself, holding her tightly by the hand while he greeted me. 'Hey, Tania. The other guests are here,' he told me. 'It's time to party.'

Zoran's infinity pool was hidden away from the main complex, built on a ledge overlooking the high peaks of the Bitterroot Range. The pool was as luxurious as you would expect, with a large hot tub bubbling on one side, but it was the panoramic view that took your breath away.

Black Eagle Lodge stood at around 8,000 feet. From here we looked out at snow-capped mountains reaching 14,000 feet, where the ice never melts and the clouds meet the land in luminous banks that take your eye higher still, above even the misty violet mountains into an intense blue canopy. Beneath it, the jagged peaks roll on, layer after layer, growing fainter, as far as you can see.

'Awesome, huh?' Daniel sought me out and joined me on the terrace beside the pool.

'But not good for someone with vertigo,' I told him. If I moved any closer to the edge, my head would start to spin and my knees go weak for sure.

He took up a protective position between me and the sheer drop down the mountain. 'I'd forgotten that about you. But don't worry, I won't let you fall.'

I never discussed my fear of falling with you in the first place, I thought. Why does this keep on happening with you people?

Daniel's smile was serene. 'Actually, this is my favourite place. I sit here evenings and watch the sun go down.'

'It's a big, big space,' I murmured. Totally awesome was what it was. With my back to the party guests and with guitar music playing low in the background, there was a moment of perfect, immense silence before a short yelp and a splash behind me broke it. When I turned, I saw that someone had plunged into the pool and was swimming underwater, his body pale and fluid. A second guest came to the pool edge, ready to dive, then a third and a fourth. Soon a dozen people were swimming, laughing and fooling in the deep-blue water. Tanned bodies plunged and vanished, dripping heads and shoulders soon emerging out of the depths, plunging again and kicking up spray in the faces of people standing nearby.

'You want to swim?' Daniel asked amid the light-hearted cries of protest.

I shook my head. 'Thanks, I like what I'm looking at right now.'

'The sun sets over Carlsbad Mountain, which is the highest peak in the range,' Daniel explained, coming behind me to get into my line of vision. He wrapped one arm around my waist to keep me safe then pointed with the other hand. The close contact brought the same shiver down my spine as the earlier kiss. But I picked out the mountain he meant. It had a conical peak and glaciers running in thin white stripes from the summit. 'On a clear day you see Carlsbad turn fiery red. The sun hits the peak and sinks behind it like a stone.'

'You're so busy with the mustangs and whatever else you do out here for Zoran, I'm surprised you find time to watch the sun set.' Take it back to boring, bland, everyday stuff; don't get lost in Daniel's word picture, his soft voice, his hand resting now on your shoulder.

'That's the thing about Black Eagle Lodge – there's always time.'

'To party?' I forced myself to step away, turning to two guys playing guitar under an awning at the far side of the pool and recognizing them as the guitarists from the Heavenly Bodies gig. They were both in their thirties with dark hair curling over the collars, giving them an artistic, perhaps Romany look, which figured considering Zoran's background.

Today, for this intimate gathering, there were no electric guitars and big sound system, only acoustic instruments, which sounded mellow, the notes floating up into a clear blue sky. Guests sat drinking and chatting at nearby tables – I noticed Lewis sitting at one of them with Cristal and Aaron's preppy, fair-haired replacement, Oliver. As yet there was no sign of Grace and Ezra, I noticed.

The host was absent too, though this didn't surprise me. From past experience, I knew that Zoran favoured a big entrance after everyone had gathered.

'If you won't swim, how about something to eat?' It was Daniel again, determined to take care of me and be a good host among strangers. He took my hand and led me down steps to a lower wooden deck where there was already a full-blown barbecue, steaks sizzling and big bowls of fruit punch being served from a bar built into the rock. 'No?' he asked as he felt me hesitate.

'No, thanks.'

'Then back to the music,' he suggested, retracing our steps up to the pool.

And now here was Grace, with Ezra at her side. She had a drink in her hand and still the scary expression of hyper-delight on her face, deep in conversation with Cristal, with Lewis, with everyone who would pay her any attention as she swayed to the music and tilted and spilled her drink until Ezra took it from her. Spotting me across the pool, she threw her arms wide and cried, 'Hey, Tania, let's dance!'

'Later,' I told her.

'Now!' she insisted, still raising her voice across the water and attracting attention. 'Loosen up, dance with me.'

Ezra put down the drink and wrapped his arm around her waist, partly to steady her, partly – it seemed to me – to take control. He spoke into her ear and right away she dropped the manic behaviour, turning her back and forgetting me completely.

I watched from a distance, wondering how come Grace was drunk so early in the evening and should I step in to help her sober up?

'She's OK,' Daniel assured me. 'Ezra will take care of her.'

I wasn't convinced, but I was distracted by more diving and splashing and then by Cristal's new guy, who stood up suddenly and walked to the sheer drop at the edge of the terrace, seeming to stretch his arms as if he meant to dive into space. Teetering on the brink, he bent his knees and crouched forward until suddenly Cristal appeared at his side, said something and the blond boy straightened up. Without a word he walked back to the table, sat down and stared straight ahead.

'Did you see that?' I asked Daniel, who nodded and smiled. 'Am I the only one around here who thought that was an incredibly dangerous thing to do?'

'Probably a joke,' he said, 'or a dare. Something like that.'

'So not funny,' I muttered. The kid looked very young, skinny and vulnerable in his swimming shorts. And what really bothered me, apart from everything else, was that both Grace and the fair-haired kid were acting like zombies, with Ezra and Cristal the ones who were pushing their buttons.

'What song would you like the guys to play next?' Daniel asked me, taking me by the hand again.

'You choose,' I said, resisting and pulling free.

As Daniel left me to talk to the guitarists, I had a chance to look around again. Gorgeous Cristal was now leaning over the table for a laughing kiss from the blond guy, Lewis was standing up ready to dive in the pool, and Ezra was engaged in a smoochy poolside dance with Grace. Everything seemed cool. My anxiety eased. Maybe, after all, I did need to loosen up.

I sat on a nearby lounger and looked around some more and saw twenty or so chilled party guests, sitting at tables or lying back on poolside chairs, or else playing in the water. The sun was going down, the shadows were cool. What was not to enjoy?

Relax! I told myself as the guitarists broke into a new, up-tempo song and Daniel breezed back.

'Ready?' he asked.

And before I had the chance to ask, 'Ready for what?', a hundred underwater lights came on and changed the colour of the rippling water from blue to green then purple and back to blue. The music built, all heads turned towards the infinity edge to see a figure rise slowly as if by magic.

No steps or ordinary, everyday form of elevation would do for rock legend Zoran Brancusi. No – he was on a small platform raised by a hydraulic lift from the deck below. Caught with the mountains as a spectacular backdrop, with arms outstretched and in the last rays of afternoon sun, he stood as if suspended in mid-air and began to sing.

'Our kisses taste of danger/ Every lover knows a broken heart.' His voice was a hoarse whisper, the rhythm slow and sad. 'Nothing we make is perfect/ You knew that from the start . . .'

It was a song I had never heard before, the sort that digs under your ribs, tugs at your heartstrings and makes you want to cry. The image of Orlando's clear grey eyes staring longingly into mine flashed into my head. 'Is this new?' I murmured to Daniel.

He shook his head. 'No, it's from way back. Don't look sad – it's only a song.'

But the message drew me in. It was about the fragility of love, the fading of dreams, and it made me zone in on me and Orlando, who would go to Dallas without me, and this time next year I would be in Europe and the connection between us would stretch and stretch until it finally broke.

Zoran understood – love hurts.

His voice grew clearer and louder. He stepped from the platform dressed in dark jeans but stripped to the waist. His smooth skin looked tanned in the evening light and he wore a heavy gold ornament – green eyes glinting in a snake-head pendant. It was Mochtezuma's serpent, suspended around Zoran's neck on a thin leather strap.

And once I saw the primitive head, I couldn't take my eyes off it. Its grotesque face sparkled as it swung hypnotically from the strap.

'Tears when the dream is shattered/ Though the longing never dies/ Looking back in anger/ To the heartbreak and the lies.'

*The snake's head smiles and grimaces, the jaws seem to open. And when I look again at Zoran's face, it has become the serpent, teeth bared, with forked tongue lolling. His eyes are emeralds.*

*I turn to Daniel. He is the red and black Aztec god of the underworld, the mask that shattered and re-formed itself. I gasp and step away, want to run but find that my feet won't move and my legs won't bear me up. I sink to the floor.*

When I woke, I was alone with Daniel by the pool. He was himself again, looking down at me with caring eyes.

'You gave me a big scare,' he murmured, stroking my forehead as I lay back on one of the loungers. All around was silent and dark, except for a huge moon hanging low over the mountains. 'What is this, Tania – do you suffer from some kind of seizures?'

'No. It only happens when I'm here . . . I have no idea.' Raising my head, I found that it felt light and empty and my vision was unfocused. 'Where is everybody?'

Daniel seemed genuinely concerned. 'The party moved indoors. Describe it to me – the sensation before you pass out.'

'It's nothing.' A snake's-head ornament comes alive. You turn into a savage god. 'I'm kind of confused. I guess I haven't been eating or sleeping well.'

'Callum, our medic here, thinks you should have it checked out when you get back home. Will you do that for me? Here, drink some water.'

I sipped from the glass he gave me then felt a stab of panic in my stomach. Do I trust you? Should I have taken that drink?

'Can you get up?' Daniel asked, offering me his hand. 'Callum thinks it may be a neurological condition linked to hypersensitivity to flashing lights. Does that figure?'

'Maybe.' Here we go again – being told I was super-sensitive and never in a good way. I struggled to stand. 'Anyway, I'm OK now. Where did the others go exactly?'

'Let me help you. Maybe we should stay here a while longer?'

'No, really, I'd rather . . . I'm still stressing over Grace.'

'You want to see her?' he offered, raising me to my feet and keeping his arm around my waist. 'Promise me you'll take it easy.'

'I'm good, thanks.' After the laughter and noisy pool play, the music and the song, the dark silence of the mountains felt vast. 'Did Grace drive her car up here or did Ezra bring her?'

'I'd be lying if I said I knew,' he shrugged, stroking back stray strands of hair from my cheek. 'Don't worry, after the party I'll drive you both back home.'

'So let's find her,' I insisted.

And Daniel said, 'Come with me,' and I followed him across the yard.

It didn't look anything like a normal chapel and there were guests dancing and music playing so it took me a while to realize where Daniel had brought me.

We were in a high, bare room with a platform at the far end and small, narrow windows high on the walls. The floor was black granite and the walls were painted with primitive representations of mythical beasts – creatures who were half man with the heads of buffalos, or human from the waist up, but with the legs and cloven feet of goats or deer. They were heavily outlined in black and coloured in shades of ochre and blood-red, like cave drawings that I'd only ever seen represented in books.

'*Now* will you dance?' Grace cried, appearing at my side and dragging me into the centre of the room. She

175

kept hold of my hand among the swaying dancers, and when she found a space she smiled at me so brightly that I smiled back and squeezed her hand.

'Are you OK?' I asked, mouthing the words clearly so she could make out what I said above the music.

'Totally!' she replied. Her long fair hair was loose around her shoulders, a plain black robe had replaced the short flowered one. 'This is my big celebration – it was Oliver's yesterday and now it's mine. And I'm having the best time, Tania. It's so cool!'

Grace's mood – her joy, that's all I can call it – was infectious. I felt a pang of sympathy and my fears lifted again. I began to dance with her under swirling coloured lights.

'I'll tell you a secret about why we're celebrating,' Grace said, putting her lips close to my ear and pausing before she made her big announcement. 'I've decided to stay here. I'm never going to leave!'

A fresh shock ran through my entire body. 'Seriously – you're planning to live here?'

'For ever.' The music slowed, dancers drifted to the side of the room and Grace and I were left standing alone on the sparkling granite floor. 'It's everything I want – to live in this beautiful place with Ezra and with Zoran. And now that you have Daniel, you should come and live here too.'

'Now that I have Daniel?' I echoed.

'Sure,' she said brightly. 'And Oliver has Cristal. Aaron could have had all this too, but he turned his back.' She said 'all this' and gestured around the chapel to the unlit platform, the decorated walls and the shadowy figures standing at the edge of the room waiting for the next song to start.

In the dim light and deep shadows I had a shuddering sensation that the paintings on the wall had slipped from their places and morphed into living, breathing beings among the expectant guests. I closed my eyes, tried to overcome the by-now familiar sensation of slipping and reeling into unreality. 'Aaron's problem was he didn't dare to believe.' Grace came out with her favourite phrase, which seemed to becoming a kind of mantra.

I fought to get a grip on what was happening. 'But do you know what you're saying?' My words sounded weak, even as I spoke them, but I was driven to put up some kind of argument. 'This is huge. You're telling me that you plan to turn your back on everything in your old life – your folks, your friends, Jude . . .'

'Don't mention his name,' she snapped. 'I told you, I'm not interested in my old life. I don't want to discuss it.' For a split second the hyper-delighted expression vanished from Grace's face and she looked pale, crushed and broken. But she took one sharp breath then she was back on her high – eyes wide, lips parted in the strange, ecstatic smile.

'This is too sudden, too much for me to take in,' I told her, desperate to hold her attention.

'Because part of your mind is still closed,' she insisted as her gaze flicked around the room. 'I have to go now, but stick around, Tania. Listen to what Daniel tells you. Watch what happens and see what you think. I guarantee you'll be impressed.'

'Grace, wait . . .' My instinct was to grab hold of her, literally to pull her down and keep her feet on the ground.

'We'll talk later,' she said.

And she was gone, slipping off into the shadows.

The music began again. Dancers returned to the centre of the chapel floor, the beat quickened, Daniel was by my side and Zoran had appeared on the raised platform to begin another song.

This time things happened so fast I didn't even take in the words.

*His voice leaps from deep in his throat, strong and fast, soaring into the vaulted roof. Dancers stamp out the rhythm and jump into the air, hair flying, arms flung wide. Zoran throws back his head, glides across the stage, turns, glides again under a bright yellow light. His skin is golden, his body sinuous like a snake as he slides from the platform on to the floor.*

*Suddenly there is smoke in my lungs; I smell fire. The flickering lights glow orange and red. Why? Why the fire memories? Why now, when I'm trying to focus on what is happening to my friend Grace?*

*Zoran weaves among the guests. His eyes are green and glittering, his teeth are bared.*

*An infant cries. Flames rise. A voice cries out a name. Aimee. Do you mean me? What is it you are trying to tell me?*

*Zoran is here, in my space. He sings and towers over me in serpent shape, holds me helpless in his ugly, beautiful, glittering gaze, leans in to clutch my throat with his flickering forked tongue. Then he slithers on by. His voice is a wave of sound, crashing over the dance floor, forcing dancers to their knees, casting them aside until he finds the one he is looking for.*

*It is Grace. Zoran raises her and carries her in her black robe to the platform. She rests in his arms like a child, head back, golden hair swinging down.*

*Smoke fills my lungs. I see flames leap up the chapel walls. I am no longer Tania Ionescu. I know what I am – I am the infant Aimee, reincarnated.*

*Grace is alone with Zoran under a vivid green light. She stands mesmerized, arms by her sides, gazing into his emerald eyes. He is gold and glittering. He speaks over fading music.*

*'Daughter Grace, you will come with me.'*

*She doesn't speak. There is a look of ecstasy on her face as she spreads both arms in voluntary submission. He clasps her wrists.*

*The guests are drawn to the stage. They stand in darkness staring up at the light.*

*'You will walk with me,' Zoran tells Grace. 'Where I go, you will go. You will not leave my side.'*

*Guests murmur. A fresh spotlight shines on Ezra, whose raised face wears a smile of victory. I struggle for breath and stare at Grace. She seems to be sleepwalking out of her old life into unknown, infinite danger.*

*'I am your dark lord,' Zoran hisses. He clasps her by the wrist and they rise above the ground together. He is immensely strong. He dazzles. She is empty, she sees nothing. 'I grow strong as you grow weak. I rise as you fall.'*

*I choke in the flames and try to run out of the chapel towards the pure, clear voice that calls my name – 'Aimee!' But the vision in the chapel draws me back.*

*Monstrous creatures are alive among us. Minotaur eyes glint from under great curved horns; their bull breath is hot on*

180

my skin. Daniel is the god of the underworld and he is taking me by the hand.

'Aimee!' The pure voice sounds far away. I wrench free, I try not to look at Grace surrounded by flames, I am blocking out Zoran's voice but his words force themselves on me.

'Your suffering eases my pain,' he hisses, his face close to his victim's. 'I snatch you from your earthly lover's paradise to make you my own. And so I grow, I thrive!'

A drum beats slowly in the background – two thuds, silence; two thuds and on.

My own god of the underworld snatches my hand. Resist. Breathe. Flee, find a shelter, pray that the flames leap over you. A hot gust of wind, a fireball directly above my head. Breathe, breathe, breathe.

I am outside under the night sky. Daniel halts at the chapel door. I leave Grace behind and run on, up the black mountain.

# 8

*I run into darkness. A wind blows in my face and sucks at my breath, the crackling heat of forest fire chokes me.*

*Ahead, a low wall of orange flame consumes the thorn bushes. A man in a yellow helmet and jacket reaches out his hand from the far side of the blaze. The indistinct figure shimmers, but I know the hand is a life saver, a signal that says 'follow me'. It gives me the courage to crouch low and force my way through the blaze. Breathe, run, breathe.*

*I feel the firefighter's hand grasp mine, hear a man's voice tell me I am safe.*

*I stumble, I collapse to the ground. A woman cradles me, rocks me and tells me I am safe.*

'Tania, thank God!' Orlando held me as if he would never let me go. 'I thought I'd lost you.' I clung to him; I sobbed. 'You're everything to me, you know that?' His arms were around me. I felt his heart beat against mine.

The flames died away, the firefighter, the woman and child – all gone. Instead I was in Orlando's arms and the air was clear, the sky pitch-black.

'I've been searching for hours,' he told me. 'I'd almost given up.'

Everything, not only the sky, was black. There were huge, ragged holes in my memory. 'Where am I?' I asked. 'What time is it?'

'It's late,' Orlando muttered, his arms still tight around me. 'We're on Black Rock in the middle of the night. What happened to your phone, Tania? I've been going out of my mind trying to call you.'

'I was at Zoran's place, with Grace. I guess I was out of signal.'

'That was my guess too. I came up the mountain and tried to get in there but the security guys at the gate threw me out.' Loosening his hold, he studied my face. 'You're freaked out, Tania. What is it? What happened?'

'Another party. Something awful – they've got Grace!' Clinging to the sleeves of Orlando's jacket, I made a sound between a sigh and a groan. 'They've got her and they're not going to let her go.'

An image broke through my hazy recollection of Zoran lifting Grace and carrying her to the platform under a swirl of moving, dancing, coloured lights, the thudding drumbeat behind the voice of the dark lord chanting, 'I rise when you fall.'

That was it – evil Zoran was hell bent on destruction.

'She's trapped,' I whispered as I tugged at Orlando's jacket, willing him back down the mountain in the direction of Black Eagle Lodge.

He gathered me again and held me close. 'Right now, it's you I'm worried about. I spoke with Holly – she agreed I should drive up the mountain and bring you home.'

I leaned against him, let his arms enfold me and tried to push the monstrous images from my mind. They clung ferociously, those minotaurs with their massive horns, the cloven hooves of the goat-men, the golden snake with the glittering green eyes that was Zoran. And now the grey dogs without names that loped up the hill towards me and Orlando.

'Lie down!' a man's voice cried.

The two Black Eagle lurchers ignored the command and raced on up the mountain, caught in the bright beam of a flashlight. They were lean and muscular, with sharp muzzles and bared teeth – Zoran's hunting dogs, sent to snatch at me, tear my flesh and drag me down.

'Down!' the voice repeated. It didn't sound like Daniel.

184

A man strode after the dogs, his flashlight waving unsteadily across the thorn bushes and boulders, his feet crunching over the grit and granite.

This time the dogs obeyed. They lay growling at our feet. It turned out the guy giving the orders was Callum, the Black Eagle medic.

'Tania, is everything OK?' he asked, pointing the flashlight into our faces. 'I heard you might need some help.'

Orlando raised an arm to protect my eyes. 'Take the light away from her face,' he told the newcomer.

Callum redirected the beam. The dogs still lay panting and waiting for the next order. 'You're Tania's boyfriend, right?' he checked with Orlando. 'It's good to meet you. I'm Callum Ramsay, the medical doctor on Zoran's team. We're a little concerned about Tania. I'd advise her to fix an appointment with a neurologist right away.'

'Just back off, hold it right there,' Orlando cut in. 'I find my girlfriend alone and scared half to death on a mountain in the middle of the night. She's being chased by two dogs and a guy with a flashlight. And you're telling me she needs to see a doctor!'

'Thank you!' I breathed, shutting my eyes and taking deep breaths. Believe in me, don't let him tell you I'm crazy!

'I've seen it before,' Callum went on without a pause. 'It's a neurological reaction to strobe lighting, flashlight photography – quite common.'

'Meaning what?' Orlando looked like he was about to use his heavy hiking boot to kick out at the growling dogs then thought better of it.

'It causes an epileptic seizure in the brain. The patient passes out. When they come round, the memory part of the brain is scrambled. They can suffer from memory loss, confusion, delusion—'

'I hear you.' Again Orlando cut Callum off. 'So let me run that by you again. You figure Tania is seriously sick and still you let her run up here alone?'

'Dan— *We* couldn't stop her,' Callum explained, checking himself quickly. 'We're having a small celebration; things got pretty wild.'

'I've heard about your "celebrations". They're getting a bad name around here,' Orlando muttered as he began to steer me around the crouching dogs. He took a flashlight from his own pocket and shone the beam down the slope. 'Come on, Tania, we're out of here.'

Callum nodded then stood back and kept the dogs to heel. Probably he watched us pick our way between the rocks and bushes. Then, as soon as we were out of sight, he must have headed back to the lodge.

'Are you doing OK?' Orlando kept checking me all the way down to the spot where he'd parked his car. He hadn't picked up on Callum's half-mention of Daniel's name and for this I was grateful. 'You're still shaking like a leaf. Watch this rock up ahead. Take my hand. Here's a low branch – bend your head. Not far now.'

He was strong, he was there for me. I held his hand and began to think more clearly, already planning ahead and working out what I had to do next to save Grace.

The World Wide Web is a wonderful thing.

Saturday morning, after a night's sleep, breakfast with my parents and at least six messages from Orlando, I sat on the porch with my laptop.

'Honey, I'd like you to stay home today,' Mom had said, which is as forceful and direct as she ever gets.

'You need rest,' Dad had agreed.

This was after Orlando had given them his midnight version of what had happened on Black Rock and I'd laid down my no-doctor condition. 'The problem is not with me,' I'd insisted. 'It's with those guys up at the lodge.'

I wasn't sure how far they believed me, but my parents knew me well enough not to pressurize me. They realized that stay home and rest was the best promise they could extract for the present.

By the way, the six Orlando messages were wonderfully repetitive: I luv u with ever increasing hugs and kisses.

There were two things I wanted to check on the Internet, and thank you to Wikipedia for the following.

First I searched 'psychic powers' and came up with this explanation. A psychic connects us with unseen parallel worlds. He or she (more often she) has unusual *sensitivity* to the occult. My italics. This type of medium goes way back in history and used to be called a shaman in other cultures. Big, big point – they can communicate with the spirit world.

I stopped reading and took a deep breath – this was my own personal dare-to-believe moment. Psychics connect with the other side, the astral plane, and can voice prophecies, predict the future and heal by the laying-on of hands. Another deep breath. They experience visions that make them the channel between the material world and the spirit world. Oh, and they can guard against ghosts and bad spirits, like sentries on duty at the gates of hell.

'Tania, would you like coffee?' Mom asked through the kitchen window.

'No thanks.' I was too busy mind-juggling with spiritualist concepts like the existence of the eternal soul, free will and karma, plus the ever increasing possibility that I was seeing dead people and hearing dead voices.

Dad came on to the porch and sat down with his latest brick-sized hardback – a study of the lives of Scott and Zelda Fitzgerald.

'What happened to gold cross?' he asked, looking closely at my necklace.

My hand went to my throat. I felt Orlando's heart locket there but not the family crucifix. 'I must have lost it!'

Dad looked disappointed. 'You know when, where?'

'Some time yesterday.' I remembered Zoran glancing at it, saying it was pretty. Maybe I'd lost it by the pool – it could be on the terrace, even in the water, who knew? Then I had another memory of Zoran slithering towards me in the chapel, leaning in to clutch at my throat . . .

'Maybe you find,' Dad sighed as he opened his book.

Putting the loss to the back of my mind, I cleared my screen then googled again: epileptic seizures.

OK, so there are dozens of types of seizure caused by an interruption of electric signals in the brain, either as a result of brain injury or else it's genetic.

'Tell me something – did you drop me on the head when I was a baby?' I broke off my reading to check with my dad.

'Not that I recall,' was his mumbled answer.

189

Read on. You can get the electrical interruption in different hemispheres and lobes. Frontal lobe disconnect leads to the sensation of a wave passing through the head, twitching in an arm or a hand, et cetera. Nope. Temporal lobe means you get an unusual smell or taste; you feel intense, unexplained joy or fear. Check. Parietal lobe – numbness or tingling, occipital lobe – visual disturbance and hallucinations. Check, make a note. That would be a Simple Partial Seizure (SPS) in occipital lobe.

Complex Partial Seizure (CPS) – confusion, loss of memory. Check, check. Generalized seizures send you unconscious. Check again. Triggers include lack of sleep, stress, alcohol and flickering lights, which is called photosensitive epilepsy and is the type Callum was describing.

I took in as much information as I could in one sitting then logged off and sat for a while staring out of the window and down over the town.

OK, so I was both a psychic who could connect with the astral plane, be reincarnated and get chosen to stand guard against evil spirits, or my brain cells were misfiring like old automobile spark plugs. Face it – neither of these are immediately appealing.

'Scott put Zelda in high-security psychiatric

190

institution,' Dad informed me without looking up from his page. 'If not crazy before, for sure after.'

Later that morning I had visitors.

Holly showed up first with a stack of CDs and magazines. 'Are you sick?' she asked. 'Or just totally hungover?'

'Neither.' I was shaky as hell and my head was hurting but I wasn't admitting my symptoms to anyone.

'Orlando said he found you going midnight walkabout on Black Rock. That sounds like an alcohol-related activity to me.'

'Sit down,' I told her, making room on the porch swing. 'But no more comments, OK?'

'I guessed the patient might like to listen to these while she convalesces.' Holly grinned as she tipped the CD cases into my lap. 'So what exactly did I miss?'

'Nothing. Just another party at the lodge.' I've said before – it's best to tread carefully with Holly, in case she lets rip with her scornful tongue.

She pursed her lips. 'Any more weird stuff?'

'Maybe. What did Orlando tell you?'

'He said, yeah – more hippie-tripping.'

'Is that what he said word for word?' Traitor – I trusted you.

191

'No. It's how I read it. He mentioned you went through a repeat of the heavenly bodies experience – freaking out and having hallucinations. And that makes me think drugs again. Maybe not Rohypnol this time, but hey, there's a whole pharmacy of mind-bending pills and powders out there that could be investigated.'

'"Don't worry, guys; Holly Randle is on the case!"' God, it made me feel tired just to look at her firm, tight, tanned face, to hear the fresh conviction in her voice.

'I mean it, Tania. If Zoran Brancusi is heavily into drugs, the authorities in Bitterroot need to do something.'

'All rock stars are into drugs.' Studying the plastic CD cases, I sighed and shook my head.

'Sorry,' she said after a long pause. 'I'm confused and I'm not handling this well. I honestly don't mean to make things worse.'

I revise what I said much earlier. Scratch the surface and you find deeper things about Holly's personality that would make me want to be her friend even if she wasn't my next-door neighbour. 'That's OK. It's cool.'

'Seriously, I'm freaked out by what I'm hearing.'

'You and me both. Did Orlando mention Grace?' I asked.

'That she decided to join Zoran's commune? Yeah.'

'Grace shut us out,' I told Holly with sudden, hot tears

in my eyes. 'We've been buddies all our lives, but now she doesn't want to know.'

'I don't get it. Doesn't she care about how much pain this is causing – to Jude, her parents, to us?'

'I know – I've talked to her about it but she blanks me. It's so totally not like the Grace we know.'

'I've been thinking,' Holly said after another pause. 'About what happened to Aaron. It's OK – we're back together better than before and he explained to me about Cristal.'

'He did?' I swallowed my surprise, trying to guess where this was leading.

'Aaron dropped her name into a conversation we were having about Black Eagle Lodge and I picked up in a nanosecond he had a thing for her.'

'Did he admit it?'

'I forced it out of him.'

Ouch! 'He didn't . . . I'm certain they didn't . . .' I ground to an embarrassed halt.

'It's OK, Tania – I know they didn't. Anyway, who could blame him? Apparently she's the total package. And sure, I was jealous when he told me he spent a morning with Cristal at Zoran's place. Who wouldn't be? It seems she offered to show him the recording studio. Well, you only have to be a beautiful woman talking bass levels and speaker balance to most guys, and they're putty, Aaron included. He said the equipment was amazing.' She raised her eyebrows at the innuendo and smiled. 'After the studio, he got a guided tour of the house, the pool, even the chapel.'

'Me too. I saw the chapel,' I said faintly, without enough emphasis to stop Holly in her tracks.

'And then he says you showed up with Zoran,' she went on. 'Right after that, the lights went out on my boyfriend's budding romance. In other words, Cristal dumped him. Aaron thinks it must have been something *you* said, so thank you, Tania. You're my buddy.'

'He blames me?' I thought back and came up with a different conclusion. 'Actually, all I said to Zoran was that you and Aaron weren't all loved up like you usually were. In fact, I told him you were taking a break, which is what he passed on to Cristal, because I actually heard him say it. He said Aaron wasn't a good fit.'

'How does that figure?' Holly grabbed back a CD and tapped it impatiently against her knee. 'Cristal dumps him *because* he doesn't currently have a girlfriend?'

'Whereas Grace does have a serious boyfriend in Jude, though you wouldn't know it to see her with Ezra now.'

'And you too – you're a member of the loved-up

division. Does Daniel know you're still hitched up with Orlando?'

'He does; I told him right at the start.' My answer was too quick, too definite. 'Holly, you have to promise me something. Don't tell Orlando about Daniel – not right now, because we tried to talk it through before and Orlando didn't understand. We had a big fight, OK?'

'I promise,' she said grudgingly. 'It's not the way I would handle it, but hey, what do I know? But anyway, let's look more closely at this! Cristal dumps Aaron because he's *not* in love. Ezra grabs Grace because she is. Likewise Daniel makes a big play for you.'

'I don't know. Maybe it's coincidence. Can you establish a pattern out of a sample of three?' I told Holly it wasn't good science.

'But say I'm right – just for once.' Now it was my knee that she leaned forward to tap with the edge of the case. She gave a short, self-mocking laugh then grew serious again. 'I do have a brain inside this thick skull, so hear me out. Zoran's guys – the original members of the cult – they only go after people who are currently in a relationship, like it's a kind of bet they make, a game they're playing. That's the reason Cristal dropped Aaron the second she heard he was single.'

I thought for a while and accepted Holly might be on

to something. 'But why?' I asked. 'It doesn't make any sense – unless Zoran gives the order for his followers to wreck as many lives as possible out of sheer boredom.'

'Spite,' Holly added.

'For his weird idea of fun.'

'Because he can.'

Or because he's evil and the monsters, the shape-shifting, the nightmares are true. *The green-eyed serpent opens its mouth and hisses. It coils around my body and presses against my heart.*

'Tania, are you OK?' Holly asked, laying her hand over mine.

'One thing's for sure,' I whispered. 'Whatever is happening here, you should let Aaron know he had one lucky escape.'

Second on my list of visitors that morning was Jude. He brought me flowers.

'These are beautiful,' I told him, finding a vase and setting them on the kitchen table. 'Who told you I was sick?'

'Orlando. We cycled out along Prayer River before breakfast. He told me about last night.'

'Well, I'm good now – especially when a hot guy brings me roses.' I could say stuff like this to Jude and he wouldn't ever take it the wrong way. He just is the sweetest guy. 'Seriously, you don't have to worry about me.'

'Tell that to Orlando.' Accepting coffee, Jude sat at the table. His hands were shaking, I noticed, and his face looked drawn. 'You freaked him out, Tania.'

'I know. But he was amazing – my knight in shining armour.'

'I told him I wish I'd been there with him.'

'To rescue Grace?' I asked quietly. 'Yeah, right now she needs her own Sir Galahad.'

It was turning into a morning of visitors and pauses. A lot of thinking was going on. 'This situation is what my parents always warned me about. They said right from the start to watch out for Grace – she's the type to break your heart.'

I sprang to my friend's defence. 'No way! Grace isn't like that. She's sweet natured and generous . . .' I was halfway through this sentence before I realized the hundred wrong things about what I was saying and particularly my use of the present tense. I stopped short.

'Well, it looks like they were right,' Jude murmured. 'They said girls like her – girls who are too picture-perfect – they have too many temptations thrown in their path. You can't trust them.'

'I still want to say that's not true. I mean, how can you generalize?'

'Maybe they picked up on something I didn't. My parents are pretty smart people in their own way. Besides, they're older. They lived through a lot when they were young.'

'No, don't believe it. Grace and you – you were perfect together.'

Jude shrugged and thought for a long time. 'I *thought* we were.'

'She does love you, Jude.'

'Make that past tense.'

'OK, so she's going through something right now that we can't explain, that makes her cut off from the rest of us. But it doesn't mean we should say, go ahead, Grace – do what you like up there on Black Rock. We shouldn't abandon her.'

This thought didn't get through because Jude was fixated on his next question, the one that had wormed its way into his heart and was eating him alive. 'Did she come right out and tell you she wanted to stay?'

I nodded. 'But it wasn't her voice, it was someone else. Do you know what I'm saying?'

Jude was staring at me, his brown eyes begging for scraps of comfort even while his mouth ran away with him. 'This guy – Ezra. What does Grace see in him?'

'I'm not going to tell you he's ugly,' I said softly, reaching out to put my hand on Jude's arm. 'He's three, maybe four years older than us, he works for Zoran – I guess that's part of it; the glamour, the guys he mixes with. But it's more than that.' Now it was my turn to create the silence, wondering how much more I could tell Jude without freaking him out. Should I even begin to describe the ceremony in the chapel?

'How – more than that?'

'I don't know exactly. Something happens when you're there at Black Eagle Lodge; you get sucked in.'

'What is it, some kind of sect? Are we talking weird religion, brainwashing techniques?' Though I'd run through the possibility with Holly, this idea was new to Jude and he grabbed it with both hands. 'Zoran is leading a cult. They all have to follow him and do exactly what he tells them. Jeez, Tania, is that what you're saying?'

'Anyway, that or drugs is what Holly suspects. Either way, it's a type of mind control.'

'God, why didn't I think of that? It's obvious Grace would never have acted the way she is!' Jude was striding around the room, ready to explode into action. 'I hate myself. I've been totally stupid not to see it before now.'

'Wait,' I pleaded. I could see him shaking and growing

short of breath and recognized the signs of a major asthma attack. 'We need to stay calm, think this through—'

'She needs me, Tanya, and I couldn't see it. We're running out of time. I have to go up Black Rock and find her, get her out of there!' Each word came short and jerked out through harsh, shallow breaths as he dug in his jeans pocket for his inhaler. Fumbling, he let it drop to the floor.

Quickly I stooped and picked it up, put it in his palm and wrapped his fingers around it, guided it to his mouth, helped him hold it there. 'Breathe in,' I told him.

He swayed then sucked hard. When he tried to speak, I shook my head and ordered him to breathe again.

I heard Dad come in from the garden and straight away he assessed the situation. 'Shall I call 911?' he asked.

Jude signalled no, he was good. A couple more breaths through the inhaler and he would be able to speak again.

But by this time Mom had opened her study door. 'I'll tell your folks,' she decided. And she made the call before Jude could stop her. 'Your dad is on his way,' she reported back.

I led Jude to the nearest chair and sat him down. 'Don't do anything about Black Eagle Lodge,' I warned as we all fussed and fretted. 'I know how you're feeling, but don't act right away.'

'What have you two been discussing?' Mom asked in wary, tiger-mom mode. 'Tanya, I asked you to stay home today. I especially don't want you to go back up the mountain, you hear me?'

I turned to her, palms up, with a look of injured innocence. 'Which is why I'm telling Jude, stay away! If he wants to make contact with Grace, he should try texting, or send an email, set up a meeting . . .'

'How is it, Jude?' Dad asked. 'You can breathe?'

He nodded. He looked like he'd collided with a truck, but he was insisting he was good.

'Here's your dad,' Mom said, going out on to the porch to meet Dr Medina. Doctor, as in astral physics professor, not medical. Jude's dad is an expert in black holes. His wife works in federal taxation, which I guess goes some way to explaining their suspicion of their son's 'superficial' relationship with glamorous Grace, which also, I guess, betrays my own prejudices about seriously brainy geeks.

My dad, on the other hand, has a brain but is not a geek. He came to this country as an outsider and he made good. He learned the language, loved the free life and when he found jobs in construction he got made supervisor in every company he joined. Now he works for one of the biggest in America.

Every day he gets out of bed and wants to do something new, to learn something from books, from the landscape, from people.

'It says here that Zoran Brancusi owns biggest private collection of religious art in America,' he told me after lunch. He was logged on to Zoran's website, looking for anything that would help us understand what was happening to Grace on Black Rock. 'From Mexico, from Europe, from India.'

'I believe it. He showed me his Aztec stuff. It was stunning.'

Dad read on. 'Look here – last month interview in *Time* magazine. With pictures.'

I looked at the screen. The photographer, who must have worked his way around the no-pictures clauses in Zoran's insurance policies, had taken interior shots of the house, with captions that listed gold-inlaid Greek icons and Renaissance pietas among the treasures on show at his 'isolated mountain hideaway'. The owner was there too, standing next to a fifteenth century painting of the Archangel Gabriel. Our art collector was dark and stern beside the angel with the gold halo and he was staring straight at camera. 'And this one – this is *Angel of Death*,' Dad said, stabbing a finger at the final image, a nightmarish painting of a black-winged figure crouching astride the jaws of a burning hell.

'Creepy,' I shuddered. 'What is he thinking when he buys these things?'

'Says here, he studies myths, says everybody in history needs to believe in higher power. Angels are messengers from God.'

'I reckon it went to his head,' I muttered. 'What's it called when you identify with creatures in mythology and you start believing you're actually part of it?'

'Does it have name?' Dad asked.

'Delusional psychosis,' Mom suggested, appearing suddenly with a jug of freshly squeezed, iced orange juice.

'Don't take Tania anywhere near the crazy guy on the mountain.' Mom had laid down the law to Orlando when he came to visit.

I'd called him and said I wanted to drive, to listen to music, eat ice cream – be normal.

'How about I take her to the hot springs?' he'd laughed.

'Perfect,' she'd agreed.

If there's one thing about Bitterroot that I totally love it's the natural springs that rise from deep in the earth's crust and bubble to the surface in clear, swirling jets in the valley between town and Turner Lake. They're incredibly pure and warm, and I ask myself, how can anything so pleasant actually be healthy too?

You sit in a specially constructed pool up to your neck in bubbles. You chat with your friends, you gaze up at the Bitterroot range. It sure beats mountain biking, which is the other health reason for tourists to visit.

'You and Jude went cycling by Prayer River?' I asked Orlando as we relaxed in the late afternoon sun.

He nodded. 'But he couldn't do the hills. We had to turn around.'

'He didn't tell me that.' And I described Jude's morning visit, including the roses, and Orlando faked jealousy for about ten seconds, while I thought guiltily and silently about Daniel's kiss and all the reasons Orlando might have to be truly hurt.

'Jude's a fast worker,' he joked. 'How many days is it since Grace dumped him? Now he makes a move on you!'

'No, really – you know Jude's like a brother to me.' I moved on quickly to the asthma attack. 'He wants to go up the mountain and rescue Grace,' I explained.

'Did you warn him about the two guard dogs and the security guys?'

A high white cloud drifted across the sun, casting the lightest of shadows across the surface of the pool. 'Actually, I didn't tell him much. But now he's convinced Grace has been brainwashed and he wants to get her out of there.'

'I've been thinking,' Orlando began in a strained voice. 'I reckon we should forget the cult and the brainwashing theory. Maybe there's a different angle.'

'Do we have to talk about this?' I sighed. The sun was back out and beautifully warm on my face. Jets of hot water soothed and caressed my whole body. And I'd had enough theories and angles to consider for one day, thank you.

Orlando kissed my cheek.

'I get it. You want me to "hear you out"?' I lowered my voice two octaves to imitate his.

He grinned and kissed me again.

'OK, I'm listening.' I leaned my head back against the arm he had wrapped around my shoulder.

'All this flashing light and loud music stuff you describe at Zoran's parties, and the fancy dress heavenly bodies, et cetera – it fits in with what he's always been good at, which is performance.'

'He's a rock star, yeah.' I was listening. In the sunlight, far away from Black Eagle Lodge, I was even willing to believe.

'So, once a performer, always a performer. OK, so he's retired from the music business – he says.'

'Yeah, Mom doesn't believe him either. She reckons he's planning a comeback.'

'And he still has the money to stage a big event, even if it's for private guests instead of thousands of fans in a giant stadium.' Orlando was in full flow, totally into his own theory. 'He plans the whole thing – the costumes, the light show, even the hydraulic lifts to raise him up. You know how these stars are into illusions – you just have to download their videos.'

'I can see that,' I sighed. I'd closed my eyes and could make out tiny orange hexagons floating on the backs of my eyelids. I loved the weight of Orlando's wet arm along my shoulder. 'You're saying the whole thing is pure theatre.'

It's extraordinary how the human brain operates. Or *my* brain. I can swing from one point of view to the extreme opposite in seconds. One moment I'm believing Zoran is the devil incarnate, next thing he's a showman staging a theatrical event. All I could think was – yeah, what a relief!

Then Orlando has to go and spoil things.

'And with someone like you, Tania – someone with a vivid imagination, plus a sensitivity to flashing lights – that's all it takes to throw you into major meltdown, end of story.'

# 9

Someone like me! This was the phrase that did it – the reason why Orlando and I had our biggest fight ever.

Skip the details. They were spectacularly immature and vicious, and neither of us came out in an even halfway decent light. It blasted at full volume from the changing rooms at the hot springs through the drive back into town, all the way to his house, which was empty at the time.

Then we made love. Either that or split for ever.

The making love threw us back together like we were both whirling inside a giant metal drum, emotionally bruised and battered by what had been said, yelled and spat out until a centrifugal force flung us into the centre and we clung to each other in desperation then in lust.

There were no words, only gestures, an intertwining of our bodies, hot limbs locked, eyes closed, my head thrown back against the pillow, Orlando's weight on top of me.

And nothing was said for a long time after, as we lay on our backs staring up at the ceiling, waiting for our fragmented thoughts to piece themselves back together.

'I don't ever want to lose you,' he sighed at last.

I turned into him, rested my arm across his chest, kissed him gently.

'What are we going to do?'

'Nothing.' I kissed him again.

'When I go to Dallas, when you're in Europe, what are we going to do?'

'I'll still love you.'

'Yeah, but will you?'

I could tell he was thinking about all the slick Italian slimeballs, intense French painters and angst-ridden British poets I would meet. In my mind I had a picture of the stick-thin fashion models and boho fabric designers he would be getting creative with in Texas. 'Yes, I will,' I promised. For what could possibly beat lying in his arms staring up at his white ceiling dappled with evening sunlight and shadows?

The real world drags you back. Monday was school, with Holly and Aaron, Leo and Tarsha and a whole group of classmates cornering me, Jude and Orlando for gory details about Grace.

'Where exactly is she?' 'Why does she want to stay?' 'Is she out of her mind?' 'What do her parents plan to do about it?' These were the sort of questions fired at us.

Orlando was our spokesperson. 'Back off, guys. Grace has done what she's done. She's old enough to make up her own mind.'

'But shouldn't we get her out of there, find her some counselling?' Tarsha wanted to know. Dig beneath her alternative styling – strands of shocking-pink hair falling over one eye, lip piercings, regulation black skinny jeans and tops with goth emblems – and you find a practical, grounded core. 'Grace needs help, she really does.'

'That's my plan,' Jude said quietly. Today he looked more tired and ill than ever, as if the least physical effort would be too much.

'I think it should be Mr and Mrs Montrose taking that action,' Leo said.

Holly and Aaron agreed. They said they both knew something about the pull of Black Eagle Lodge and the power that Zoran Brancusi seemed to hold over the members of his commune. They'd experienced it first hand.

'How do we know the Montroses haven't tried it already?' Tarsha asked. 'Listen, if it was me deciding to quit school early to join a sect that nobody knew anything about, my parents would be the first people hammering on their door.'

'But it might take more than that to change Grace's mind. There's a history of stuff like this,' Aaron said. 'Remember Waco and the cult leader guy?'

'David Koresh,' Tarsha reminded him. 'He took child brides and brainwashed entire families. They held out against a government siege until everyone was dead. Is that what this is? Are we really talking Scientologists, Moonies – a dangerous cult right here on our doorstep?'

'I don't think we should assume anything.' Orlando spoke up with his latest theory about Zoran using Black Eagle Lodge as a spectacular stage set to rehearse and promote a world comeback tour. 'Grace has fallen for the whole rock-star lifestyle, and unfortunately she also met a guy named Ezra up there.'

'That's news to me.' Leo hadn't been in the loop and he sounded pissed. 'So this is all about a guy?'

Orlando shrugged. 'Sorry you have to hear this, Jude, but I'd say that plays a major part in what's happening with Grace right now.'

'Then, hey, what can we do?' Losing interest, Leo and Tarsha drifted on into their science class and we followed.

Today's hot topic for discussion: is it possible for a Creationist to use scientific method to disprove Darwin's Theory of Evolution?

I was getting through the week, recovering from Black Rock, blocking the voices and dropping the psychic speculation. In other words, I was siding with Orlando about my Friday night experience. We were good together, sharing special times, trying hard not to think about the future.

There was only one small crash on the hard drive: the time when we were biking out one evening along the cycle track by the river and Orlando said out of nowhere, 'I feel bad for Jude.'

'Me too.' Through sudden lack of concentration I hit a snaking tree root, took off and landed hard on my front wheel with a thud that jarred my wrists and elbows.

'He looks like he lost ten pounds.'

'I know. What can we do?'

'I guess I'm lucky.' Slowing down to my pace, Orlando narrowed his eyes and seemed to concentrate on the shimmering water in the middle distance.

'In what way, lucky?' I couldn't escape asking the question even though I didn't like the way this conversation might be going. Twigs snapped and gravel crunched under our wheels.

'That *you* didn't reply to that text.'

'Which text?' I almost yelped.

'From that Daniel guy. I'm lucky he's not turned into another Ezra.'

'Yeah,' I gasped. My sun god seemed to hover above my head. He cast a deep, dark shadow, making me veer to the left, hit another root then steady myself before I hit a tree.

Orlando didn't say another word. But he'd mentioned Daniel's name and he'd been probing for sure. And I hadn't come up with the necessary reassurances, the heartfelt protests and protestations. No, I'd almost crashed my bike then come up with a lame 'Yeah', for God's sake.

I've come to a definite conclusion – no way am I good at deceit.

Thursday night I was home alone. Dad had flown out to Wyoming for two days to cost out a new construction project and Mom was visiting *her* mom in Miami. Orlando was pleading work, always a red rag to a bull with me – 'Tania, I have to read Mimi Rossi's biography of Coco Chanel. How will it look if they invite me for interview and I haven't read her book?'

So the knock on the door just before eight brought me running downstairs in the hope that he'd abandoned Coco for me; I was disappointed at first to find a forlorn Mike and Alice Montrose standing on my doorstep instead.

'We're sorry to disturb you, Tania,' Mrs Montrose began.

They looked awful, both of them. Sure, they were putting on a dignified pretence in their smart casuals, with fixed social smiles, but inside they were broken.

'Come in,' I said. I led them into the sitting room, moved a couple of Dad's doorstop histories from the sofa and plumped up the cushions. 'Sit down. Would you like a drink?'

'No, thanks.' Grace's mom was the one doing the talking. Her husband sat silent and staring throughout, like a small animal fixed in your headlights the second before he becomes road kill. 'We thought long and hard about coming here,' Alice sighed. She placed her hands neatly in her lap, one on top of the other. Her ankles were crossed. 'It didn't seem fair to put you under pressure, Tania.'

'It's no pressure. Are you sure you don't want a drink – beer, wine, coffee?'

She shook her head. 'We understand from Jude that

214

you had a traumatic experience yourself last week on Black Rock. We sure don't want to make that worse.'

It breaks your heart when decent people continue to be decent when all they want to do is cry and tear out their hair, fight somebody tooth and claw to get their daughter back. 'How can I help?' I said.

'Grace didn't even say goodbye,' Alice sighed. 'If there was a note – some kind of explanation – maybe we would understand. But she just took off; she didn't say who she was going to meet, where she was going. And she never came back.'

*'Aimee!' The woman's voice is wailing her daughter's name, knowing that she's gone for ever. Trees around the log cabin crackle and burn.*

This was weird and getting weirder. I wanted to reply to my ghostly voice, to tell her I was OK. But instead I blocked my ears and made myself focus on the here and now.

'I'm sure Grace will call you,' I tried to argue but even I wasn't convinced. 'Give her time.'

'You've been to Zoran Brancusi's lodge, Tania,' Grace's mom went on. 'Can you help us understand what has happened here?'

'It's difficult to describe. There are lots of things that might make you want to stay. It's a fabulous house, for a start, with a recording studio and priceless art on the walls. And Zoran – he's charismatic. Then there is this guy called Ezra.'

'Tell us about him,' Mrs Montrose pleaded.

*'I'm coming, Aimee. Don't be scared!' She runs into the flames, disappears inside the burning house.*

I fought to keep my pulse rate steady, tried to block the images, the despair.

'The first time Grace saw him he was in costume for the Heavenly Bodies party – his face was painted and he had dreamcatchers hanging from his belt.'

'What type of costume is that?' She frowned in prim non-comprehension.

'Some kind of shaman – Native American. He was really romantic-looking. His eyes are kind of almond-shaped, with long, dark lashes, and his hair falls down over his forehead.'

'Not like Jude then.' It was the first time Mike Montrose had spoken and we turned our heads sharply towards him. 'Jude is grounded, sensible. He wouldn't mess with face paints and stuff.'

'Ezra's exact opposites with Jude,' I agreed.

'Why did he hit on Grace?'

I shrugged. 'She's gorgeous – you know.' Botticelli angel, Venus rising from the waves. Lots of fathers refuse to acknowledge that their daughters are out of braces and braids and into training bras. Mike Montrose has always been one of these.

Grace's mom spoke, right on target. 'Do you think this Ezra guy cares for her? Will he make her happy?'

'The last time I saw her she seemed . . . elated.' I struggled to find the right word. 'The relationship is new, so it's pretty intense.'

'And?'

'In between the highs she seems to dip down a little. So no, I wouldn't say Grace is happy exactly.' Maybe I should have softened this, I thought later, remembering the stricken looks on both their faces. With this comment I'd confirmed the bipolar thing in their minds.

'Last question, Tania,' Alice said after the longest time. 'We want your honest opinion. Should we drive up there to Black Eagle Lodge and try to speak with our daughter?'

'Would it make things better or worse?' Grace's dad added quickly.

*A second figure is silhouetted in the burning doorway. He doesn't speak, just raises an arm to shield his face then runs into the flames to rescue his wife and daughter. I rise from the ashes. I am Aimee incarnate.*

'I think you should try,' I said quietly.

217

'The security team wouldn't even let them through the gate,' Jude told me two days later. 'They gave the Montroses the message loud and clear – Grace doesn't want to see them.'

We were sitting round the table – me, Jude and Dad. Jude hadn't been in school for two days, his asthma was so bad again.

'And she won't answer phone?' Dad checked.

'She's out of signal, or else she has it switched off.' Jude knew this all too well. I think he'd given up trying even to text Grace.

'So is it true she doesn't want to see them?' Dad insisted. 'Or do they *want* you to believe this? I know Grace long time. She is not this sort of girl.'

'You haven't seen her lately,' I reminded him. 'She's definitely changed.'

'Her dad went crazy,' Jude told us. 'You know what a quiet, easy-going guy he is? Well, he tried to drive his car clean through the barrier until one of the security team fired a bullet into his tyre. They said to turn around or else they'd call the cops.'

'They fired at the Montroses?' I gasped. 'Is it legal? Can they do that?'

'Zoran owns thousands of acres up there. Apparently

he can do whatever's needed to keep out intruders.'

'And Grace doesn't want to talk for sure?' Dad was still stuck on this.

'I guess the only way we could find out is if we decided to drop in there like Bobby Mackey and his smokejumper guys.' I was only half joking as I pictured white parachutes opening out and floating down from a clear blue sky. We'd be swaying in harnesses, gazing down at the tree canopy, seeking out the helipad for a smooth landing.

'Don't even think about it,' Dad warned. 'And you, Jude – you don't try driving up there alone. And, Tania – you too. Men with guns. Security cameras. All bad.'

'So what do we do?' Jude wanted to know.

'We wait. Grace will come out when ready.' It was the best Dad could do as he went outside to answer a phone call from Mom, though obviously not good enough for Jude, and not good enough for me either.

Jude was gone when Dad came back after his phone call. 'How you feeling?' he asked me, clearing a space on the coffee table for him to sit down on the couch, take off his boots and put his feet up.

I was in for one of his long talks, the type we'd had ever since I can remember. We don't have the usual parent–kid dynamic, not buddy–buddy either, but definitely equal in a thoughtful, considerate way. 'Not good,' I confessed with a sigh.

Dad patted the couch and I sat down next to him. 'You find gold cross?' he asked.

I shook my head. 'Honestly, Dad, I guess I lost it up at Black Eagle Lodge that last time.'

'Then is lost for good,' he decided, then switched topics. 'You and Orlando – you OK?'

'Yeah, cool.' We were – I wasn't lying, just so long as I kept Daniel out of the equation.

'So it's Black Rock – this is why you don't smile?'

'Grace, yeah.' Dad is tall and broad-shouldered. He wears thick, knitted socks and Cat boots. I totally love that he's my dad.

'So tell me.'

Where should I start? Afternoon sun slanted in through the low windows; the aspens that Dad had planted after the forest fire were now taller than the house and cast a dappled shade. 'Sometimes I think like Orlando – that this is down to Grace and nobody else. She made up her own mind, end of story.'

'And other times?'

'I'm scared she doesn't have a mind to make up any more, that she's kind of bewitched. Does that sound stupid?'

Dad shook his head, waited for more.

'What if she's not actually choosing to stay? Can you think of anything – I mean, other than actual witchcraft, which we don't believe in, obviously, in the twenty-first century – which would make someone do things against their will?'

'Hypnosis. Power of suggestion,' he offered.

'Do we believe in that either?' To me, hypnosis means men in capes lined with red silk twirling their vaudeville moustaches and swinging a pocket watch to and fro.

'Don't know. Can't be sure.' Laying his head back against a cushion and staring up at the ceiling, Dad ran through other alternatives. 'Brainwashing. I read about this. Famous experiment where ordinary, everyday guys use electricity to hurt others.'

'Because they're told their victims are dangerous spies who are a threat to national security. Yeah, we learned about it in psychology.'

'Maybe they tell Grace that world is bad place; only safe if she stays with Zoran.'

'But she'd already have to be seriously paranoid to believe that. And Grace was the least paranoid person . . .'

'Drugs,' Dad went on to suggest. 'Drugs that twist brain – LSD, acid, E, heroin, cocaine, marijuana.' The list went on.

'That's actually Holly's theory. She thinks those guys spike people's drinks.'

'And you?'

'Maybe.' I paused before I took another plunge into unknown territory. 'You can tell me something and I won't tell anyone else, I promise.'

Dad gave me a sideways look and a puzzled grin.

'When you were young, did you mess around with stuff like that?'

His face cleared and his answer was open and matter of fact. 'Everybody did; we smoke dope, drop acid. You want to compare notes?'

I nodded.

'Acid – LSD – was worst. Marijuana not so much. LSD messes with brain – world goes weird.'

'Do objects move around without anyone touching them? Do people change shape?' I wanted to know. Masks falling apart and fixing themselves, murals on chapel walls coming alive.

'It can happen. Bad trip brings monster faces, trees turn into snakes, ground opens up like ocean and swallows you.'

'You lose your inhibitions?' I was seeing Grace's face with its look of wild elation, remembering how she threw herself at Ezra, danced with everyone, let Zoran lift her and carry her on to the sacrificial altar. And of course I was living again the nightmare of the golden, green-eyed serpent, the minotaur men and those Aztec gods who spread their wings and rose in the air.

Dad turned his head towards me and studied me deeply. 'Is this truth? This is happening to Grace?'

'Maybe,' I said again.

'You tell me everything?' he quizzed.

'Everything,' I swore.

Everything except Daniel and Callum's suspicion that I was suffering from episodes of epileptic seizure. Worse, as far as Dad was concerned, that I was a medium for dead spirits, maybe even a dead person reborn. It's called a sin of omission when you tell part of the truth but not all of it and what you miss out makes you the worst kind of deceiver because you break the trust of people who love you. I never fully understood this until now.

Anyway, I papered over these particular cracks, promised Dad I wasn't into drugs even if Grace was (true) and agreed with him that I would let Grace's parents make the decision about what to do next (untrue). Because actually I already knew I was going to go ahead and meet up with Jude early on Saturday morning.

'We need to get past those guys on the gate.' Jude may

223

have been totally messed up and confused but he was clear about this one thing.

We were determined to go together up on to Black Rock and make contact with Grace. I didn't tell my parents or even Orlando, because how would I handle the situation if we ran into Daniel while we were up there? Yeah, I know this is short-term reasoning and extremely flawed, but I was acting under duress.

When I say 'make contact', what I really wanted to do was to lock back into the lost, crushed expression I'd seen on Grace's face when I'd mentioned Jude's name the last time I saw her. Perhaps if we went up there and she met him face to face she would all of a sudden see what she was losing by turning her back on her old life and then maybe reconsider.

Failing that, Jude and I would have to kidnap her and bring her safely home. Ambitious and a touch unrealistic, huh? But Jude was by this time desperate and I had it on my conscience that the last time I'd seen Grace, she was being offered up to high priest Brancusi like a sacrifice and, coward that I was, I'd wimped out and left her.

'There are guard dogs too,' I warned Jude. 'And I reckon Zoran has security cameras covering every metre of his boundary.'

Over the last week Jude had developed a crazy-stubborn, jaw-set expression that I'd never seen before. It made him look years older, despite his skinny-kid frame. 'If they catch us on camera, what's the worst they can do?' he muttered.

'Charge us with unlawful entry, set the dogs on us, shoot us,' I suggested, checking off items on my fingers.

'Do you want to do this or not?' he grunted.

I nodded. 'I'm only telling you it won't be easy.'

Then again, it was early enough in the day to hope that we could beat Zoran's security surveillance system, especially if there had been partying on the Friday night and there were the usual hangovers and morning-after memory lapses. The best scenario was that Jude and I could drive high on to Black Rock and make our way down to the lodge without being spotted. 'And are you certain you can do this?' I checked. 'There's walking involved, maybe even climbing.'

Even the nod that he gave me brought on a short fit of coughing. He patted his jacket pocket. 'I'm carrying my inhaler.'

The magic medicine, the legal chemical kick. 'Then we should go.'

Of course, the driving part was easy. We used Jude's Jeep Cherokee and got up the dirt road to Black Rock, no problem. But by the time we reached the end of the track and were ready to park the car, we'd already hit a snag.

'Is that mist high in the canyon, or smoke?' I asked, pointing north towards the craggy summit.

Jude shielded his eyes and tried to identify the source of a white cloud lingering between two peaks. 'Smoke,' he decided. 'I guess the fire crews are up there building their fireline.'

This was bad news because, though the artificial fuel break might safeguard against the spread of future wildfires, the clearing and burning out of vegetation would be likely to send smoke down the mountain in our direction. 'You want to turn back?' I suggested to Jude. 'Come again when the smoke has cleared?'

'No, I'm good,' he said through gritted teeth. Maybe he was hoping that the wind would change direction before the smoke reached us, or maybe he was just fixated on our task and wouldn't consider any change of plan. Anyway, it was a risk he insisted on taking. 'Let's go.'

So we left the Jeep and walked on up a steep incline between worn and weathered fingers of granite that stood like giant chess men on guard at the entrance to a narrow draw. Twenty metres into the cleft in the rock face, we found that it was a dead end, so we retraced our steps, skirted wide around the chess men and began to scramble up a slope of loose scree. Stones dislodged under our boots and peppered down the mountain, scaring three mule deer, a momma and two babies, hidden in a thorn thicket. We saw them leap from the bushes and bound down the slope into some aspens, out of sight.

'Where now?' Jude asked as we reached a ridge and he had to pause for breath.

'I reckon Black Eagle Canyon is east of here. We won't see the lodge until we get to within a couple of hundred metres – it's built right into the mountain.' Of course, I was worried about him – the way he was panting and finding it difficult to draw breath. We were up at eight thousand feet, remember, and by now we could actually smell smoke in the air. I could also hear the Forest Service chainsaws and a mechanical digger churning the thin soil to make their ditch.

'Just our luck that they decided to work on that fireline today of all days,' I muttered.

Jude coughed and collected phlegm.

'Go ahead, spit,' I told him.

He bent forward and cleared his mouth. 'Sorry – not pretty. But I'm cool, let's keep going.' He set off along the ridge until we met another barrier of rock and we were forced to descend a hundred feet or so.

'Stop again,' I told him. The white smoke hadn't changed direction – in fact it was heading our way. Already our vision was limited and the smell of burning filled our nostrils. Normally this would have been enough to freak me out and for the dead voices and visions to begin, but today all my concern was fixed on Jude, so I managed to keep them at bay. 'We should get out of here. Let's come back tomorrow. Those guys won't work Sundays.'

'No, I see something – look!' Coughing again, he pointed through the billowing clouds to a white fence and a long, low structure that I recognized as Zoran's new arena and barn. 'The smoke gives us some cover. We can sneak in without being picked up by the security cameras.'

As I watched him set off towards the barn, I felt more and more scared. This seemed too easy. Where were the cameras, where were the dogs? 'Wait!' I warned.

Jude shook his head, plunged into some thorn bushes and struggled on. By now, the thickening smoke almost hid him from view.

I ran after him, right through the thorns – what else could I do? The bushes caught at my legs, pierced through my jeans to my bare flesh. When I came out the other side, I stumbled right into Jude. 'That hurt!' I complained, picking a thorn out of my forearm. 'Why did you stop?'

'Horses in the arena,' he whispered.

I heard them before I saw them – Zoran's wild mustangs exploding out of the barn and thundering into the round pen, neighing shrilly through the smoke. Horses hate fire more than any other phenomenon. They'd rather be in hurricane-force winds or face lashing rain and rising rivers; anything rather than run the risk of being burned alive. I expected them any second to break right through the new fence and stampede across the brush.

There they were, emerging from a cloud of white smoke, bunched together and galloping crazily and out of control inside the arena. An alpha male led the group – a brown and white Appaloosa with a ragged dark mane and tail. His ears were flattened, eyes rolling and nostrils flared. Once more around the arena, past the dark entrance to the barn, where a solitary man stood, they turned again towards Jude and me, charging straight at the fence without stopping, crashing through the wood, splintering it and stamping it underfoot.

Then they were galloping towards us – about twenty horses running for their lives, acting as one terrified unit, chest muscles straining as they sucked in air, hooves striking rock and sending up yellow, orange, red sparks.

I threw myself behind a rock, dragging Jude with me. But I couldn't hold on to him as the mustangs passed to either side, felt him twist from my grasp and lost him as the horses' hooves raised dust and gravel. I felt the ground shake under my feet, smelled their sweat and their fear.

'Jude!' I cried after they'd thundered by. I had grit in my eyes, the smoke was thicker and he was nowhere to be seen.

'Who's there?' another voice cried. It came from the patch of thorn and brush that we'd just crossed. Instinctively I hid again behind my rock.

'Did you hear that?' a second voice yelled above the receding hooves.

The first man's voice, deep and rough: 'Yeah, it was a girl. Where is she?'

I crouched down, kept quiet, wished to hell that Jude had stayed with me.

'Is someone there? Are you OK?' It was the second voice again.

Seven or eight stocky figures were beginning to emerge through the smoke. I peered round my rock and spotted their bright-yellow jackets. Forest Service firefighters were coming down the mountain carrying heavy chainsaws, shovels and axes. I stepped out of my hiding place to wave both arms above my head and speak with them.

'There she is!' The leading firefighter cut across the scrubland towards me. He had broad, Hispanic features, and thick black hair escaped from under his helmet. Black-rimmed goggles protected his eyes from the smoke.

'I'm OK!' I yelled. 'Those horses broke out of the arena at Black Eagle Lodge. I lost a friend of mine when they ran by.'

'What are you doing up here anyway?' the crew leader asked me as he drew near. He took off his goggles to get a better look at me. 'It's early to be out hiking.'

I didn't have time to frame an answer before I noticed that two members of the team were carrying what looked like a heavy stretcher covered with a bright-blue tarp. 'Did someone get hurt?'

'OK, here's the deal.' The leader took my arm and gently but insistently held me back as the rest of the crew stepped clear of the thorn bushes. 'You tell me your business then I tell you mine.'

'We're hiking,' I insisted.

'You and your buddy – no third party?'

I nodded. The guys with the stretcher were passing close by just as a strong gust of wind lifted the smoke

231

cloud to give me a clearer view. The tarp was humped over what could only be a human body. 'Just the two of us,' I confirmed with a shudder.

'Then I guess this young guy must be from the lodge.' Jerking his thumb towards the stretcher, the firefighter loosened his grip on my arm. 'He hadn't been up there long when we found him.'

'Is he dead?' I whispered, watching the tarp shift and slip to one side. One of the stretcher-bearers roughly pulled it back into place.

The leader nodded.

'Where did you find him?'

'Down a sink hole, half covered by earth. You could've walked right on by and not spotted him, only we were digging a ditch for our fireline – darned near put a shovel through his skull.'

I shuddered again.

'You want us to swing by Brancusi's place on our way down to the truck?' someone yelled as the wind died and left long curls of smoke drifting at ground level.

'You do that,' their team leader agreed. 'Go ahead and warn them that we need identification.'

So a guy split off to head for the lodge while the others rested. My own mind raced, wondering why anyone from Black Eagle Lodge would be hiking alone and getting himself killed by falling down a sink hole. 'You really reckon he's from the lodge?' I asked.

'Maybe.' The chief firefighter came across like someone who'd seen many wildfires, many deaths – not exactly hardened but in no way shocked by the discovery of their latest corpse. 'He could also be from town – a high school student. He's a teenager for sure, someone around your own age.'

'You want me to take a look?' My question caught me by surprise and I stared uneasily at the long shape under the tarp.

'No obligation,' one of the other firefighters reminded me. His lean face was streaked with dirt and he wore a loose red neckerchief around his throat.

'No, I'll do it,' I said, taking a deep breath.

The chief nodded and walked me across to the stretcher. The guy with the neckerchief stood by, ready to fold back one corner of the tarp.

When he eased the blue cover to one side, I saw that the face underneath was pale but not disfigured. The eyes were closed, the mouth half open. He looked unmarked but more than asleep – kind of absent – and it was by his blond hair that I recognized him.

'You know him?' the chief firefighter prompted.

I nodded. 'Yeah, your first guess was good. He's not a

233

school student, he's from Black Eagle Lodge.'

Last seen by the side of the pool, gazing into Cristal's green eyes, leaning forward to be kissed. 'His name's Oliver. That's all I know.'

# 10

I went straight from identifying the body on the mountain to Black Eagle Lodge with Ricki Suarez, the leader of the Forest Service firefighting team.

The tall pines sighed in the wind, threads of white smoke wound down the hillside towards Bitterroot. And I was seeing ghosts, hearing voices again. *Aimee, take care. Mind you don't fall and hurt yourself.* Drifting on the breeze, sighing through the pines.

'You OK?' Ricki paused within a hundred metres of Zoran's place. 'You're certain you don't want one of my guys to drive you home?'

I shook my head, cleared out the whispering spirits. 'Thanks, but I need to find my hiking buddy. He has asthma – he doesn't do well at this altitude.'

'Let's hope he headed this way.'

We approached the broken fence and stepped over

the smashed rails, me leading the way and of course looking out for Daniel, guessing that he was the figure standing helpless in the doorway when the mustangs broke out. 'Zoran just built this facility,' I explained. 'He adopts horses from the Californian desert.'

'Zoran?' Ricki echoed. 'You're on first-name terms?'

'I've been here a couple of times.' I felt my face colour up, sensing some disapproval.

'Your parents know this?'

'Sure. Why?'

'I won't let my daughter near the place,' he muttered, taking the lead now as we entered the barn. 'Not after the reports I heard.'

'My parents don't lay down those types of boundaries.' I was only half concentrating and didn't care if I came over like a spoiled brat. How come the guys from the lodge hadn't set out to bring the mustangs back? And shouldn't Daniel be in charge of the search? Daniel . . . Daniel! The closer I got to the lodge, the more I obsessed. Following Ricki past feed stalls and a grain store, we came out of a smaller door at the far side of the barn. 'Anyway, what reports?'

'About the way Brancusi runs this place. I hear he likes to be in control.'

'No more than you would expect,' I argued. Oddly,

whatever thoughts and suspicions I was personally experiencing, I didn't appreciate it when outsiders picked up rumours and ran with them. 'Think about it – a guy in his position, he needs to protect his privacy.'

'I hear you. But, to be honest, the Forest Service doesn't like it when a wealthy individual buys up half a mountain. These multimillionaires, they're not necessarily into land conservation and management. We'd like to bring it all under federal ownership – that's our ultimate aim. So which is the main house?' he asked, stopping at the edge of Zoran's helipad and scanning the various doorways – entrances into the studio, staff living quarters and Zoran's own house.

'Can I help?' Someone had followed us out of the barn. It wasn't Daniel and I couldn't place him at first in jeans and T-shirt, but then I recognized that this was Lewis, Holly's god of youth in the feathered cloak and heavy gold collar.

My companion introduced himself. 'Ricki Suarez, Carlsbad County Forest Service. We're currently setting backfires, creating a fireline.'

'And you're here because . . . ?' Lewis stood in the narrow doorway with arms crossed, viewing us suspiciously and giving no sign that he recognized me.

'I want to speak with Mr Brancusi,' Ricki told him.

'Mr Brancusi is currently busy. I'm Lewis Mullins. You can speak with me.'

'Mr Mullins, let's cut to the chase.' Ricki's tone conveyed controlled hostility. 'This is official Forest Service business. We could save some valuable time if you let Mr Brancusi know I'm here.'

'Let me be equally plain,' Lewis said without moving an inch. 'You guys start tearing up the ground with heavy machinery, you set fires that stampede our horses, and you expect us to break off from what we're doing and welcome you with open arms?'

'This is important.' I forced my way in between the two guys' locked horns. 'They found a body down a sink hole. I think I identified him.'

'Hey, Tania.' Lewis directed his cool gaze towards me and acknowledged me at last. The word 'body' seemed to have no impact whatsoever. 'Are you looking for Jude?'

'We got separated. He was in trouble. Have you seen him?'

'I haven't. But Callum has and he told me he was in bad shape. Don't worry, he took care of him.'

'Thank God! Do you know where Jude is now? Can I see him?'

'Hold it!' Ricki Suarez refused to waste another second. 'First things first. Does the name Oliver mean anything?'

Lewis tilted his head to one side. 'Sure. Oliver Knight. What about him?'

'Does he live here in the complex?'

'Not any more.' Lewis had moved out of the doorway and joined us in the centre of the helipad. 'Oliver arrived here a couple of weeks back, hung around a while then decided to bale out.'

'He left?' Ricki checked. 'When, exactly?'

'Let me see – it was last night after supper. These kids come and go. Oliver came to the Heavenly Bodies party with a couple of guys from Bitterroot and decided to stay on. He was from out of town, here on vacation. I guess it became time for him to go home.'

Ricki's hostile frown didn't lift. 'Well, he didn't make it,' he grunted. And he filled Lewis in on the location of the sink hole where they'd found Oliver's body. 'It would help us, Mr Mullins, if you would confirm Tania's identification of the body so that we can go ahead and contact the boy's family.'

Lewis nodded. 'Last time I saw Callum, he was in the studio,' he informed me as he turned to follow Ricki back through the barn. 'He can tell you more about Jude.'

I thanked him and gave the team leader my number. 'If you need to contact me again,' I explained. Then I turned and ran to find Jude.

* * *

At first I thought the studio was empty, though the main door was open and the lights were on. I looked around at the complicated sound boards and cubicles, trod carefully over coils of cable and past heavy metal stands until I saw the man himself – Zoran in headphones, his back turned, hunched over a desk and listening intently.

I had a moment to study him – that tall, wiry figure, the grey stubble covering his scalp – before he said without turning around, 'Tania, go back and press the button to close the door then come and listen to this.'

As always, I did as he told me and when I reached the desk he handed me a pair of headphones. 'Something new,' he explained. 'What's your opinion?'

It was a song not about love this time but about the price of fame, how it tempts you and draws you in though you know that beneath the bright, glittering surface it's worthless. Zoran's voice was echoey and slow, backed only by an acoustic guitar. The chorus used the image of a precarious tower that topples and ends up as rubble, taking a host of famous names with it.

'I think I like it,' I said hesitantly. I loved the voice, the melody, but the lyrics had unsettled me.

'You're not sure?'

'It's too sad. It makes me feel that life may not be worth anything.'

'Don't worry – your opinion is in line with Cristal, Daniel and Lewis; they say it's not commercial.'

'Maybe you know what sells better than we do.' I handed back the headphones with a shrug. 'I thought Cristal would approve. Didn't she want new songs from you?'

'Just not this one,' he smiled. 'But you agree with the sentiment – that these days it's easy to get famous but hard to live with the consequences?'

'I don't know.' Again, he lived in that world and I didn't.

'Believe me,' he insisted. 'People who chase fame and then have to live with it are often disillusioned. They start to find they can't walk down the street without a bodyguard, they can't eat in a restaurant, go to see a show without a dozen cameramen popping flashlights in their faces. Maybe that doesn't seem to you like a very high price to pay for a million-dollar pay cheque, I don't know.'

'Honestly, I can't judge.'

'Come with me,' Zoran told me, making an unexpected move out of the studio and down a corridor that seemed to tunnel underground until it finally connected with the main house. We came out in the large room where he'd hosted his private gathering on the night of the Heavenly Bodies party. He reached under a big glass coffee table to pull out a portfolio of colourful prints. 'You know Andy Warhol's work? What do you think of these?'

I leafed through the prints – multiple Marilyns, Elizabeth Taylors, Jackie Os, plus one of mop-haired, owlish Warhol himself. Iconic. Brilliant. Amazing. 'Are they genuine?' I gasped.

Zoran laughed in my face then apologized. 'No, you're right – with Warhol it's difficult to be sure, even if the signature appears real. But the dealer I bought them from had them authenticated by The Studio in New York and I paid top dollar, so let's hope they're the real deal. Which ones do you like the best?'

'The Marilyns,' I replied instantly. 'Warhol gets everything about her, the fact that she was on every billboard and magazine cover all over the world, that she was glossy and beautiful . . .'

'Yeah, beautiful,' he repeated, passing his fingertips over Marilyn's face then glancing up at me. 'And so vulnerable.' Closing the portfolio, he started to ask me about my own artistic ambitions. 'Did you use the photographs you took of the mountain?'

'Not yet. Actually, I lost the images from my camera. I need to take some more.'

He gave a nod of what appeared to be satisfaction. 'And you have a studio to work in?'

'I'm lucky – my dad converted part of the garage. I'd like to spend more time in there.'

'But life keeps getting in the way. Believe me, I know how that is. Classes to attend, friends who need you, lovers . . .'

'I came to find Jude,' I said, before the conversation got too personal. 'Lewis said Callum took care of his asthma attack.'

'Yeah, I get the reason you were on the mountain,' he said casually. 'Jude wanted to check on Grace. I don't blame him for that, considering their history, though I think you might have used the front entrance!'

'I – we didn't think we'd get through security.'

Zoran faked hurt feelings then smiled. 'Look at me, Tania. Do you see me objecting to your visit? No, I'm always pleased to see you. And any friend of yours is a friend of mine.'

As ever, he threw me completely off balance. Here was the rock god shaking his head at me and grinning, acting like the whole world misunderstood him. He, Zoran Brancusi, who wanted only to open his home and share his gifts and treasures with anyone who was genuinely interested. And yet . . .

'Actually, I'm sad for your friend Jude,' he went on, scooping up my doubts into an invisible box and putting a lid on them. 'Love hurts, we all know that. Like the words of my song – you open up and make yourself vulnerable, and when it ends it feels like your whole world has come crashing down. I do understand what Jude's going through.'

. . . And yet Zoran's security guards fired a pistol at Mike Montrose's car tyres, there are secret cameras covering every inch of the property, and a kid has just walked out of here to a lonely death on Black Rock.

'Look at Oliver,' he went on, catching my thought in another of those uncanny mind-reading moments. 'One glance at Cristal and the kid was transfixed. I mean, seriously, the second he saw her, he was smitten.'

I said I wasn't surprised. Girls didn't come more gorgeous than Cristal. 'How about her? Did she feel the same way?'

'What do you think?' he countered.

I remembered watching Cristal and Oliver at the pool party – how he was drawn like a moth to a flame, how she sat without reacting when he went to the edge of the pool and made as if to dive over the edge. 'I think, no way.'

'Give me reasons,' Zoran invited. 'Apart from the obvious ones that she is so beautiful she can have the pick of any man she meets.'

Including Holly's Aaron, whom she also dropped without a second thought. 'Yeah, right,' I murmured. 'Why choose Oliver?'

'Before Oliver there was a boy named Aaron,' Zoran recollected breezily, forcing me into yet another double-take. 'Before that there was a boy she met in the airport, and before that too many even to recall.'

'So she wasn't in love with Oliver and she won't be too sad about what happened to him?' I checked.

For once it seemed that the main man wasn't up to speed. 'Why, what did happen?' he quizzed.

'You seriously don't know?'

'Cristal told me he was going through a personal crisis and last night he decided to go back home. Did you hear something different?'

'He didn't go home,' I reported, deliberately delaying and playing with my solitary moment of information-supremacy over Zoran Brancusi.

'Where did he go?' A wariness had come into his expression; those dark eyes were searching my face.

'Whatever crisis he was going through, Oliver didn't head for town. He did the exact opposite – he went up the mountain and got lost out there. The firefighters found him early this morning.'

'Dead?' Zoran asked, still wary, holding his breath and waiting for my answer.

I nodded. 'No one knows exactly what happened. He was buried down a sink hole when they found him. There wasn't a mark on him to show how he died.'

'Poor boy,' he said after a long, piercing stare. 'He was a good kid. I'll miss him.'

They were formulaic words, without any emotional content – no shock, no curiosity. Even when Zoran promised me that he would help the family any way he could, there was nothing I could identify, except perhaps a silent satisfaction that it had all worked out the way he'd planned.

Zoran's next move was to contact Lewis, who had been quick to confirm with Ricki Suarez that the dead kid was Oliver Knight and had come straight back to the barn.

'Come over to the studio,' Zoran instructed down the phone. 'Send Callum here to the house. Tell him Tania's here, looking for Jude.'

And Daniel, I thought, though of course I didn't admit

246

this. I kept expecting, maybe even hoping to bump into him any moment, or better still, for Daniel to hear that I was around and come looking for me.

I also expected to run into Grace and Ezra, but my feelings here were even more mixed. I didn't know if I could stand the tension of seeing my old friend in one of her manic, elated phases; or else bewildered, sad and scared like a little girl lost in a fairy-tale forest – the one where the stepmother wants to have her secretly killed and put in a pie then fed to her father. Or did I make up that gruesome stuff? Anyway, I mean that I thought of Grace these days as a child in the grip of something evil – the spellbound kid with the splinter of ice in his eye in *The Snow Queen* may be a better comparison.

In any case, Zoran trusted me with the Warhols as he made arrangements then left the house by the main door and I stayed where I was until Callum and Jude came to find me.

'Hey, Tania.' In fact, Callum showed up alone. Like all of the personnel at Black Eagle Lodge, he was exceptionally laid back, never out of jeans and T-shirt unless in costume for one of the big events. Now, as I looked up from an art magazine left on Zoran's coffee table, he struck me as easily hot enough for a lead role in a long-running TV show about doctors rather than the real thing.

'Where's Jude?' I asked with a note of panic in my voice. 'Is he still sick?'

'Take it easy,' Callum advised. 'It's true he wasn't in good shape when he got here – it was a bad attack. But I knew his history so I gave him intravenous medication – a shot to help him breathe.'

'So he's OK?' I was looking beyond Callum, still hoping that Jude would be following.

'I sent him to the hospital to get checked out by his own physician.'

'You didn't let him drive?' I protested.

'What kind of doctor would I be?' he smiled. 'No, Cristal drove him there. Take it easy, Tania – Jude is going to be OK.'

'Thanks,' I gasped, taking a deep breath. 'So Cristal – she hasn't heard the news about Oliver?'

'That poor kid.' Just like his boss, Callum seemed to say the words without meaning them. 'I knew he suffered from depressive episodes and he was pretty close to the edge when he arrived here. Actually, I prescribed medication to help him.'

'What are you saying?'

'We see his type a lot. Kids who don't relate well to their peer group – lonely, lost individuals without too many social skills. They drop out of the mainstream and gravitate to charismatic figures like Zoran. There was a serious case of hero-worship going on there.'

'Which you didn't discourage.' I grew angry and I let it show. 'In fact, I'd say that you guys work hard at getting people like Oliver to stay here. The parties and those celebrations in the chapel. They turn a lot of heads; it happened with Grace, Oliver and I would guess a whole lot more.'

'Oh, Tania,' Callum sighed. 'Why not come clean about what's bugging you? You believe we're creating a cult here, that we brainwash people, don't you?'

'The thought had crossed my mind,' I muttered, though the second he brought it out into the open it began to look flaky and absurd.

'Yeah, it's how a lot of people view us, so what's new? It's something Zoran has learned to live with over the years – accusations about his motives, the bad effect he has on his fans. He's studied the Michael Jackson phenomenon and he knows his enemies won't let this stuff drop. By the way, Tania, did you take my advice about seeing a neurologist?'

So here I was, suddenly wrong footed again, just like on the tennis court when Holly sends a sly passing shot down the line and I'm stretching wildly for a return. 'Actually, I looked it up on the Internet,' I muttered.

'And?'

'I didn't follow it through. I've been totally fine since then, thanks.'

'Yeah, because you didn't encounter any flashing lights. That's the trigger with photosensitive epilepsy, remember.' Just then Callum's phone rang and he answered it. 'Hey, Daniel . . .'

I heard the name and took a sharp breath, listened on.

'. . . Good job,' Callum said. 'You brought them all back? Cool. Is Zoran with you?'

The talk went on and I gathered that Daniel had been out on Black Rock to round up the runaway mustangs. None had been injured and they were presently being led into their feed stalls. I also heard that the smoke from the Forest Service fireline was dispersing and all was well.

'Did Zoran tell you about the kid?' Callum asked Daniel as I faked an interest in the art magazine while drinking in every syllable of the conversation. 'The Forest Service guys stretchered him off the mountain. They'll deal with the family, so we don't have to. Yeah, I guess the cops will want to check it out. There'll be an autopsy to establish cause of death.'

I was busy pretending to study a reproduction of a Brancusi sculpture and my vision took me by surprise.

There was the usual supernatural warning – a hot, suffocating blast of air – then the voice.

'*Come with me.*' *The woman in my dreams reaches out her hand to a slender, fair-haired kid. She is kind. She offers to lead him off Black Rock, away from the towering smoke and flames. I see her face more clearly. She has hazel eyes with heavy lids, rose-pink lips and softly curling fair hair. She reaches out but the blond kid doesn't respond. He walks past her through the drifting smoke towards other, darker and more sinister figures waiting further up the mountain.*

Tuned into my waking dream – or whatever you want to call it – I blanked the cool, uncaring talk between Callum and Daniel.

'Daniel says hi,' Callum told me as he came off the phone. 'And Zoran said you should talk with Grace while you're here.'

'Sure!' I jumped at the chance. Even though Jude had failed in his mission, it seemed I was being given the chance to speak for him.

'She's by the pool. Do you know your way?'

I nodded. Up in the elevator, out through the main door and down on to the terrace, where I'd stood with Daniel and he'd told me about the sun setting behind Carlsbad, with his arm around my waist, close enough to feel his breath on my cheek. 'Does Grace know Jude was here?' I checked.

Callum was already on his way out of the room ahead of me. 'Why don't you ask her? I have to go now, Tania, but you take your time, OK?'

So he strode off down the corridor and disappeared into one of the side rooms, leaving me to find Grace.

I dealt with the elevator and the automatic doors, hit daylight, dipped into my pocket for my sunglasses, put them on and made my way on to the pool terrace.

The sun was shining and there was music playing – the fast, hard-hitting track called 'You Don't Know Me'. 'You don't know me though you see my face/ My name is lost in time and space.' There was a row of empty loungers down either side of the bright-blue pool. A white robe was flung over one at the near end, one corner trailing in the water – typical Grace. She herself was in the pool at the infinity edge, looking out over the mountains.

'Grace!' I called. My stomach tightened to see her so close to the edge.

'Hey!' She twisted round, saw me and waved, started swimming towards me. 'Did you bring your swimsuit?'

'No. Come and talk to me.' I picked up a towel ready to hand it to her, noticing how skinny she'd become, how her ribs showed and her always slim hips were now positively bony.

Grace wrapped the towel around her shoulders and shook out her wet hair.

'Good to see you,' she told me. 'I hoped you'd come back to visit.'

I nodded, decided not to mention Jude yet. 'How have you been?'

'Good. I missed you after the celebration. It was my big day and I wanted you to share it with me.' She took another towel from a neatly stacked pile and wrapped it turban-style round her head. Then she sat on one of the loungers. 'Come sit. Didn't you think the whole thing – the chapel, the music, the dancing – was so cool?'

'I was scared for you,' I confessed. 'I didn't even know what you were celebrating.'

'Just being here!' she sighed. 'I'd made my decision to stay on with Ezra. That's a big deal. The celebration is Zoran's way of saying welcome.'

'So that's it?' I stared in disbelief, recalling with a shudder Zoran's satanic power-fest in the chapel. 'No going back.'

Grace smiled and nodded. 'It's my best decision ever. I'm so happy here. Ezra is amazing and he totally loves me.'

'So what do you do all day?' I was still staring at her, watching for any expression or movement to suggest this wasn't the paradise she was describing.

'I live, I breathe, I do whatever Ezra wants to do. Sometimes we walk on the mountain, sometimes we study.'

'What do you study?'

'History, philosophy, religion.' She kept her answers brief and they seemed to me deliberately vague. There was a small shrug, a moment when her hand flew nervously to her cheek. Then she resumed her bright smile.

'And who's your teacher?'

'Ezra. He's a psychology major.'

'Yeah, I heard.' I interrupted, not knowing where I was headed, only that my time was limited. 'Listen, Grace, I don't understand how you got here.'

'Because you refuse to listen,' she said simply, with a sigh that was full of regret.

'How you got here to this place in your life where you make this big decision to cut yourself off and step across into a world none of us knows anything about.' Ignoring her sorrowful gaze, I ploughed on. 'All I know is – and I've told you before – you're hurting people.'

She frowned, stroked her cheek, turned her head away

and when she spoke, it was in a flat, detached tone. 'Tania, I've tried to explain.'

'No! You've spouted stuff about moving planets around and changing the weather . . . daring to believe, but that doesn't justify what you're doing to your parents, to Jude.'

'Every time you come here I tell you not to mention that name,' she warned, picking up the robe and drawing it around her then walking the length of the pool.

I followed her to the infinity edge. The mountains were misty blue, the sheer drop at our feet terrifying. 'Jude came here to find you today.'

Grace didn't react to my news.

'You don't know me though you see my face.' The track played insistently. 'My name is lost in time and space.'

'Grace, we don't know anything about these people, but every time I come here something bad happens – something weird and twisted. And it's not just me. Ask Holly, she'll tell you the same thing.'

'I knew Holly would never understand,' Grace sighed, turning to me with the same sad look. 'The doors in her mind are all shut tight. But you, Tania – I hoped you would get it.'

'I try, I honestly do. But it is just so scary. Things

happen to me when I'm here; my brain stops making sense of what I see.'

'Because you won't open your mind,' she sighed.

'No. I see things – inanimate objects – move without anyone touching them. I get pains in my hands; I lose things – my necklace for instance. I go dizzy and black out. Worst of all, people change shape, turn into creatures that don't exist. Do you understand what I'm saying?'

'And why does that scare you?'

'Because it can't be real,' I cried. I got the usual feeling of wanting to grab her by the wrists, to drag her out of here back into reality and make her safe. 'You talk to me about moving planets around the universe – show me, show me!'

'We don't have to do that. We have nothing to prove,' she replied calmly. 'Ezra says that those without the courage to join us don't matter. All that matters is that *we* know it's true.'

I shook my head at the catch-22 and changed track. 'So, Jude,' I went on. 'What happened to the feelings you had for him? Don't you care what you did to him?'

Grace's eyes widened, she spread her palms upwards. 'What did I do? How am I responsible for the way Jude chooses to react to my moving on?'

Ouch, ouch and ouch! 'He's sick, Grace, and getting

sicker. He practically risked his life to find you today. Don't you even care?'

'Nobody told me he was here,' she said with the first break in her voice – the one I was looking for.

I seized my chance. 'Of course they didn't! The last thing they want is for you to meet the guy who truly loves you, has loved you for two whole years and will do anything to get you back. Are you still listening to me, Grace? Am I finally getting through?'

'Where's Jude now?' she whispered with tears in her eyes.

At last, a glimpse of the old, empathetic Grace. 'He had an asthma attack. Cristal drove him to the hospital.'

As she closed her eyes, the tears brimmed over and trickled down. 'I didn't know that.'

'He was here – literally here – and they didn't tell you. How does that make you feel? What does it tell you about what these people are trying to do to you?'

She swayed and took a step closer to the edge.

'And Oliver – did you hear what they did to him? He died, Grace. He had a major breakdown then he walked out of here and he died on the mountain. And guess what – they don't even care!'

'No! They— *We're* not responsible!' she cried. 'People choose their own courses of action.'

'So Oliver wasn't brave enough and that's why he died?'

She nodded, choked back the tears and stepped away from the edge. 'It's down to you, what you choose to believe, Tania. I was hoping I could explain, but obviously it's going to take more time.'

'*You* wanted to convert *me*?' I gasped, following her back down the side of the pool and laughing at the irony of the situation. Only this wasn't funny and my old Grace was disappearing fast. 'Won't you meet with Jude? Please – just once!'

She kept her head turned away, looked up and saw Ezra coming down the steps to join us. Quickly she dipped her hand into the pocket of her robe. 'I found something that belongs to you,' she said quietly, handing it to me without letting Ezra see. 'I know it means a lot.'

I glanced down and saw my gold cross nestling in the palm of my hand, glinting gold and red. I closed my fingers over it and thanked her.

'I found it on the floor of the chapel,' she whispered. 'Don't tell Ezra I gave it back.'

So Grace had a secret too – a tiny doubt, an area of mistrust. It was the one hope I still held out for her as I said goodbye, left Black Eagle Lodge and made my way back down to Bitterroot.

# 11

I walked down from Black Rock at the same time as Zoran rose above it. At least, it was his private helicopter taking off from the helipad and so I assumed that he was in it, rising into the sky and gazing down on us mere mortals crawling like ants across the landscape. The force of the churning blades flattened the feathery grass, a wind whipped through the silver aspens as the machine gained height and banked off to the south.

I pictured Zoran at the controls, a co-pilot at his side, swooping off the mountain into the valley below. And a heavy weight lifted. I felt I could breathe easier now that he was gone.

'Hey, you found crucifix!' were Dad's first words when I went into the house.

I'd hung the family heirloom back on its gold chain, next to Orlando's heart, soon after Grace had smuggled it from her pocket into my palm. It felt cool and smooth at my throat, back where it belonged.

Dad's next words, spoken emphatically and with a serious expression, were, 'Facebook news. Come see.'

So I followed him into his small office at the back of the house and waited while he clicked on to an exchange in Romanian with a friend listed as Dr Stefan Bibesco.

'Who's this doctor guy?' I asked.

'Cousin,' Dad replied, busy finding the right click to translate the entries into English for me. 'Father's sister's kid. Works at Spitalul de Urgenta Floreasca in Bucharest. The Emergency Hospital. Now read.'

I stooped to read the screen.

Hey, Stefan, Dad had begun. Long time no speak. Say hi to your father, mother and sisters. Hope all is good with you. Do you still work in the Floreasca hospital? If so, I want to ask you a few questions.

Hey, Andrey, came the reply. Look who crawled out of the woodwork! How is life in the US? How are Karen and Tania? And yes, I'm still at the clinic, overworked and underpaid. Anyway, feel free and ask away.

OK, Stefan. The question goes back a couple of years. You remember when big star Zoran Brancusi smashed up his

Porsche and came to your hospital? Were you on duty that day? Do you recall any medical details?

I stood back and exchanged glances with Dad. 'What are you up to?' I asked.

'Read!' he insisted.

Unexpected line of questioning, Andrey – Sure. I was there. Crash happened on mountain road. They airlifted Brancusi out of there – multiple injuries to skull, spine and internal organs. X-rays of head and full body scan, then emergency surgical procedure to release build-up of pressure from bleeding inside the skull. Why do you ask?

Thanks for the detailed reply, Stefan. Recently Brancusi came to live in America. He built a home near us – did you know?

I read about it. How do you like your new neighbour?

Not a whole lot. But here's my main question – what happened in the operating theatre? And how come there were rumours that he died?

More than rumours, Andrey. The surgeon, Mihail Cantemis, is a friend of mine. The bleed out into the brain was massive, and there were other complications. Cantemis told me they lost the heartbeat then attempted to resuscitate for thirty-five minutes before they finally declared Brancusi dead.

I shook my head, reread this part at least three times: they finally declared Brancusi dead.

Dad had sent one last Facebook message: Hey, Stefan. So what exactly are we talking about here? Was this a medical miracle, or what?

And my Romanian relative came back with one more enlightening reply: Immediately on declaration of death, corpse was taken by a member of Brancusi's personal staff in helicopter to private clinic. Any miracle performed took place there.

But I tell you, at Floreasca we were more shocked than anyone by the reports that he was still alive. In medical terms it was considered impossible – the guy who left our operating table had definitely bled out. His lungs, his heart, his brain, had ceased to function. End of story.

I sat down at Dad's desk and put my head in my hands. 'Oh my God!'

'I know. Wasn't end of story, was it? This guy on mountain came back from dead.'

'Dad, don't! I can't handle it.' I was shaking all over, feeling dizzy and my palms were clammy with sweat. 'There has to be some explanation, some technique they didn't try in the main hospital.'

'Such as?'

'I don't know – freezing the body until they found a

specialist surgeon who could stop the bleeding into the brain. Cryonics or whatever.'

'We can send man to moon but not deep-freeze whole human being and bring back to life again, not yet.'

'OK. What about keyhole techniques? A neurosurgeon? They can do amazing things.'

'Lungs, heart, brain – all dead,' Dad insisted.

I breathed out loudly, emitting something that sounded like a groan. 'So who is the Zoran on Black Rock? Is he a double?'

'Secret twin,' Dad murmured.

'Or a guy who was prepared to have surgery to change his face and look like Zoran. There are plastic surgeons who would do that.'

'But why?'

'To fool everybody into thinking that a rock star, an actor, a politician, a world leader is still alive. If you have enough money, I'm sure you can do it.' I was clutching at straws, trying to find a reasonable scenario, but inside I was riddled with fear. Who or what exactly was the guy on Black Rock with all the power and the Satan-complex, with the ability to make you think you were crazy whenever you visited?

'So they make Zoran double so he can make more records, sing more concerts?'

'Yes,' I insisted. 'He's a cash cow; he can still earn them millions.'

'But Zoran stopped singing, remember.' Dad leaned over my shoulder to log off and I watched the screen go blank. 'He didn't make more records.'

'Then he's a ghost,' I sighed. 'He's something supernatural, and let's stop right now because I don't even want to go there!'

That night I couldn't sleep, of course. I lay awake and heard the woman's voice, felt her spine-tingling presence in my room.

*'Sleep,' she sighs. Her fingers brush my forehead.*

I gasped then held my breath, felt myself melt and become one with the child who had died.

*The walls of my room are pink, stencilled with lilac butterflies – a baby girl's nursery. There is the scent of soap, the tinkling of a mobile toy above my bed.*

*'Go to sleep,' the woman murmurs as she leans in to stroke my cheek.*

*I lie until the sun rises and shines through the slats of the blind, wrapped in silence and love.*

'Did you sleep well?' Mom asked when I went down for breakfast. Obviously Dad had told her his cousin's news from the Bucharest clinic and she already knew I'd been on the mountain when they discovered Oliver Knight's body, so she was on edge as she cooked bacon, watching me like a hawk.

'Actually, yes!' I said.

'No nightmares?' She flipped the bacon from the pan on to a plate, put it between two slices of bread and handed Dad his usual start to Sunday.

'No. My dreams were good for a change.'

'Glad to hear it.' Her hand trembled as it hovered over the loaf of bread, knife in hand. She doesn't express her anxieties, she bottles them up. That's the problem with my mom.

In this way she and Orlando are pretty similar – great when the going is good, but distant and withdrawn when it gets rocky. I guess it's why she hasn't especially warmed to him.

'What did I do?' Orlando asked me after he'd come to the house on his mountain bike and we'd set off for the lake together. His face and arms were tanned, his hair newly washed. One quick glance and I knew just why I adored him. I gave myself a short lecture – remember this, OK? Don't let Daniel happen!

'Nothing. What do you mean?' I said.

'Karen hardly talked to me the whole time I was there.'

'That was because Dad was too busy telling you about his cousin in Bucharest and Zoran's rising-from-the-dead trick. Mom couldn't get a word in edgeways.'

'So it's not that she doesn't think I'm good enough for her daughter and she wishes I'd get the hell out of your life?' he quipped.

'Ha-ha, no. Don't exaggerate.'

'I'm not. Your mom is one scary lady, did you know?'

We cycled for a while in silence. 'I could talk to her, ask her to be nice,' I suggested.

'No thanks, I can handle it.' Picking up speed, Orlando zigzagged across the narrow track then carried out a tricky one-wheeled manoeuvre as if he needed to boost his macho image.

'Stop – I'm impressed already!' I laughed. 'Did you finish reading about Coco Chanel?'

'Yeah. And I got a date for an interview.'

'When?' This was big news, dropped in like a small pebble hardly breaking the surface.

'End of this week. Friday the twentieth.'

'Why didn't you tell me?'

'I just did.' Back by my side and cycling sensibly, his blown-back hair and rosy cheeks made him look younger. 'I heard yesterday, but you've been busy.'

'I know, I'm sorry. You should have texted.'

'No signal on Black Rock, remember.' He rode ahead again, head down, staring at the dirt track.

Here was an ego that needed massaging, I realized, so I cycled hard to join him. 'I'm happy for you – you know that. And you'll be great at the interview, with your fabulous portfolio and all the theory to back it up. They're so going to want you!' Inside, part of me was thinking, So ask me how it was to identify a dead body! Ask me what a corpse looks like and explain how it feels. I'll tell you – scared, shook up, confused; coming up against Death face to face.

'Yeah well, I'll still be nervous,' he confessed. 'I fly out to Dallas Thursday.'

'Cool. I can drive you to the airport.'

'Mom already offered,' he cut in before I'd finished. 'You don't mind about that, do you?'

'No, it's cool,' I lied. OK, so if you don't want to talk dead bodies, at least ask me how Jude is. He is your buddy as well as mine! 'I called the Medinas,' I said. 'This morning, early.'

'How's Jude?'

Result at last! We'd reached the edge of Turner Lake where a few fishermen's vehicles were parked and we got off our bikes and leaned them against a fire-hazard warning notice. I slid my arm around his waist. 'He's in hospital. They kept him overnight again.'

'Yeah, I bet the Medinas really love you, taking him up Black Rock.'

I stepped away and frowned. Why are you doing this to me? Why are you blaming me and making me feel bad? 'I didn't take him – he took me. And we didn't know the Forest Service would be up there digging firelines until the smoke started coming down the mountain.'

'Bad timing.'

'Very. And you're right – Dr and Mrs Medina made it clear they didn't want me to help Jude try and contact Grace again.'

'No one wants anyone going near Zoran's place until the cops clear up the body-in-the-sink-hole story,' Orlando pointed out. 'They think it's linked to bad stuff that goes on up there, and who can blame them?'

'I know. Imagine how the Montroses must look at it.' This lakeside conversation was making me feel like I was engaged in an awkward ballroom dance where neither of us quite knew the steps and the rhythm was jerky and slow. We'd covered the topics of Oliver and Jude without showing a glimpse of how we really felt. 'I'm sorry, I can't do this any more!' I faltered and turned away.

'What?' Orlando stepped round in front of me, caught me by the arm. 'What, Tania? What can't you do?'

'I need you to ask me how I'm doing,' I cried. 'I can't bear it when you push me away.'

'Because!' he said, staring fiercely at me. 'Because you went up the mountain without telling me, why do you think? And because that guy, Daniel, lives up there! How do you think that makes *me* feel?'

'I sometimes figure it would be better to be alone.'

This pearl fell from Holly's lips late Sunday afternoon, after I'd spent the whole day telling Orlando that I hadn't even seen Daniel up at the lodge, that the guy meant nothing to me and my only interest in being on the mountain was in connection with Grace. All true, but not the whole truth.

We were sitting in the sun on a lawn by the side of a tennis court, watching the guys play. 'Alone! What makes you say that?' I asked.

'I mean it's tough to be in love,' she pointed out. 'Look at the day you've had.'

'It's been hard work,' I sighed. 'I've been tying myself in knots trying to convince my boyfriend that I love him.'

'Sometimes,' she went on after the longest pause, 'I think it's not love but fear.'

'Fear of what?'

'Of *being* alone. That's what we're all scared of, isn't it? Of being left out, not chosen, feeling nobody wants us.'

'I guess,' I sighed. Orlando was playing well. He was partnering Leo and they were beating Aaron and a kid called Nathan, who was Leo's cousin from out of town. Nathan was the type who looked like he'd grown six inches in a year – all wrists and elbows, bony knees and ankles. He looked as if a strong wind would knock him flat. 'Terror of being alone. So that's why I'm fighting for my relationship with Orlando?'

Holly lay back on the grass, her arms behind her head. 'I hate that moment when Aaron and I split – each time it happens, and it happens a lot. He storms off, or I walk out on him and I have a split second where I feel I've lost my grip, I'm falling off the edge of the world, I'm yelling, "Help!" and no one hears me. I'm alone. But later, when you get a distance and you start to think it through, it feels like it might not be so bad.'

Nathan reached an overhead lob from Orlando and smashed it back. Orlando had forgotten that the new kid was seven feet tall. Six foot four, actually.

'There'd be no more compromises,' Holly insisted. 'And I'd be my own boss again.'

'Free?'

270

'Yeah – so maybe we should all give up on love and get on with everything else,' she sighed. She turned her head towards me and squinted through the glare of the sun. 'Why don't we?'

'Because we can't.' I watched Orlando throw the ball high, swing his racket behind his back then bring it up and over for a crashing serve. Poetry in motion.

'Because we love them.' Holly came full circle and we laughed and put the philosophical stuff to one side. 'So did Orlando believe you when you told him Daniel means nothing to you?'

'I don't know. I tried everything.' Reasoned argument, tears, kisses – and the rest.

Holly raised one hand and tried to put it over my mouth. 'Too much information,' she said quickly. 'And is it true?' she demanded, sitting up and wrapping her tanned arms around her knees. 'Daniel is just a guy who has the hots for you but there's nothing in you that returns the compliment?'

'Exactly,' I told her. Orlando and Leo had won the set. All four boys were walking off the court towards us. 'He knows I love Orlando. I made that absolutely clear.'

Try talking to a guy about the way he feels and you get awkward silence, or "I'm hungry. What shall we eat?"

Give him a scientific conundrum and he'll happily spend an hour over it.

'So how can Zoran be pronounced dead in the hospital then resuscitated in a private clinic?' I asked over cold drinks in the clubhouse. And I explained what Stefan Bibesco had told my dad.

'You're sure you got your facts straight?' Leo checked. He was wearing his version of tennis gear – baggy white shorts, a vest top and a black bandanna with a death's-head motif.

'The guy's my dad's cousin. He was on duty at the Floreasca, plus he's best buddies with the surgeon who worked on Zoran.'

'But you know how these rumours spread.' Right away Aaron showed his boy colours. 'Plus there's the language barrier.'

'My dad's first language is Romanian,' I reminded him. 'There was no doubt: the doctors gave up on him and signed over the body.'

'Maybe they missed something,' Leo said, assuming the scientific position. 'A patient with bleeding into the brain cavity can go into a deep coma. It can look like he's brain dead.'

Our jaws dropped in mock amazement then Holly quizzed him and it turned out he'd read an article in *USA Today*. In such cases they keep the patient artificially unconscious for weeks until the bleeding and the swelling stop.

'So the Floreasca guy made the wrong call.' Aaron talked as if Leo had nailed it. 'Lucky for Zoran, his guys took him to the right place. They saved his life.'

'Yeah, he does have a medical guy on his team,' Holly told them. 'Maybe he was the one Zoran has to thank.'

I realized that neither Orlando or I had contributed and at this point I caught his eye. He looked stonily back at me as he stood up. 'Who cares?' he muttered, swinging his heavy bag on to his shoulder. 'Honestly – I liked this town a whole lot better before Zoran Brancusi ever built his place on Black Rock. Who cares about this crap? Not me. I'm out of here.'

Back at home, alone in my room, my phone rang and when I saw it was from Daniel I let it ring out.

He texted me straight after. Tania, please pick up. Will call again.

I put down my phone and stared at it like an unexploded grenade. I had it on silent, so when it began to vibrate I jumped for cover and let it ring out a second time. But on the third attempt my nerve broke and I answered.

'Tania?' His voice sounded calm, though my own heart was thumping.

'Hey, Daniel.'

'I thought for a moment there I must have hurt your feelings by not saying hi yesterday.'

'No, you didn't.' Thump-thump-thump – just his voice was enough to do this to me.

'There was the crisis with the mustangs, remember. I had my hands pretty full.'

'I know. It doesn't matter – really.'

'Anyhow, it worked out. We rounded them all up, no problem. Actually, I've just been working in the arena with Zoran's sorrel mare. She's doing good. So how are you?'

'I'm cool.'

'The smoke didn't bother you? I heard Jude wasn't so lucky.'

'No. He had another attack.'

'Cristal told me. That's partly why I'm calling you.'

'Sorry, I haven't been able to visit him so I can't update you. His parents—'

'No, that's not what I mean. I'm actually calling to update *you* on his condition. Cristal just came from the hospital. He knew you'd be worried so he told her to tell you he's doing OK.'

'Cristal?' I echoed. 'Oh, OK. Cool, thanks.' Of course she would want to visit him, I told myself. She was the one who drove him down from Black Rock. It was just that somehow I didn't see her as the angel of mercy type.

'Well, I told her I'd pass on the message because there was something else I wanted to talk to you about.'

Before he could go any further, I leaped in. 'Look, Daniel, if you're going to ask me to meet up again, I really can't – OK?'

There was a short silence then, 'That's not what I planned to say. Actually, this isn't about you and me, it's about your experience with the fire team.'

'Sorry, I shouldn't have . . .' Shouldn't have assumed anything, shouldn't have put both big feet in it, should have bitten my tongue right off before I'd made such a fool of myself!

'No, that's OK. It's Orlando's feelings you're protecting. It's difficult for you – I understand. So anyway, Oliver.'

'Yeah, Oliver – sorry.'

'No need to apologize, honestly, Tania. The cops came by earlier today. A guy called Sheriff Hanson and his sidekick.'

'And?'

'They're still waiting for autopsy reports, but they

contacted Oliver's parents – actually, his mom. His dad is off the scene, travelling somewhere – Thailand or Cambodia. His mom took the news badly. Oliver was her only son. The sheriff told her they're not currently treating the thing as suspicious, depending on further reports – toxicology, blood tests, et cetera.'

'What does that mean – they don't think anyone else was involved?'

'Right. The cops think the poor kid had a freak accident up there on Black Rock, which is what we said all along. An accident, pure and simple. Since you were the one who identified the body, Zoran and I . . . we thought you'd like to know.'

'Yes – thanks. Really, thanks, Daniel.'

There was another silence – a little longer this time. 'So you'll call me?' he asked. 'If you hear any more news on the cause of death from your end.'

'Oh, yeah, for sure – I definitely will.'

'And if you and Orlando . . . Tania, if you ever want that coffee and someone to talk to—'

'Thanks – bye!' I said quickly. I pressed the button; end of call, but found no button in my brain that said Delete. Oh no, Daniel stayed right there in pole position with his Formula One voice and brilliant steering, easily outmanoeuvring all the opposition.

* * *

That night we had a freak storm. A warm wind came in from the east, hit the cooler mountain air and produced the whole summer spectacular – brooding blue clouds over the Bitterroot peaks that rolled down the valleys bringing lightning, thunder and blast after blast of cold rain. I lay in bed watching forks of lightning crack open the sky, waiting for the roll of thunder and hearing raindrops batter against my window pane, and just as I was picturing what it must be like to be out on Black Rock in this kind of storm, my special voice began to whisper.

'*Aimee, don't cry. It's only a storm. I'm here. I won't let it harm you.*'

I half wanted to block it out. The wild storm had already spooked me and I wasn't ready to take on board more messages from beyond the grave. Then again, given the current Grace–Ezra–Zoran situation, I totally needed help. So I reluctantly tuned into my voice.

*The wind rattles the window. Down below, a door bangs. The voice sounds a long way off, growing louder.*

'*Baby, baby, don't cry.*' *The woman bends over me, her grey eyes tender.*

*Thunder cracks and rumbles on towards the town. Here on Becker Hill, the wind whips through the aspens, tearing green leaves from the branches. Maia Witney holds me close.*

*Lightning flashes. There's a disconnect, like in a dream. And now I see Maia standing by the window, and there's no infant in the room – only me and her. I blink then stare.*

*She's wearing a sky-blue tunic over jeans, silver hoop earrings, silver bracelets at her wrist. I'm trembling, I can hardly breathe.*

*'Tania, don't be afraid,' she says.*

*My chest tightens. There's another clap of thunder and the rain still batters at the window.*

*'Take my hand,' Maia murmurs. A glow surrounds her – not moon or starlight – it's soft and silver like nothing I've ever seen.*

*I walk towards her, only my feet don't touch the floor. It's as if I'm floating as I take her insubstantial hand.*

*'I've waited so long,' she sighs. Her bracelets jingle as her fingers close over mine. 'Ever since the fire – through the weeks, the months, the years.'*

*I don't ask who she is because I already know. And I have an all-over, tingling sensation, of my body melting away to leave me pure spirit, pure soul. Maia's soft voice fills the room; her silver light shines. 'You must know, Tania, that you exist as two spirits, side by side.'*

*As the boundaries melt, I'm gripped again by fear. I try to withdraw my hand, but she holds me tight.*

'Look inside yourself,' she insists.

I shake my head. 'It's too hard. I don't know if I even want this.'

She gives me a sad look. 'Yet part of you always searches. The part that is Aimee pleads for me to come.'

I let out a sigh. It's true – I am two spirits.

'You see, you are twinned with Aimee. It's how we all continue. We are multiple, layer upon layer.'

Her soft, slow words gradually soothe me. 'That night – the night of the fire, when Aimee died and I was born – that was the moment when this happened?'

She nods and smiles. 'I watched your father raise new timbers in the ashes, heard him work with saw and hammer. I saw you play where my child had played, with your dark hair framing your beautiful face, your eyes flecked with colours of the fall.'

'And what now?' I want to know. I realize we've been building to this through all my childhood dreams and fears.

Maia's mood changes, becomes more urgent as we share her silver light. 'Now you must play your part,' she confides.

'Is this connected with Zoran and all the stuff at Black Rock?'

She nods and suddenly the talk grows cosmic – so much so that, although I've lately begun to expect the unexpected, I'm still shocked by what she tells me.

'Do you believe in evil?' she asks.

Immediately I see in my mind's eye Zoran slither across the chapel floor, his snake eyes gleaming. I see him onstage, spreading his dark-angel wings. 'Yes,' I whisper.

'Then know that the whole universe is a battleground, good versus evil. An army of fallen angels, devils in torment, is ranked against the spirits of light.'

'Like you?' I check. Of course like her – glowing, gentle and good. She doesn't need to reply.

No – what she wants to make me understand is the fallen angel thing. 'They are full of hatred and the desire for revenge. Evil – evil for its own sake – drives them on.'

Evil. I don't know about you, but I don't often use the word. It's too big. Place a 'd' in front of it and 'devil' is what you get. Put into the context of what you see on the news channels, on the streets of your neighbourhood, and it's all the murderers, rapists, assassins, war lords, ticking suicide bombers rolled into one.

The fact is, there's evil wherever you turn and the knowledge terrifies me. I try my best to focus and take in what Maia says.

'We keep up a constant guard,' she explains. 'But sometimes the dark angels pierce the barrier set up to keep them out of this world.'

I take a hard swallow as I imagine shining archangels and

burning devils, their swords clashing and sparking in the dark heavens. Maybe that's how come we see falling stars, comets trailing fiery light. 'You're telling me that this is what happened with Zoran?' I ask.

'Yes. He's cunning and cruel. He forced his way back, hunting for new recruits to swell his devil army.'

'You mean Grace, Oliver . . . me!' I shudder. I'm sick with fear again.

She nods. 'So that one day, when he has claimed enough innocent souls, they – the dark angels – will outnumber the angels of light. They will have ultimate power.'

'And?'

'And then darkness and chaos,' she says simply. 'All light will disappear.'

Apocalypse. I totally see it, and it fits with everything I've seen on Black Rock.

'Summon your strength to fight Zoran,' Maia urges. She touches the crucifix hanging around my neck. Then she steps back.

Devil images dance in the shadows. 'You're leaving!' I realize.

'Think about what I've told you. Arm yourself.'

'Don't go!' I need her here, I can't be alone.

'I'm always with you,' she promises.

And there's no way I can stop her. Her light fades. She's in

281

*the shadows with the devils and angels. Maia's pale, beautiful face is the last part to fade and disappear.*

# 12

*Now I am certain, now I am truly afraid. This is too big for me to handle – a cosmos torn apart by warring spirits, and I'm so small and weak.*

I have my 'why me?' moment, flop down on my bed and cry hot, salty tears.

Monday dawned and life went on – Mom left for another three-day work trip to Europe, Dad went back to supervise the construction project in Utah – but nothing was as normal. *I* wasn't normal. I was a bridge, a channel for good or evil – whichever tried to claim me, a soul twinned with a baby who burned to death in a wildfire and with God knows how many souls before that. Of course, it hadn't taken Maia to appear to me in a halo of soft, supernatural light. Actually, as I say, somewhere deep in my psyche I'd known this all along, ever since the day I was born.

'Tania, you take care, OK?' Mom was concerned as she stood in the hallway with her suitcase. 'And remember, you can reach me by text or call me whenever you want.'

'Thanks, I'm cool.' I attempted a smile but didn't do a good job.

'You're sure you'll be OK alone in the house?'

'Totally.'

'So call me.'

'I'm OK. Now, go!'

She wheeled her bag to her car, turned and smiled tentatively back at me. 'Did you and Orlando have a fight?' she asked.

'No. Go!' I waved and made as if to close the door.

'Something's wrong. What is it?'

'Nothing. I'm good. Leave now or you'll miss your plane.'

She looked at me a long time. The usual working-mom thoughts went through her head, I knew. Should I stay and take care of my daughter? What do I tell my boss? Tania's not a kid any more – leave her to sort out her own life. Something's not right – I know it. All the familiar torn-apart feelings.

'Bye!' I insisted.

Mom sighed then waved and got in the car. She drove

away. I felt more scared than I had ever been in my life.

Zoran was evil. I had the evidence for it now. He was a devil from hell, exploding back into the material world on his dark, destructive mission in which he was obviously succeeding – first Oliver, next Grace, and who knows who would be after that . . . me or Jude, or someone I hadn't thought of yet? Anyway, we were all in his grasp; innocent victims ready to swell that dark cosmic army of fallen angels.

And how come I hadn't been ready to see this clearly before now, from the moment when he appeared on stage at the Heavenly Bodies party with his angel wings and evil expression, gliding, whirling, singing?

I remembered how he'd been, up there under the flashing lights. How tall and wiry he was, how scary with his shaven skull and plume of black feathers, his intense gaze. Then there was his bare torso and angel wing tattoo, his satanic wings.

'You spoke my name,' he sang. 'I came/ In the dark, dark valley/ You call my name.'

And we'd been drawn in from that moment – me, Grace and Holly, along with a thousand others. We'd loved the wild thrill of it, the beat of the drums, the whining guitars. 'You don't know me/ You never will.'

Yes, I did – I knew him now for the dark angel he was – shape-shifting, whirling in front of us, preparing to drag us into chaos.

And he'd risen up, levitated in that slash of green light. He was beyond beast, pure evil.

It was Monday and the sun was up as usual. The house was empty.

'Hey, honey. Am flying out to Salt Lake City.' Dad had left me a note on the kitchen table. 'Had to leave early. Looked in while you were sleeping. Said goodbye.'

Oh, I needed him. I needed to hear his solid footsteps coming down the stairs, to know that he was out on the porch, reading about the 1890 massacre of Big Foot and his Miniconjou Lakotas at Wounded Knee.

But there were no footsteps, no thousand-page tome with Dad's unique bookmark slotted in – a laminated picture of me tilting back my head and grinning at the camera when I was five years old and in kindergarten – my first official school photo. The house was empty, uninhabited, and the sun was rising but nothing was as it should be.

I emailed my dad's cousin Stefan in Bucharest. I'd thought it through and decided it was the only practical way forward.

Hi, Stefan. Tania here with a follow up to Dad's query about the Zoran Brancusi mystery. I know – not that old thing again! I guess you all grew sick of answering questions about him. But here's another one for you. Do you recall the name of the guy who took the corpse away from the hospital? I ask because we figure something weird is going on up at Zoran's new place and I'm wondering if the same person is still in the picture – specifically a guy by the name of Ezra, or Lewis, or Daniel. Or possibly even a medic called Callum. Oh, and a girl who goes by the name of Cristal. Do any of these ring a bell? Sorry to bother you, but it's important. Bye for now.

Tania.


I pressed Send and stared at the screen until my phone rang.

'Hey, Tania, where are you?' It was Holly, demanding to know why I wasn't in school.

'I stayed home. I don't feel so good.'

'What is it – stomach cramps, sinus, headache?'

'Yeah,' I sighed.

'Which? Wait, girl – I get it. You had another fight with Orlando.'

'No.'

'He showed me his portfolio. How talented is he!'

'I know.'

'He'll wow them at his interview on Friday, you know that?'

'Yeah. Listen, Holly, I've got to go.'

'OK. I'll drop by after school. You sound like you need someone.'

'Thanks. See you later. Bye.' I ended the call, tried to calculate the time difference between me and Romania, figured it would be late in the day over there. I stared at the screen.

Lunchtime came and went. I closed my laptop, went out on to the porch, stared at the young pine trees and pictured Becker Hill burning. *Yellow flames lick at tall black trunks; they roar up into the canopy. Firebrands leap through the smoke-filled air. Breathe, breathe, go back inside.*

'*I am here,*' Maia murmurs. *A fleeting breath, a reminder.*

When I log on again, there is a message from Stefan.

Hey, Tania. Don't worry, I expected more questions from you or Andrey. I sensed something was wrong and anyhow I love a good mystery as much as the next person. So I checked on the details you asked me about and our hospital records show that the guy who took possession of the body went by the name of

288

Malach. No first name and his signature was kind of scrawly and hard to decipher. No Ezras or Daniels, and definitely not a Cristal. Sorry I can't give you more and I hope this helps in any case. Say hi to the rest of your family, Love, Stefan.

I typed, Hey, Stefan. This guy, Malach, how did he look?

The answer came right back.

Sorry, Tania – I didn't see him in the flesh. And the record is incomplete – no contact number or address. I'm afraid this is where the trail goes cold. Plus, my bleeper just went – I have to go now. Stefan.

I read and reread the two messages, feeling frustration settle on me and confine me like a straitjacket. However long I stared at the name, Malach meant nothing to me. I thought so long and hard that the letters seemed to shift and twist under my gaze. What to do now, I wondered.

It wasn't much of an answer, but I drove down to the hospital to visit Jude.

I guess I thought I would warn him about Cristal. Stick to plain facts, I told myself as I parked my car. Don't get into angels and devils – he'll think you're crazy. Tell him Cristal uses guys then dumps them. Remember what happened to Oliver and how fast she moved on? It proves she has no conscience.

I'd hoped Dr and Mrs Medina wouldn't be bedside when I arrived but there they were, fussing over their son, packing his bag and getting ready to leave.

Dr Medina was crouched beside Jude, helping him on with his shoes. He looked up at me as I stood in the doorway. 'OK, Tania, that's as far as you get.'

'Look, I'm sorry but it wasn't my fault. I didn't mean for Jude to get sick,' I said. 'He was the one who wanted to go up Black Rock – it was his idea.'

Jude stooped to put on his own shoes. His dad frowned then straightened up, deliberately ignoring me.

Mrs Medina zipped the overnight bag closed. 'I believe you,' she told me. In her own mind she had everything clearly worked out. 'This was probably the result of Jude's obsession with the Montrose girl. We warned him she was no good for him way back, and now look what's happened. Not only does Grace ditch Jude without any explanation but within hours she's moved on to some hippie dropout living in a mountain commune.'

'Jude?' I said, doing my best not to react. 'How are you doing?'

'Good,' he grunted. He was thinner than ever, his features shadowed and drawn. And I noticed that he avoided looking me in the eye. 'They gave me a new type of antibiotic, plus a different type of inhaler – what can I say?'

'He is not doing well!' Dr Medina stepped in. 'Can't you see? Now, if you don't mind, Tania, we'll just get him out of here and home safe before we have another incident.'

I always knew the Medinas were overprotective but I'd never seen them in overdrive before. They were acting like Jude was five years old, for Christ's sake. 'Jude?' I said again. And if I thought the situation was already bad, it was about to get worse.

'Ready?' Mrs Medina asked, literally pushing me aside. She was out of the room and in the corridor when Cristal arrived.

My mouth fell open – I couldn't help it.

'Hey, Jude.' Cristal's smile was all for him. She ignored everyone else completely.

His face lit up in response. 'Hey,' he said softly.

Here she was in his room, dressed in her usual green – this time in a close-fitting top that was a subtle shade of jade, plus tight blue jeans and black, heeled boots. Her flame-red hair was tied back and she wore dangling silver earrings.

'Thanks for calling me to let me know they were ready to discharge you,' she murmured as her long fingers brushed his shoulder.

'Thanks for driving me down here to begin with and saving my life,' he countered, his smile softening his face and making him look more like his old self. It was clear to everyone that he couldn't take his eyes off her.

'Jude, your mom's waiting,' Dr Medina reminded him stiffly.

'It's OK, you two go ahead,' Jude replied without tearing the direction of his glance away from Cristal. 'This is my ride home. That's why I called Cristal – so I could thank her and ask her to drive me home.'

'Sure thing, and I'll bring him back safe,' she promised the Medinas. Those full, smiling lips, those green eyes, that pale, smooth skin also held other unspoken promises.

For once Dr Medina was silenced. Even he could see the attraction.

'He doesn't need you to drive him home,' Mrs Medina argued. 'We're here to do that.'

'I'll ride with Cristal,' Jude said firmly.

Oh, I'd seen that goofy look, those doting eyes before – on Oliver Knight when he was sitting by the pool across the table from the beautiful, the adorable, the magnetically attractive Cristal.

She carried on smiling through the glowering expressions of the parents. 'So glad you're well again,' she told Jude. She took his hand and held it, leaned forward to brush his cheek with her lips.

And how could I warn him now? Now that he was holding Cristal's hand and he was spellbound once more?

'So quick bright things come to confusion.'

I stepped aside to let them out of the room, glanced at the Medinas and followed Jude and Cristal down the corridor.

'Good to see you, Tania,' Cristal called over her shoulder. 'Why not join us for a cup of coffee?'

I could only see the back of Jude's head so I couldn't tell what he thought about this. And the offer took me by surprise. 'Oh, no, thanks. I'm good.'

'No, really,' she insisted. 'My car is parked by the exit gate. We'll wait for you there.' She gave me no time to object. The parents were marching close behind as she whisked Jude out through the glass doors, and I was sidelined – sandwiched helplessly in between what felt like newly-formed arch-enemies of the Medinas versus Cristal.

So I did look for her by the gate, waved when I saw

Jude sitting next to her in the passenger seat and slowly followed Cristal's car out of the parking lot, thinking maybe somewhere, somehow I could still warn Jude to stay away, not to have anything to do with anyone connected with Zoran and Black Eagle Lodge.

We drank coffee in a small diner on Bitterroot's Main Street.

*Take care. Be aware of what you're getting into*, guardian Maia whispers in my ear. I look round for a woman dressed in dressed in a sky-blue tunic and jeans. The only other person in Starbucks late on a Monday morning is an unshaven, heavy-set guy in a thick plaid shirt and a grey baseball cap that has once been white.

'So do you still plan on seeing Grace?' I threw Jude a curve ball, hoping that it would drag his attention away from the green-eyed goddess sitting opposite.

He only shrugged and went on staring.

'Jude can see Grace any time he likes,' Cristal said, returning the ball with a curving, spinning, dipping vengeance. 'I talked with her last night and I reckon she's over not wanting to meet with him. In fact, she made it plain she'd be happy to.'

I jerked forward in my seat. Grace wanted to see Jude! 'So what was the problem before now?'

'The usual stuff that happens just after a relationship breaks down. Unresolved issues like who's to blame, who said what to whom and in what circumstances. It takes a little time to process that.'

So now Cristal was part relationship counsellor, part goddess. Christ, did this woman bug me! So much so that I temporarily forgot how dangerous she was. 'It wasn't that Grace was feeling downright guilty for what she did to Jude?' I challenged.

She pressed the tip of her tongue against her teeth and made a small tutting sound. 'We don't know the details,' she reminded me. 'It's impossible to guess what goes on between couples when we're only looking from the outside.'

'That's true.' Jude's hands were wrapped around his mug and his eyes had developed a faraway look. 'In the first place, I should never have let Grace go to Zoran's party alone.'

'But you were sick,' I pointed out. 'That was so not your fault!'

'I let her go without me. I should have said no, stay home with me.'

'Like, that would've worked,' I muttered, thinking of the old, lively, party-loving Grace.

'Yeah, then she would have known I didn't want her

going into any situation where a guy could think she was single and hit on her. I should have made it clear that I cared about her too much to let her do that.'

'Jude, did I hear you right? What century are we living in here?'

'I wasn't strong, I wasn't there for her,' he insisted, his voice fading as he seemed to lose interest in the topic. 'Anyway, it's history.'

'So you still want to see her, or not?'

'Sure he does,' Cristal said for him. And before I spotted the next danger she went straight on. 'Jude, I think you should drive up to the lodge with me right now, right this minute, so you and Grace can get closure.'

'No!' I gasped, standing up and almost spilling my coffee. 'Your folks are expecting you back home. They'll be worried.'

'Send them a text,' Cristal told him, smiling and honey-sweet. 'Come on, let's go.'

'I'll come too,' I said before I had time to think. I was in a panic about what would happen to Jude if I let him out of my sight.

'Cool. I'll drive you both,' Cristal offered, still smiling and sailing serenely on.

All the way along the highway and up the dirt road to

Black Eagle Lodge my heart hammered at my ribs. Cristal's car jolted and rattled over the washboard surface, the tyres kicked up gravel and I stared out of the back seat at a near-vertical drop into the dry gorge below. When a deer leaped out from behind a rock and stood on the track in front of us, that was it – my pounding heart broke free of its cage.

What am I doing? I asked myself. If . . . no, not *if* but *when* . . . things go wrong, how do I get out of this?

Cristal braked hard to avoid the deer, which finally took off into some bushes. I was thrown forward against the back of Jude's seat but I didn't care. At least the squealing tyres masked the sound of my hammering heart.

Now I know how gladiators felt way back, I thought. And at least they had a shield and a sword to protect themselves. What do I have? Nothing!

*You have me*, Maia whispers. *You have me and the cosmic force for good to tap into. I'm here. Don't forget.*

Jude turned to me still with that distant, dreamy look. 'Don't you just love this ride?' he asked. 'This mountain, Prayer River and Turner Lake below, the big sky above? I mean, can't you see exactly why Zoran built Black Eagle Lodge where he did?'

I stared back at him, wondering why he'd suddenly

begun to talk like a realtor. No, not like he was selling the place, but like he was in love with it, like it was paradise. And this was because it was where Cristal lived, I realized. All I could do was try and drag his mind back to the reality of visiting Grace. 'Will Ezra be around when Jude and Grace have their talk?' I asked Cristal. 'Or will he stay away?'

'I'm sure Grace has nothing to hide from Ezra,' she said calmly.

'No but maybe Jude would feel more comfortable if—'

'I don't care who's there,' he interrupted. 'As a matter of fact, Cristal, I want you to be there too.'

'Sure,' she said. 'And, Tania, I know Daniel will be around. We should all six of us get together, have this talk out in the open so everyone is clear about what's going on.'

I went along with the plan because I had no choice. I mean, I'd accepted a ride in Cristal's car; we were driving across the cattle guard into Black Eagle Lodge. The clang of metal as the tyres hit the bars sounded like the cell of a prison door closing.

And Zoran was standing in the yard to greet us, dressed in his usual black T- and jeans, the dome of his skull looking barer than ever though his chin had two days' stubble. Here comes the devil, I reminded myself with a shudder. His two grey lurchers bounded towards us then straight past into the thorn bushes and sage brush.

'Chasing rabbits,' Cristal explained.

I heard the dogs rustle and snuffle unseen.

'Hey, good to see you!' Zoran extended his hand to Jude as we stepped out of the car. Then he looked my way. 'You too, Tania. How's your dad?'

'Good. He's in Utah.' Damn – the question caught me off guard and I gave away a fact when I didn't need to. Be more careful. Don't let him know that I'm home alone.

'My compadre, my Bucharest buddy,' Zoran grinned, shaking my hand and exposing the angel tattoo.

It was a wolfish grin – lean and sharp. I did my best to put aside what Maia had told me and to smile back.

Zoran led the way over to the arena where six or seven mustangs were gathered in a huddle around a feed stall. The horses' heads were down; you could hear their teeth munching and grinding the alfalfa. 'You know they broke free?' he asked me.

'I was here,' I reminded him as I looked around, expecting, maybe hoping for Daniel to walk out of the barn any moment.

'It was definitely the fire they set high on the mountain. The smoke drifted down and panicked the horses.' Zoran was smooth and relaxed, leaning on the fence rail watching the mustangs eat. His dogs emerged from the brush, one with a rabbit hanging limp from its jaws. 'And you, Jude – how are you feeling?'

'Good, thanks.' Jude stuck close to Cristal as if on an invisible leash. He gave her a shy, embarrassed grin – the characteristic smile I'd known from junior school that made him who he was, but it was reserved now for Cristal and no one else.

'We were worried for you. But Callum was here. He always knows what to do.' Bringing the subject to a close, Zoran turned away from the arena, put a hand on my shoulder and walked me towards the house. 'How often does your dad take a trip back home?' he asked me.

'To Bucharest?' I asked. Stay on guard. This time resist the urge to tell too much of the truth.

'Yes. Does he still have family there?'

'Some. He hardly ever goes back though.' We lost the dogs and went through the sliding doors, which opened as if by magic. They closed behind us and we were sealed in.

Zoran looked closely at me and I had the uncomfortable feeling that he knew about today's emails to Stefan. But how could he? Unless he'd hacked into my Facebook messages. But then, *why* would he?

'I'd like to meet your dad,' Zoran said. 'We have a lot in common. Why not let me know when he gets back from the desert?'

We crossed the mirrored, marble hallway, took the elevator and headed down the corridor past the rooms to left and right, walking underground past the row of ethnic masks on the wall. I was developing the uneasy sensation that any second now these walls and ceilings could collapse and bury us alive. I felt a new anxiety, a feeling of ribs being crushed by rock, of lungs emptying. Steady yourself; breathe easy. I glanced round at Jude and Cristal walking silently behind.

'He and I can talk about the old country,' Zoran said pleasantly. 'Does he share your interest in art, Tania? Tell him I have two Brancusi sculptures to show him if he would like.'

And so he chatted, and every step we took I felt more pressurized, more trapped.

'Tania!' We'd reached the big room where Zoran had first received the chosen ones during his party and Daniel was there, standing up from a couch to greet me.

I took a sharp breath, tried to stop my pulse from

racing. He was walking towards me, leaning forward and doing the double European kiss, first one cheek then the other. I felt the scratchiness of his stubble, felt myself melt under his bright-blue gaze.

'Long time, no see.'

I blushed then nodded and tried to picture Maia at my shoulder clothed in her mystical light.

Don't fall for it, I told myself – those dazzling eyes, the clean lines of jaw and cheekbones, the perfect proportions of nose and mouth. But equally, don't let him know that your defences are up. Smile back, play the game.

I remembered what Maia said about the forces of good and evil and devils in torment and tried to bring to mind a picture of Daniel, Zoran, Cristal and the rest fighting their way back from the spirit world, finding their links, claiming innocent souls. But today, right now, they looked so normal, so human in their jeans and Ts, and so beautiful. As I looked at Daniel, my heart fluttered and I felt myself falter.

'Jude decided he still wanted to talk with Grace,' I told him. 'I happened to be there, so I came along too.'

'I understand,' he said quietly. But there was amusement in his eyes, as if we were sharing a joke and he and I both knew I was really here to see him – that I simply couldn't resist.

He shouldn't have done that; the flicker of arrogance annoyed me. I rebuilt my defences.

And then, as Zoran bowed out and left us to it, Grace walked into the room with Ezra.

I was shocked all over again. Wearing a shapeless grey sweater and jeans, with her fair hair hanging limp, she was like the shell of Grace but not Grace. Her face was pale, her eyes big and blank and she moved slowly and stiffly, as if she had to consciously remind her body what to do. I noticed a bruise on her right forearm and a small one on her face, just under her left eye. Ezra shadowed her as she drifted towards Jude.

'You came,' she breathed.

Jude stared at her uncertainly. He glanced at Cristal, who reassured him with her smile, and turned back to Grace. 'You're ready to talk?'

Her eyes widened then flickered shut, opened again. Her pupils were dark and huge, leaving just a rim of grey iris. 'I'm glad you're OK,' she murmured to Jude.

Ezra stood at her shoulder, a dark figure with long, black hair curling against his neck – Grace's dreamcatcher, her jailer.

'I'm fine.' Jude gave a ghost of his usual smile. 'I came to see how you were.'

'Cool,' she whispered.

He checked with Cristal. Was this it? Was there anything left to say?

'It's good that you two can still be friends,' she said easily – too easily. 'No jealousy, no regrets.'

Slowly they both nodded.

'It makes you free to move on. The door opens.'

Daniel took up this piece of wisdom and ran with it, bringing his arm around my shoulder as he spoke. 'Regrets are what hold us back,' he agreed. 'We have to learn that what is past is past. There's no sadness in that, only peace.'

Jude and Grace nodded again. I was fixated on the bruise under her eye, obsessing about how she got it. Had she grown dizzy and fallen? Had she bumped into something? Or had she been hit, by Ezra or someone else? But then I told myself that she didn't look afraid – only vacant.

Empty, not even there any more. I asked myself yet again – where, for Christ's sake, was the sunny, vibrant Grace, the Grace with the touch of vanity, the love of dressing up and partying, my outgoing, golden Grace?

My attention switched from the bruise to her dark, expressionless eyes. Drugs! Briefly I thought again about Rohypnol, cocaine, heroin and, though I was way too scared to ever go near those mind-altering substances, I wished I had at least tuned into the heroin-chic subculture thing. Now I needed an expert to confirm that, yes, over time this was the effect – weight loss, lack of energy, absence of will. For a moment I was in denial and actually wished with all my heart that this was the plain, straightforward chemical answer.

'Are you ready to move on?' Grace asked Jude. Slowly she bent her arm then extended it in a gesture that suggested opening a door.

He turned to Cristal for an answer.

She smiled and nodded. 'That's why he came.'

And I knew with a pitter-pattering, sinking heart that really it wasn't drugs, it was the force of evil hiding behind those smiles and glances, strong spirits growing stronger as Maia had told me, dark angels bursting through hell's barriers back into the material world.

Could I do it? Did I have the guts to stay here and fight for Grace and Jude?

After Ezra had taken Grace away and Zoran had reappeared to send Jude off with Cristal and Daniel to get something to eat, he and I were left alone in a vast room close to the original party room.

Here the theme was medieval. The stone walls were decorated with spears and pieces of medieval armour and

305

a stuffed stag's head hung over a big open fireplace. Opposite it was a huge tapestry featuring a forest with huntsmen on horseback.

'So, Tania, tell me your dreams,' Zoran invited, patting the place beside him on the crimson couch. 'Where are you at in your life?'

I sat next to him, totally afraid. Surely he could feel me shake and tremble.

'Relax,' he smiled. 'Try to forget who I am, who I was – you know what I mean, all the rock-star shit.'

Swallowing hard, I nodded, determined to keep the barriers up. Man becomes beast, beast becomes devil. Remember!

*An image leaps from the medieval tapestry opposite the fireplace. It's the enormously enlarged face of a grey lurcher, fangs bared, mouth dripping blood, snarling and drooling. It explodes out of the picture, whooshes in on me with a loud roar then it retreats, vanishes back within the frame.*

'So what's next for you, after your boyfriend gets his college place in Dallas?'

*The dog snarls again. It bursts out and comes within centimetres of my face.*

'Catch the devil by the throat, fight him down.' *It's Maia's voice I hear, crystal clear, and the words get etched in my brain. Catch the devil by the throat.*

'I take a year out,' I reminded Zoran as coolly as I could. If he already knew every detail of my life, then surely he must know this.

'And will you join Orlando in Dallas?'

'I guess not. I don't know.'

'But he would like for you to be there with him?'

'Maybe.' I tried my hardest to deflect the ongoing, uncomfortable interest in my love life. But when I met Zoran's gaze, it was fixed on my face, reading every nuance. His pupils were huge under those heavy, straight brows.

'It's tough being in love,' he empathized, unconsciously taking up Holly's riff at the country club. 'Especially at your age, when everything is so intense.'

*Why* the interest? How did it link in with what Zoran was doing here? I stared back without speaking, letting certain things slot together in my mind.

OK – this guy's mission was to step over from the spirit world on to the material side to claim souls. Maia had told me that as plain as anything. He aimed to snatch young victims and draw them on to the dark side – and Holly and I had already decided that the more unspoiled and innocent, the more in love they were the better.

The more in love! I reworked the evidence. Hadn't Zoran specifically checked via Ezra that I was in love when he first met me at the Heavenly Bodies party? Ditto with Grace. And hadn't he allowed Aaron to slip through the net when he'd learned they had had a fight? After that he was no longer suitable. I felt my eyes widen with shock. That's it! He has to steal his victims from the arms of people they love. He is the love thief! He feeds off their love.

'*Good, Tania!*' *Maia breathes, sweet as honey. My skin tingles and I am bathed in her light.*

'What?' he said, smiling and unsuspecting. 'Come on, Tania, share!'

I shook my head, looked away.

Zoran waited a while then spoke again, tempting me and drawing me in like before. 'So if you don't go to Dallas for your gap year, maybe you can spend time here with us?'

I drew a sharp breath and closed my eyes for a moment. 'I plan to go to Europe,' I mumbled.

'Oh, but Daniel would love for you to join us on Black Rock.' He came right out with it, no frills. 'It's no secret, Tania – he adores you, has done from the moment he set eyes on you at my party.'

'Don't,' I sighed. My protest was weak – it wouldn't even put a dent in Zoran's ongoing pitch.

'And how much do you really mean to Orlando, deep

down? Is he the kind of guy who would give up everything for you?'

I should have objected – back off, mind your own business – but instead I made a case for my boyfriend, gave the reasonable response. 'Well, obviously I wouldn't expect him to not have a career. He has to go to college.'

'Even if it involves leaving you behind?'

'It's cool. We're strong enough to take it.' I spoke the words but into my mind crept the old seeds of doubt. Would Orlando still find time for me in his life once he got to college, or would it be out of sight out of mind? Zoran's questions watered my insecurities and made them shoot, twist their tendrils around my heart. Which was exactly his plan, I realized.

'Daniel would never abandon you that way,' he insisted. 'He believes in soul mates, in sharing everything. It's part of our philosophy here at the lodge. By the way, Daniel hasn't asked me to sit here and talk to you about this. He respects your right to make your own choices.'

'Sure. Thanks – I know that.'

'But I'm older than he is. I know the way the world works. Daniel loves you but he won't put any pressure on you, whereas I tell him, don't hold back – seize the day!'

That was true, I thought, as the tendrils of doubt

gripped me. Daniel hadn't crowded me. He'd told me he understood about Orlando.

'And at your age, everything is so fluid.' Zoran sat beside me dropping pearls of what masqueraded as wisdom. Except that he wasn't who he said he was. He was a dead man walking, and his motive couldn't be anything but evil.

I felt Maia's presence – an opposing force here in the antique-stuffed room with the dogs snarling from the tapestry on the wall, alongside horse riders in fur-trimmed robes, against tall trees in the background, with white daisies in a green meadow at their feet.

'The heart shifts, nothing is stable – you in Europe, Orlando in college.' Zoran again.

'And you want me to come here and join Grace and Jude?' I asked.

'Sure. The door is open. What's not to like?'

A millionaire spread on a mountain with pool and helipad, with art and culture, and my own old buddies to keep me company. And godlike Daniel. Look at the package, the place, the guy. Who in their right mind would say no?

'Let me explain.' Zoran lowered his voice and hesitated as if he was digging deep to help me understand the offer. 'Listen, Tania, I know you've heard and read a lot about me, and not all of it good. It's the nature of the world I live in – people are jealous, they envy my success. So you get wild rumours, things are written.'

I looked directly at him for the first time in a while and found myself paying close attention. In the here and now, without taking anything else into consideration, the guy did come across as totally genuine.

'They say I've set up some kind of cult, that I must have weird motives for luring kids up here on to Black Rock. I know – it's a stupid rumour because you've seen the way it works, Tania, and you can tell everyone in Bitterroot, hand on heart, that we don't use any kind of force to make people stay. Grace is here purely because she wants to be, the same with Jude.'

He looked earnestly at me, waiting for my slow nod of agreement.

'And we do have a philosophy, it's true – one that particularly appeals to young people, based on discovering what's important to you as an individual and following that through with study and guidance from the guys who've been here a while.

'Take you, for example. We know how passionate you are about art and we can provide you with materials that will allow you to develop as a painter and an art historian. No, wait,' he said, seeing that I was about to speak and raising a finger to stop me in my tracks. 'It's more than practical help that's on offer. It's the whole atmosphere here, out of the mainstream, which lets you develop at your own pace, which opens doors and expands your mind. You know what I'm saying?'

I took a deep breath then nodded again. As he'd said – what's not to like?

'Why do I do this?' he went on, plausible as ever. Zoran Brancusi could have been a politician. 'Because I believe in you kids. I want you to have the best possible chance in life. My aim is to take you a step beyond what you can achieve elsewhere.'

'If we dare to believe?' I murmured, at this point almost ready to forget my fears and just do it. But mouthing the mantra jerked me back on to a different level. I connected it with Grace and her dark, empty gaze and I shivered.

'Exactly,' Zoran said, sensing my change of mood and abruptly ditching his ad-man pitch. Instead he stood up and obviously expected me to follow him out of the room. 'Are you cold, Tania? Would you like an extra jacket?'

'No, I'm good, thanks.'

He led the way, out from under the snarling dog tapestry, along the corridor past the carved masks, up in the elevator to the big hallway and the exit into the fresh air. 'It's almost evening. The temperature has dropped and I didn't install heating in the chapel.'

The chapel? The main doors opened and cold air hit me. I almost had to run to keep up with Zoran as he crossed the yard.

'It's time,' he told me. 'Jude has agreed to become one of us. Come and see.'

# 13

Zoran's chapel was the place for ceremony, for welcoming people to the dark side. It was where I'd lost Grace for good, where she'd travelled beyond my reach in her black sacrificial robe.

Before her it must have been Oliver, and now it was Jude's turn.

What exactly had happened with Oliver, I had time to wonder as I entered the chapel. Why had he left the lodge and wandered on to the mountain? Is that the way it worked once Zoran and his crew had snatched a soul and dragged it on to the dark side? Once Cristal's mission had been effortlessly accomplished, did they cast away what was left like junk?

Yes – it was only the hollow shell of Oliver that had walked away, found a blackened sink hole, a scorched underground chamber where he could curl into the foetal position and die.

This was how they did it – the honeyed web of entrapment, the snatching of his soul, the triumph for the dark side, all sparked by the welcoming ceremony I was about to witness.

A ceremony, a victory parade, with Cristal at its head.

I went into the high chapel with its cave-drawing murals and immediately started to tremble.

'Here, take my coat.' Now Daniel was with me, offering me warmth, wrapping his jacket round my shoulders.

I shook, I shuddered. The half-men, half-beast paintings seemed to shift in the shadows. *Catch the devil by the throat . . .*

'People are only afraid of the unfamiliar, the unknown.' Daniel was calm. He led me by the hand through a small crowd of people gathered expectantly. In the dim lighting and the deep shadows, I picked out Callum, who gave me a reassuring smile. Next to him was Lewis, beyond them Grace and Ezra.

'Cool – you stayed to watch.' Grace came over to me without Ezra for a change. 'Tania, this is going to be amazing! Zoran will open up a whole new world for Jude. I can't describe it. But just you watch!'

She spoke as the music began – a Zoran track – and I soon recognized the tune as the early number 'Stardust' even before the familiar voice came in surround-sound from powerful speakers high on the walls.

'Come with me/ Fly with me/You're stardust, you're heavenly!'

The familiar song exploded around us, the drumbeat rapid, guitars thrusting on behind the soaring vocals.

'Wait – watch!' Grace breathed.

The lights dimmed. We stood in darkness and held our breaths.

'You're forever in my arms/You're heavenly.' Zoran's voice filled the chapel. A single white spotlight lit the raised area at the far end of the chapel, then with one of those illusions that Zoran loved, we saw him rise through the floor.

And even I, who was prepared, who had seen it all before and had learned how this dark angel could shape-shift and mesmerize and overwhelm his victims, still I wasn't prepared for this latest manifestation.

'You're stardust/You're heavenly!' he sang, head thrown back, arms outstretched as he rose.

With him came wreaths of white smoke, flickers of orange flame licking at his heels. And he looked magnificent – there's no other word – with a heavy gold chain at his neck, dressed in a medieval hunter's cloak of black fur and carrying a longbow, with a quiver of arrows strapped to his shoulder.

'Like the tapestry!' I murmured.

Somehow Zoran had rolled aside the centuries, defying history and the two-dimensional prison of the tapestry weaver's art. He let the cloak slide to the ground, where it killed the flames and settled the smoke. At his side crouched his two grey dogs, lips curled, fangs bared.

*And as flaming torches are lit on the walls of the chapel I gasp to see other transformations. Pillars supporting the roof have become tall, straight trees whose bark is smooth and silver-grey, the marble floor has turned into a carpet of green grass scattered with meadow flowers. By my side, Grace is a girl in a rose-pink gown with a sash of golden thread, her hair waving softly to her waist. Callum wears his own cloak of dark-blue velvet and ermine with a matching cap and Daniel is standing in the moonlight in an embroidered tunic of silver and black, a tiny pearl stud in one ear.*

*He looks closely at me for my reaction. 'What do you think – will Jude approve?' he asks quietly, gesturing at the scene around us.*

*'Just like the tapestry,' I say again. I'm lulled by the stylish elegance of the scene, able to pick out the exact same figures I saw woven in ancient wool; Zoran is the aristocratic huntsman in chief, Callum and Daniel his noble second and third in command. And in the shadows, between the tree trunks, I*

make out shy, fugitive animals such as deer, rabbits and foxes. For a few moments the stately pageant enchants me.

'You're for ever in my arms,' Zoran sings jubilantly.

Then Cristal glides into the chapel, leading Jude. Cristal as I've never seen her before in a long, flowing dress of Virgin Mary blue – a smooth-faced Raphael Madonna with a white linen smock gathered at her neck and long, wide, satin sleeves to her delicate fingertips. Her flame hair is covered by a fine white veil, her head is bowed.

Jude follows, eyes downcast, framed in the dark doorway. He could be a pilgrim or a monk in his long, plain black robe open at the neck, hands clasped in front, averting his gaze. Or he could be a prisoner being led to his execution.

Zoran is also in black; a woodcutter's axe leans against a tree. The dogs bare their teeth and snarl.

An executioner, and Jude is the sacrifice!

Zoran's face is bloodless and cruel, his jaw sharp as an axe blade.

Jude walks after Cristal, who raises her veil and as she passes by, close enough for me to touch, allows herself a glance of triumph.

The dogs strain at the leash. Zoran releases them and they bound forward. They part the elegant crowd, leap and sink their fangs into the flank of a roe deer. An arrow out of nowhere pierces the deer's neck; blood gushes forth. The scarlet *river runs down and the whole forest starts to rustle and roar. A snake, the old enemy, slithers through the long grass, green and slippery. A great creature roars from a cave deep in the woods. It emerges on its hind legs, twice the height of a man, with curved, flashing claws and a bucket-sized jaw. Arrows rain against its hairy hide and fail to penetrate.*

*And the whole orderly pageant disintegrates into chaos. The bear mauls its victim – a terrified female bystander who falls to the ground; the vicious dogs worry and drag down their deer. Then Zoran approaches Jude and throws his arms wide in a terrifying greeting. His face morphs into that of the bear. Man is beast again – this is not heaven after all, but hell. The chapel door flies open. Outside I see flames rage and smoke begins to suffocate – the old nightmare is back.*

*Breathe, Jude, breathe. Do not take his hand.*

*Breathe, Tania. Ask Maia for help before it's too late.*

*'I need you!' I cry.*

*Then there are figures in the doorway – three people who shouldn't be here, guests who have not been invited.*

*The bear sees them, its roar dies in its throat and it drops and crawls on all fours back into its cave.*

'A rehearsal,' Zoran explained coolly to Orlando, Holly and Aaron. 'We're making a promotional video for my greatest hits album.'

319

'Sorry. We sure didn't mean to interrupt.' Aaron was embarrassed more than shocked. He fell for Zoran's excuses, and why shouldn't he?

I stood with them out by the helipad, still too stunned to speak.

Zoran was tense but civil. 'No problem. It was only a run-through.'

'Tania, I called at your house like I said,' Holly informed me. 'You weren't in.'

'Sorry, I forgot.' The words of the Stardust song still played inside my head; the forest images of curved claws, blood and gore wouldn't go away. But here we were in broad daylight – Holly, Aaron, Orlando, me and Zoran.

'You sounded like you were really sick on the phone this morning.' She hammered her point home. 'Then when I got there the place was empty, so I stressed for a while then I called Orlando.'

'Thanks,' I muttered. 'But there was no need, honest.'

'Everyone's acting so weird lately,' she complained, giving Zoran a significant look. 'Orlando and I talked it through and decided we should come up here to look for you.'

Zoran stood patiently within the yellow circle of the helipad. He seemed normal, although maybe more reserved than usual and perhaps giving Holly and Aaron

320

more attention now that they were evidently back together. As I noted this and realized why, I felt my flesh begin to creep.

'I understand your concern,' he told them. 'We know that Tania has a few health issues that need attention. In fact it was Callum who first suggested a visit to a neurologist. But meanwhile, she knows she's welcome here any time she wants. The same goes for you too, Orlando.'

I didn't even dare risk looking at Orlando. It was still daytime but only just. The sun had already gone down behind Carlsbad and the shadows had disappeared, leaving a flat, dull grey light. And I knew word for word and without even looking at Orlando's expression what he would be thinking: You came here without telling me again, Tania. You came behind my back to visit Daniel. You betrayed me.

'So are you coming back with us or what?' Aaron asked me. He seemed totally fazed by the situation, didn't get any of it – only knew that for some reason it was gut-grindingly uncomfortable.

'No, wait.' Holly stepped in. She was her nosy, bossy self, God bless her, looking around and spotting the mustangs milling about in the arena waiting for their evening feed. Then she turned her attention back to what they'd glimpsed inside the chapel. 'That was some elaborate setting for your video,' she told Zoran. 'Really wild.'

'One of our guys studied film under a big-name professor in California. He showed a movie at the Sundance Festival last year, so he's talented.' The lies came so fast, full and easy that they sounded true. And unfortunately for me, the glib account slotted in neatly with Orlando's latest theory about the great rock star's addiction to theatre and performance. 'Problem is, we pulled in every guy we have working here to perform as extras. That's how come we had no one on the gate.'

'No security,' Aaron said. 'Yeah, we parked the car and walked right in.'

'And, Tania, you just happened to be passing?' Holly prompted sarcastically. She was focused on how this looked to Orlando. She obviously blamed me and was set on giving me a hard time.

'Well, actually she ran into Jude and Cristal in Bitterroot,' Zoran interrupted. 'They all drove up here together.'

'Jude's here?' For the first time Orlando spoke. 'Somebody tell me – how does that work?'

'He and Cristal are an item.' It was my turn to jump in, though I knew that if I gave away what I really felt about this – my fears, my terror – my whole cover was blown. 'She's the one who drove him to the hospital when he fell sick the last time we were here.'

Orlando shook his head in pure, speechless exasperation.

'Cristal and Jude – since when?' Aaron's muddled expression said it all.

'Since Grace got together with Ezra.' I kept my voice steady, didn't allow myself to raise even an eyebrow but I stared directly at Holly, hoping like hell she would read between the lines. 'Cristal came to Jude's rescue; patched him up in more ways than one.'

Aaron stumbled on. 'Cristal? The one that I—'

This time Holly dug her elbow in his ribs. 'Yeah, Aaron – that one! Grace and Ezra, Jude and Cristal. Wow, that's hunky-dory!' Even here, in this crazy situation, Holly's choice of words could force a grim smile out of me. 'So what next? Don't tell me – now Jude's saying he wants to hang out here for a while?'

'Actually, yes. And he even has a lead role in the video.' My eyebrows rose a fraction of a centimetre. Tune into what I'm saying, realize we have a huge problem, someone – please!

Suddenly the two lurchers were released from the chapel. They raced towards us, lean and muscular. For a fraction of a second Zoran's face twisted into a sneer and he gave a warning snarl, became the true beast unchained. Only I seemed to notice, however.

'*Tread carefully,*' *Maia says on the breeze blowing down from Black Rock.* '*Don't give yourself away.*'

'*Thank you for still being here,*' *I tell her silently. She's my only protection, my guardian angel.*

Had Holly picked up the problem yet? Did she suspect that what she saw as the old weird, druggy thing had started over – that Jude, like Grace, was not free to leave? Please! I prayed. Think, suspect, do something!

'I want to speak with Jude,' Orlando told Zoran, up front and in-your-face. 'I'm not happy. I need to check this out.'

Thank you, thank you! I took a deep breath and held it. At last I looked into his eyes. I love you!

But he blocked me with an angry stare. 'After I've done that and made sure he's cool, we're out of here,' he told Aaron and Holly.

'Actually, Jude is busy with the director right now,' Zoran told him. He was setting up some fresh bullshit barrier when Daniel came out of the chapel yelling for the dogs. Seeing us on the tarmac, he made his way to join us.

And for the first time I saw them standing side by side – Daniel and Orlando – in the middle of the helipad.

324

Please, God, why did it have to happen at this minute, when I needed every shred of willpower to stay calm and focused on my mission to save my friends?

With my heart running riot, I stared at them both. Orlando gave me his delinquent, rebel-without-a-cause stare that was so spectacular and had the effect of making me want to fall into his arms. Next to him, Daniel smiled. He was tanned and easy, his blue shirt open to show a triangle of white T. They were chalk and cheese.

Catching me gazing at them and making the comparisons, Holly rushed to rein me in. 'Tania, you're coming with us,' she decided, hooking her hand through my crooked elbow. 'Whether or not we get to see Jude, you're coming home.'

I thought Orlando's eyes were actually going to burn right through me when Holly gave me the ultimatum. Say yes, you'll come. Leave this Daniel guy, whoever he is, and walk away with me. Otherwise we're through! I could read it in his shadowed, angry face, though he didn't utter a word.

I knew how much it meant, knew that our relationship was on a knife edge; that what I said now, this instant, could change the rest of our lives for ever. Believe me, Orlando, I long so much to say yes.

'Tania's also involved with the video.' Zoran's voice

cut through the silence. 'She has an important role so it's not possible for her to leave right now.'

I want to but I can't! I told Orlando with my eyes, clenching my fists until my nails dug into my palms.

'It's your choice,' Orlando said through gritted teeth.

'Come on, Tania, let's go!' Holly insisted. She tugged at my arm, felt me resist.

Orlando saw me stand my ground. He gave up trying to read my intention and turned away, shoulders slumped. For him, that was it – we were through. End of story.

I murmured his name, flashed a desperate look at Holly. 'Talk to him!' I begged. Meaning, Don't leave me here alone with this situation. I have to save Jude and Grace and I can't do it alone!

But Holly glanced from me to Daniel's calm face. His head was up, his stance confident, the way a businessman is when he knows he's about to close a deal. 'Like Orlando says,' she muttered as she too turned from me, 'you made your choice.'

Aaron only shrugged. He was actually the one who led the way across the tarmac towards the main gate and the cattle guard.

Come back! I pleaded silently. Don't abandon me here!

I saw all too easily how it must look from the outside,

Daniel standing next to me, owning me.

I know how jealousy acts, how it blows your head apart.

They talked as they left, but they were too far away for me to hear their words. Aaron spoke to Holly, who shook her head and said something to Orlando. He put up his hand to stop her mid-sentence, picked up speed, didn't even look back to see if I was still there.

His car was parked under a tree fifty metres from the gate. They piled in. I heard the doors slam – one, two, three.

'Good decision,' Zoran told me as he gave me an approving smile. 'At last, Tania, you're beginning to see the light.'

That night – my first at Black Eagle Lodge – I was exhausted but I didn't sleep. Instead, I ran through the conversation I'd had with Grace after Orlando, Holly and Aaron had left.

It was not so much a conversation as a full-on attack.

'Idiots!' Grace began in a little-kid, petulant voice. We were alone in a small room in the main house, deep underground. 'If they hadn't barged in, Jude would be one of us by now.'

'So once Orlando and the others had left, why didn't

Zoran just go ahead with the ceremony?' I couldn't figure out the cancellation of the event – it had happened without a reason so far as I could see, with Callum quietly leading everyone out of the chapel and Jude and Cristal nowhere to be seen.

'Oh, Tania, you don't understand!' Flinging herself down on a couch, Grace drew her knees towards her chest and sulked like crazy. 'It has to be a certain time of day – at sunset exactly. Those morons wrecked our timing. Now we'll have to wait a whole twenty-four hours.'

I paced the room feeling trapped and claustrophobic. 'Why sunset?'

'Because! It has to be sunset – that's the way we do it.'

We. That word was aimed at me like a gun to my head, warning me off, so I tried for a more casual tone. 'So where did Jude get to after the ceremony was cancelled?'

'Jude, Jude, Jude!' Grace's scowl deepened and despite my attempt to sidestep, she turned her anger on me. 'God, Tania, you're so stupid! All you ever do is ask irrelevant questions. You never just accept and go with the flow, do you?'

I was at the opposite side of the room when I stopped pacing and took a deep breath. 'Is this what you're doing

– going with the flow?' I challenged. 'That's not how it looks to me.'

'Because you're . . .' She paused while she found the right word. 'You're so unevolved, Tania! Bang – you keep the door to your mind slammed shut to everything Zoran offers you. That's how you always react – narrow minded, bigoted, blind!'

'I'm here now, aren't I?' I pointed out, trying hard not to react to the insults. I realized this was probably one of the last opportunities I'd ever have to get through to her, that having gone through her own welcoming ceremony she was moving steadily on to the next phase that had left Oliver curled up and dead in a sink hole. Think about it, and you'll realize how desperately important this conversation was.

'Let's focus on you, shall we?' I said. 'Does going with the flow mean doing absolutely everything Ezra tells you to do, even when it's not safe?'

'It's never not safe,' she muttered, hugging her knees close to her chest.

'Isn't it?' I moved close enough to touch the bruise on her thin, bare arm. 'What happened here?' I asked. Then I touched her cheek. 'And here?'

She looked back at me with what I thought was that old flicker of panic. 'I fell.'

'Really?'

'Yes, really.'

'How did you fall?'

'I don't remember.'

'Were you and Ezra partying too hard? Did you pass out?'

The look of fear passed, the bottom lip came out in stubborn resistance. 'That's you, Tania. Losing consciousness is what *you* do, remember.'

It was no good, the fear faded and she was moving away from anything real – I'd lost her again. 'Yeah, that's me,' I sighed. 'You're not going to share how you got hurt, are you?'

'I don't remember,' she repeated, slowly stressing each syllable as she stared back at me. Then she uncurled from the couch and came close, glancing at the cross I still wore around my neck, remembering it and frowning again. 'I shouldn't have done that,' she sighed.

My hand went to the necklace to protect it.

'It was a mistake to return it to you. It was before . . .'

'Before what, Grace?'

'It was when I thought I knew you, when I still saw you as my friend.' Her words were slow and faltering, the dark faraway look came into her eyes.

'I *am* your friend,' I whispered back, my fingers still

touching the garnet-studded cross.

Grace shook her head. 'Are you?'

'I'm here!'

She leaned forward to whisper in my ear like a conspirator. 'But, Tania, the question is – why? Why are you here?'

I had to think fast, come up with something that would convince her, something that she could identify with and believe. 'For Daniel,' I confided. 'God's honest truth, Grace – I'm totally in love with the guy!'

Now, as I lay in bed staring at the ceiling, the memory of even speaking the sentence threw my fast beating heart into turmoil. I'm totally in love with the guy! Words spoken out loud have a power that they don't have if they stay locked inside your head. I'm totally in love with the guy! With Daniel.

Feeling nauseous, I sat up in the dark room, swung my legs over the edge of the bed and leaned forward.

Why not? Why not love Daniel? After all, at sunset today Orlando had walked out of my life. He didn't even look back. Slam, slam, slam! Three car doors, and the first had been his. He'd driven away with a squeal of tyres, red-devil-eye brake lights flashing.

'You didn't even try to understand,' I told the darkness.

331

'You didn't trust me, you didn't love me enough.'

This fitted exactly with what Zoran had claimed earlier – that Orlando struck him as immature and selfish, that Daniel would never abandon me that way.

I was alone and in the dark. I was scared out of my mind when Daniel came to my room.

He opened the door and came in softly, pressed a switch that turned the light on low, found me sitting on the edge of my bed. Without saying a word he put out his hands and raised me to my feet.

I was in his arms, my skin against his, almost swooning.

He kissed me on the lips, his arms held me close. He kissed my neck. I closed my eyes, breathed him in.

His lips brushed my shoulder. Turning me to face him, he kept me tight in his arms and breathed soft words into my hair. 'I love you, Tania. I've waited for this. I've been waiting since the moment I first set eyes on you.'

I turned again, kissed his mouth, sank into his embrace.

How do I describe it? Like those moments when you're standing in the sea not far from the shore, preparing for a clear, sparkling wave to swell and sweep you off your feet. You feel the ocean's power, are lifted in the surf and carried in pure delight. That's how it was with Daniel.

I was on the crest of the wave, being swept away, loving the warmth of his skin, the soft wetness of his mouth. I waited for the wave to close over me in that instant of surrender.

Until I opened my eyes and saw him in the low yellow light – his own eyes open and in sharp, glittering focus watching me, waiting for me to give in.

I pulled back. 'It's too soon,' I whispered.

His eyes flickered shut. When he opened them again his mood was different – harder but trying not to show it. 'Of course,' he murmured, keeping his arms around my waist.

'I need some time.'

'I know. I'm sorry.'

'No. Don't be.'

'I just thought . . .'

'I know. It's me. I'm being stupid.'

'I thought your staying here meant that you'd made your decision.'

'It does. I have, Daniel. But it's the first night. So much has happened.'

'And so fast,' he agreed, releasing me without moving away. 'It's OK, I understand.'

I nodded and tried to smile. I was feeling the sickening undertow, the strong pull of the ebbing tide. 'Thank you.

I knew you would. I hope you don't think . . .
I don't . . .'

Gently he put his hand over my mouth. 'It's OK,
Tania. It really is.'

It wasn't OK. It was the total opposite. I hated myself
that I'd been on the point of giving in. I tell you now –
Orlando is the only guy I ever slept with, which you
might think is unusual in this day and age, but it's the
way it is.

'What are you thinking?' Daniel asked.

I stepped back, pulled a sheet from the bed and
wrapped it around me. 'Nothing. I'm confused. I need a
little fresh air.'

'Not now. It's the middle of the night.'

'OK, I won't go outside. I'll stay in the house.'

He gave me that detached, deliberate stare. Thirty
seconds earlier he'd been sweeping me off my feet into bed
with him. 'If you need me, I'll be in my room,' he said.

The corridors were empty and silent, clean and sterile as
a hospital. Everyone slept.

My heart thumped as I walked and walked. My head
didn't stop spinning. If I was looking for clarity here in
Zoran's high-tech warren, I sure didn't find it – not when
the Aztec masks loomed up ahead and leaped from the

wall, all staring eyes and human hair, painted red and black and white. They roared and hissed in my face, fell to the floor and splintered. I trod in bare feet over the sharp fragments, turned around to see them intact and hanging from the wall as before.

Don't the others see this, I wondered. Doesn't Jude see the hunting dogs leap from the tapestry? Doesn't Grace notice when Zoran's golden snake ornament morphs and comes alive, when Daniel's eagle wings raise him from the ground? Am I the only one?

*'No, they don't. And yes, you are,' Maia reminds me in her sweet, soft voice. They don't see it because they're not looking for it. You do because your sensibilities are heightened; you were born with a special link to the invisible spirit world.'*

I walked some more and came into the main hallway just as the sun was rising.

Grace was there with Ezra.

'You're up early,' Ezra said to me. His eyes were so dark and defined I thought he must have smeared them with kohl. His pale face with its high cheekbones and honed jaw was unnaturally white.

'I couldn't sleep,' I explained.

'Yeah? Grace was the same.'

I was afraid to look at her, knowing that I would see the absence, the hollowness. When I forced myself and found that I was right, I couldn't help a gasp and a slow, sighing exhalation.

She was wearing the long black dress again, her bare arms limp at her sides. Her hair hung loose and lifeless, half covering her eyes. And she was so far gone in her trance, she didn't seem even to see me in the grey dawn light.

'Where's Daniel?' Ezra asked curtly, as if I was bound to know.

I shrugged. 'In his room.'

He frowned and turned away.

Anyway, I wondered, why were Grace and Ezra here at this time in the morning? He was glancing around as if he was waiting for someone, showed no surprise when Cristal showed up with Jude.

Jude was another ghost, another shadow of his former self. I steadied myself again, kept a lid on my fear.

'Hey, Tania,' Cristal said casually. 'Look, Jude – Tania stayed over.'

Slowly he looked at me, slowly he said hi, fuzzy and disoriented like someone waking after a deep sleep.

'We were just talking,' Cristal said brightly. 'Jude was saying he can't wait to get going with his ceremony.'

'Yeah, and this time let's hope there are no interruptions.' Ezra took up the same brisk tone, taking

Cristal to one side, perhaps to finalize arrangements for the evening.

I waited for them to be out of earshot. 'Jude!' I said, tugging at his arm. 'Look at me. Can you focus?'

'Tania?'

'Yes – listen! You don't have to go through with this!'

'What are you talking about? Where's Cristal?'

'She's over by the door. I'm asking you to listen carefully to what I'm saying. You still have a choice about tonight. You can tell them no, you want to back out.'

He looked at me as if I was speaking a foreign language and he was trying to latch on to a single familiar word.

'You can!' I pleaded. 'I'm risking a lot by telling you this. You have a choice. You can leave. Are you hearing me?'

'I hear you,' he sighed. But his brain wasn't computing – not at all.

And Cristal had quickly rounded off her talk with Ezra. She was back and dazzling Jude with her smile, telling him that we all had to go outside because Zoran was in the barn waiting for us. 'You too, Tania,' she informed me. 'Daniel's out there with him.'

The doors slid open and the cold air hit us. A sliver of sun had appeared over the mountains to the east but as yet no rays had warmed the land, and in the arena the horses huddled together, their steamy breath rising.

'Zoran's not happy,' Cristal muttered to Ezra.

He glanced sideways, caught me listening in and gave her a warning look.

Grace was behind him, half running to keep pace. When she reached my side she leaned in to whisper slyly in my ear. 'I heard what you just said to Jude,' she hissed with a flash of intense spite. 'Don't think I didn't!'

'What do you mean?' I laughed uneasily.

'Oh, yeah, little Miss Innocent!' Her look was suddenly focused and it was pure poison. Her voice was full of hate. 'I heard every word and don't think I can't repeat them to Ezra.'

'Grace – don't!' I was breathless, not from running but through fear. 'Don't tell him!'

'Ha, you don't like that, do you?' She curled her lip and sneered. 'You don't like not being in the driving seat, telling everyone what to do.'

'Come on, you two!' Cristal broke us up. She was the first to reach the arena gate where the huddle of horses shifted and scuffed their feet in the dirt. A couple, including Zoran's striking sorrel mare, broke away to linger out of the wind in the shelter of the barn door.

Then Daniel came into view carrying head stalls for the mustangs. He beckoned to me, Jude and Grace and pointed to a wooden box containing brushes and metal combs before he hurried back into the barn. 'Catch yourselves a horse and brush them down,' he told us. 'Zoran has called a staff meeting.'

Just that – nothing more. No mention of his visit to my room, no lingering romantic looks.

'You heard what he said,' I told Jude and Grace. Ignoring Grace's latest outburst, I decided I had to catch their horses for them, and handed them their brushes. Then I went across to fetch Zoran's sorrel as rays from the rising sun hit the red barn roof and a blue jay rose from the shadows. I heard voices inside the barn and froze.

'What do you mean – she said no?' Zoran snapped. He really wasn't happy, as Cristal had said. 'I thought you understood – no was not an option!'

'She said she needed more time,' Daniel explained.

'Oh, really.' Ezra's sarcastic tone made it plain whose side he took. 'So you accepted the rejection and backed off?'

Daniel tried to shrug off the criticism. 'What was I supposed to do – force her?'

Ezra laughed. 'Yeah, what's wrong with that? Anyway, you're supposed to be number-one lover boy and you're seriously asking me for advice?'

There was a pause and I pictured Daniel physically squaring up to Ezra until Zoran interrupted with, 'Enough, you two. Daniel, I gave Tania to you because I knew she was more of a challenge than the others. I saw that from the start and I thought you were up to it.'

He *gave* me to Daniel? Did I hear that right? And what was I – some kind of object to be handed around? I felt a spark of anger then a sickening thud of disgust in my belly.

'I trusted you to get it right,' Zoran insisted then waited for Daniel to defend himself, which he did.

'OK, but you can't rush Tania. And listen to me, Ezra – everyone here except you knows we only use force as a last resort. Tania should give herself of her own free will. We all know that's how it works best.'

Still they were discussing me like a deal they hadn't managed to broker and I felt sick to my stomach at how close I'd come to giving in.

'So what did happen to your famous charm?' Cristal came in with a needling voice.

'Enough again!' This time Zoran injected steely anger into his tone. 'Tania is hard to read, we all know that, and it's what makes her interesting. With the others – with Oliver especially – it was easy, like taking candy from a baby. Likewise and to a lesser extent, Jude. Grace was

340

more difficult. A little force was necessary – we accept that, Ezra.'

The bruises! Now I understood how she'd got them – at certain points she'd obviously put up a fight against Ezra's focused, cold-hearted seduction. No date-rape drugs had been involved, just pure brute force. Poor Grace. That's all I could think as I stood there and pictured the whole thing – those two words: poor Grace.

'But we need another victim, the sooner the better,' Zoran reminded everyone.

'How about the kids who were here last night?' Ezra suggested. 'There was the one called Holly.'

'No time,' Zoran decided. 'Anyway, Tania is a difficult challenge, and that's exactly the reason I want her.'

'So, Daniel, what exactly are you going to do to make it happen?' Cristal demanded, pushing him to a point when I was sure he would snap. 'Whatever it is, try and make it a double celebration with Jude. Do it tonight.'

He didn't answer and in the silence that followed I heard footsteps heading in my direction. Quickly I pulled myself together and buckled the collar around the mare's head. By the time Daniel emerged from the barn, his face dark and angry, I was alongside Jude and Grace, brushing dust from the sorrel's coat as if I'd been busy all along.

Crying inwardly for Grace, I had my back turned so I hoped no one could see that I was shaking from head to foot, that I felt battered and dirty and used, disgusted at the thought of letting Daniel lay his hands on me ever again.

# 14

In one completely new and unexpected way I was out of danger.

Never, Daniel! I thought. From now on, never in a million years!

The way they'd talked about me in the barn – like an object – the way Daniel had played me all this time with his soft words and lips made me burn with shame and fury. And to think, in spite of what I'd suspected and witnessed here at the lodge, I'd almost, *almost* fallen for it!

Stupid, dumb-ass birdbrain! Superficial, gullible schmuck, almost sweet-talked into my own destruction!

But at least, I reminded myself, I'd pulled back at the moment the wave broke. I'd said no and now I was safe. From Daniel, I mean. In every other way, I was in so much trouble I couldn't even begin to measure it.

'You like working with horses, Tania?' Zoran asked me as he strolled out of the barn after Daniel. He was back to his old jovial, *mein host* manner, playing the game.

*He spreads his wings like the blue jay, his black beak stabbing the air. He rises in a cloud of mist above the rooftop. Dark destroyer, evil incarnate. I will never look at you again without seeing the beast beneath the skin.*

'I haven't had the chance to find out,' I answered. 'This is the first time I've been this close.'

'Then you're a natural,' he told me before he ordered Grace and Jude to come into the house with him, Cristal and Ezra, which left Daniel alone with me and the mustangs.

'This is another reason why you should hang out here a while.' Daniel picked up where Zoran had left off. 'You could help me tame these wild horses. I could teach you some techniques.'

I left off brushing but didn't ease away from the mare. Somehow her warmth and strength made me feel a little safer, and the way she kept her ears flicked back towards me, paying attention to every move.

'Tania, I'm sorry about last night,' Daniel muttered, dropping into the role of overeager guy who goofed up, coming out with formulaic phrases. 'I guess I misread the situation.'

344

'Me too – I'm sorry if I gave off the wrong signals.'

'No, you have nothing to be sorry for. All I can say is, and I hope you realize this is true – it happened because I'm totally in love with you and it won't happen again because I really do respect your feelings.'

'Thank you.' I managed to look him in the eye, hoping that my own expression didn't give him any clue to my real state of mind. And I saw Daniel in the clear light of a new day – textbook-handsome, chiselled, totally gorgeous. Blink and what did I see? Corruption, darkness and ugliness oozing through every pore.

'Tania,' he murmured, reaching out to take my hand.

It was as if a creature covered in slime had crawled on to me and I had to use all my willpower not to pull away, to keep on looking steadily into his eyes.

'I'll wait until you're ready,' he promised in his softest, lowest, most seductive voice. He pulled me close, his lips brushed against my hair, my cheek.

I raised my hand and placed my fingertips against his chest. 'I won't make you wait for long,' I promised.

'How long? Have you any idea?'

I shook my head and sighed.

'Sorry,' he whispered. 'I didn't mean to pressurize . . .'

'No, it's cool.' I realized it would be good to throw him some decoy bait, to fix his attention on a specific point. I sighed again and gently pushed him away. 'After tonight's ceremony – maybe then.'

I stayed for hours with the horses in the arena, using them to keep a distance from Daniel and from what might be going on in the house, giving myself time to think. I tried to plan out how I could next get to see Grace and Jude without Ezra or Cristal being nearby, and if I could achieve that, what exactly I would say that I hadn't tried to say before.

In my feverish brain I even rehearsed a couple of variations on the kidnap-Grace scenario. I mean, by now she was so skinny and feather-light that even I could knock her off her feet and physically carry her out of the lodge, out through the gate on to Black Rock.

But then what? What about the security guys and the fact that the place was bristling with cameras? And what transport did I have to drive Grace down from the mountain? No, forget that.

OK, so I could make my own escape – find a back way out of here, deep into the canyon, scale a few rocks, disappear into the forest. It would take me maybe half a day to walk down the mountain into town, go to the cops, persuade them to come up and arrest everyone in sight. 'Mr Brancusi, you're under arrest for being a reclusive ex-rock star with a crazy dream of creating an alternative community.' OK then, no – not the cops.

So do the runner and find Holly, convince her to drive back up here and snatch Grace and Jude from Zoran's clutches. 'He's a *what*?' (I could hear the scathing incredulity in Holly's voice without even trying.) 'You're telling me that Zoran Brancusi is a spirit from beyond the grave, a dark angel who steals souls and deals in death and destruction? Tania, for God's sake, what kind of magic mushrooms do they grow up there on Black Rock?'

So not Holly either. And not my parents, and not Orlando, for obvious reasons. Anyway, let's face it – I would never get three steps beyond the ranch boundary before they unleashed those grey dogs.

So I had no plan and the sun was rising high in the sky.

'I brought you guys some coffee,' Cristal announced around eleven a.m. By 'you guys' she meant me and Daniel.

Daniel left off showing me how to gain the trust of Zoran's sorrel mare. It was all down to patience, apparently, and learning to think the way a horse thinks. 'Animals divide into two categories, Tania – fight or flight.

Horses are flight animals. They flee to survive. You present them with something new – a wooden fence, a rope around their necks – and they're convinced you're planning to drag them down and destroy them. All you have to do is convince them you're not.'

Thanks for the horse-whispering crap, Daniel. But isn't that exactly your plan for me – a metaphorical rope around my neck, a lonely death on Black Rock?

Boy, did I identify with those mustangs. Anyway, Cristal brought coffee, asked us how we were doing then gave Daniel a significant look and left.

At midday it was Ezra's turn to check up on Daniel's progress. He came out to the arena with Grace, who was deep in one of her 'absences' and didn't even seem to notice that she was outdoors among a bunch of basically wild horses.

'Don't sneak up behind them,' I warned her nervously. 'Especially the sorrel – she kicks.'

Grace didn't seem to hear, just stood among the mustangs, constantly checking to see where Ezra was and if she was acting the way he wanted her to.

'Grace has something for you,' Ezra told me. 'Go ahead, Grace – show Tania her costume.'

'For tonight's ceremony,' Daniel explained.

'Why do I need a costume?' I frowned. 'Can't I go

348

dressed the way I am?'

Ezra tutted and gave Grace a shove towards me. 'It's a celebration. You have to enter into the spirit,' he insisted. He tried to sound calm and casual but there was a scary intensity in his pale face and dark, staring eyes.

'Yeah, it's themed the way the Heavenly Bodies party was,' Grace said as she handed over a soft robe made of dark red velvet with an expensive black fur trim. 'The same theme as last night – we're all medieval hunters in the forest. It's going to be magical.'

Still frowning, I glanced at Daniel.

'Just do it,' he murmured, flashing me what he thought was his winning smile. 'For Jude – it's his big night.'

So I agreed, though my heart was heavy as lead, and drew a faint smile from Grace's pale face, as if she was relieved that she'd achieved what Ezra had instructed her to do and was off the hook for now.

'See you later,' she told me. 'It'll be fun.'

'Yeah, see you later,' I murmured back.

I watched Ezra take my ex-friend by the hand and lead her out of the arena. I was on edge again as they paused in the yard, and she said something to him and he turned back to throw a sharp glance in my direction. What was that about? Ezra looked for a moment as if he was about to retrace his steps to accuse me and I felt my stomach churn. I got ready to defend myself against anything he might be about to throw at me.

'Are you OK?' Daniel asked, resting his arm on my shoulder.

'I'm cool,' I sighed, relieved as Ezra listened again to Grace and decided not to come back into the arena. It felt like a reprieve, a small breathing space. 'I need a little time to myself – do you mind?'

A look of suspicion flitted across Daniel's amazing movie-star features but he controlled it and let his arm drop to his side. 'Sure, go ahead. Take a walk, clear your head.'

'Thanks. Is it OK if I walk up the mountain?'

He smiled. 'Walk where you like. I'll see you at lunch.'

'Thanks,' I said again, and before he could add anything, I was out of there, heading up the hill into the forest, resisting the urge to run.

The noon sun burned my skin, the heat bounced from the rock beneath my feet. All that grows under the tall pines is spiky yucca and thin yellow grass. A brown lizard sat on a pink boulder without moving.

'What do I do?' I said out loud. The iron band of doubt tightened around my chest.

There was no answer, only a breeze through the pine needles and dirt crunching under my feet. 'This is too hard – I'm going to lose the battle,' I said with tears in my eyes.

It was a dreadful fact – Grace and Jude had travelled too far on to the dark side; Zoran's hold was too strong. And I was afraid.

*My skin tingles and Maia materializes in a clearing, an oasis of green. She seems to shine golden like the sun. 'Come here,' she murmurs, and she offers me her hand. For a while I hold it and absorb the silence. Then she begins to reassure me. 'Remember – we are bound together by love, not separate, you and I.'*

*'I know. At least, I think I understand.'*

*'Whenever you look for me, I'm here.'*

*'Without you I would never have got this far.' Without a mother's voice calling through the smoke and flames, without the certain knowledge that the human spirit is stronger than any suffering that the body must endure.*

*'There will be no more wildfire,' she promises. 'Now that you know me and how I come to you, there will be no more bad dreams.'*

*'Thank you,' I whisper. I am grateful beyond belief to be relieved finally of the memory of the Becker Hill burnout.*

*'You are everything that I dreamed Aimee would be,' Maia tells me softly. 'She lives through you and I could not have hoped for more.'*

'But what can I do?' I cry now and cling more desperately to her hands. 'Every way I turn there's a wall ahead of me. I don't see how I can save Grace and Jude.'

She waits for me to calm down. 'Accept that there is no plan,' she insists. 'Know that your heart is big enough, your spirit bold enough to deal with whatever is to come.'

I'm gazing at her. Her face is radiant in the sunlight. 'Daniel can't claim me,' I tell her. 'I know him now.'

'Good, Tania. Knowledge makes you strong.' She squeezes my fingers and waits again.

'He's dark, like Zoran. He's evil.'

'He lives in Zoran's shadow,' Maia tells me.

'And Ezra – I think he raped Grace. Maybe more than once.'

Maia's eyes are filled with compassion. She doesn't contradict me.

'Tell me more about them,' I beg. 'Show me a way to defeat them.'

'I'll tell you all I can. There is a universal battle, remember – bigger than the cosmos – contained in every blade of grass, every grain of sand you see around you. Good fights against evil for each human soul, darkness against light. To gain this knowledge is to gain power.'

'I believe you,' I tell her. Two universal forces at war.

'Zoran is at the centre of this. Evil for its own sake is

*what drives him and to thrive, he must destroy.'*

*'But what's his weakness? How can I break him?' Give me a key, I beg her. Show me what to do! Despite what Maia says, I must have a plan of action.*

*'Listen,' she insists patiently. 'With Zoran, everything is false. There is no truth in him or his followers, only malice and lies. Knowing this will protect you. It will make you strong.'*

*I nod, grasp her hands and absorb every breath of her wisdom. It will be my armour, my shield.*

*'Also, you have to recognize his suffering.'*

*I stare at her in disbelief. 'His suffering? How does he suffer?'*

*'He burns in torment; he can't escape.'*

*For a moment the image takes hold in my mind and suddenly the mountain is aflame. Fire rampages through the trees, black smoke rises. It is the old nightmare. Then I look into Maia's calm, clear eyes and the fire fades.*

*'He is an angel who has fallen from grace, from light into darkness. He exists in pain – every breath he takes, every step is agony and he is driven to inflict this same suffering on others. It's pain that makes him cruel.'*

*'He's in hell.' I see this – for Zoran the whole universe is a vast, dark prison from which there is no escape. Right now I'm grasping huge concepts, my mind is wandering through the heavens, seeing planets explode into cosmic dust, watching a*

million wicked souls surrender to the forces of evil.

'Infinite darkness,' Maia confirms. 'The darkness of the soul.'

'So he looks for those who live in the light and finds a way to poison their happiness, to drag them down with him.' Like Oliver. Zoran recruited him into his army of dark, tormented souls, snatched his spirit and let his poor, discarded body wander off to its lovely death. I'm understanding now – really getting it. 'And who are the happiest, most innocent and joyful people around?'

'Lovers,' Maia confirms. 'Young lovers like you, Grace and Jude.'

Dark angel, love thief. Where there's love, Zoran brings hate. Destroy, destroy.

My angel, my other-worldly guardian spirit gazes at me for a long time. 'Now you know him fully,' she tells me, and she lets go of my hands, steps back at last. She speaks earnestly as her light dies and she fades into the forest. 'Use this knowledge against Zoran. Win this battle, Tania. Lead your friends out of the dark into the light.'


I went to look for Zoran because after Maia left me in the clearing there was only this one thing I could do. I found him with his back towards me, alone in his chapel, preparing for Jude's initiation, and when I walked through the door I was less afraid than before, inspired by my secret meeting with my angel of light, shielded by the knowledge she'd shared.

The chapel was cool and shadowy, Zoran was on his knees by the raised platform, head thrown back and arms spread wide, praying to his devils.

'In the name of darkness and all who dwell in the shadows, I kneel. I dedicate myself to the dark forces of the universe.'

His voice filled the chapel, rose to the rafters and echoed there. The sight of him dressed in black took me back to the beginning. Once more he was Zoran from the Heavenly Bodies event – winged and stripped to the waist, a plume of black feathers rising from a leather band tied around his head. I saw the angel tattoo on his arm, the razor-sharp face, the bare, domed skull.

'I am darkness, I am death,' he chanted. 'When day turns into night, when the sun sinks behind the mountain, finally I am ready!'

I held my breath, frozen in horror at the sight of this creature – no longer a man as he knelt there on the platform and his iridescent wings began to beat. Soon his features grew tighter, sharper, more birdlike until I swear he rose again from the ground, began to hover, to fly into the dark roof space – from where he looked down and saw me.

*I gaze up at him. He is a black eagle, his eyes all-seeing, his beak cruel. In a flurry of black feathers he swoops down.*

*I raise my arms to protect myself, back into a corner and huddle there, helpless under the sharp venom of his gaze. Behind him, a hundred flying creatures – part hawk, part lizard, part mythological dragon – seem to have emerged from the shadows, their dark eyes glittering, muscular tails swiping the air, hooked beaks ready to tear at my flesh.*

*Zoran raises one arm to hold them at bay. His face changes from bird to human and back again, he darts his head close to mine. I shudder and shrink back. The next time I dare to open my eyes, he is in human form.*

'Why do you always creep up on people?' he asked coolly as he stepped away and the army of airborne monsters faded back into the shadows.

'I was looking for Daniel,' I told him, struggling to find my voice.

'Well, you walked in on a private moment.' His eyes seemed to pierce through my lame excuse and hold me skewered like an insect. 'I often come into the chapel to meditate – to find inner strength.'

I nodded, afraid that anything I said would give me away.

Zoran kept me cornered; maintained his cool, considered tone. 'You and Daniel – how are you getting along?'

'Good. We're cool.'

'Really?' He took a long, deep breath, still pinning me down with his stare. 'Tell me, Tania, did anyone ever tell you that you're difficult to get to know?'

I shrugged, tried to deflect his gaze. 'I guess I'm kind of private.'

'Complex,' he agreed. 'Your friends think so too.'

I closed my eyes, suspecting that there was more to come. The blood drained from my face and I felt light-headed.

'Complex and hard to read – that's how Grace describes you.'

Grace! He'd talked with Grace! I opened my mouth to suck in air, looked towards the door in time to see it slam shut. I heard but couldn't see those winged monsters fill the dark space above my head.

'We chatted over lunch,' Zoran explained. 'You weren't there. We missed you.'

'I helped Daniel with the mustangs then I went for a walk up Black Rock. Didn't he tell you?' Keep a clear head, put up a fight, delay whatever is about to happen!

Zoran nodded. 'He was afraid you'd get lost.'

I shook my head. 'I know my way around.'

'People always say that. But these days we never know when the forest teams are going to set fires. We tell people – we told Oliver – don't walk alone on the mountain. It's not safe.'

'Maybe I'd better find Daniel and let him know I'm back,' I suggested, praying that I could find some way to reach the door, open it and walk out of there.

'Oh, he already knows,' Zoran said quietly. Then, 'The way Grace explained it to me over lunch was that you and she are not close any more, and it's because you find it hard to trust people.'

My heart beat fast, my breath came short. Treacherous Grace had spoken to Zoran and now each word that Zoran spoke fell like a hammer blow on any hope I had of walking free.

'Do you, Tania? Do you find it difficult to trust Daniel, for instance?'

'No. He and I . . . we're . . .'

'An item?' he prompted with a touch of scorn. 'I'm not sure I believe that any longer – not after what Grace told me. And how about me – do you trust me?'

His eagle beak was as sharp as a steel dagger, pecking mercilessly into the hidden corners of my mind. His black wings trapped me in that lonely corner of the chapel. 'Or is it as Grace says – you set up a stubborn barrier, you refuse to believe?'

Fake innocence, keep on playing for time, I told myself. 'I don't know what she means. What made her say that?'

Zoran eased back as if to study me from a distance. When I dared to take a step towards the door, the hovering creatures closed in on me and hemmed me in. Their wings raised a wind that pushed my hair from my face and left me exposed to Zoran's merciless stare.

'Actually, she says that you urged Jude to change his mind. Did you do that, Tania? Don't lie to me – there's no point. Did you turn traitor and tell Jude to leave the lodge?'

The wind blew cold: more figures entered through the door.

The first one I recognised was Ezra, his face striped red and white, feathered dreamcatchers hanging at his waist. He hovered at Zoran's right shoulder, killing me with his violent gaze. Then I saw Lewis in his long feathered cloak, gold discs glinting at his neck, and Cristal with her swan-pale skin, red hair aflame against pure white wings. And Callum with a dozen more dark angels, ranked behind Zoran, accusing me. And lastly Daniel, my sun god.

Daniel stepped forward. He grew in stature, towered over me in his beaked helmet and for a moment I thought I saw pity in his cool blue eyes. A moment, then it was gone.

'Take her.' Zoran's harsh voice passed sentence. 'Do what you want with her. Throw her from the mountain, crush her beneath a heavy rock, just so long as I never see Tania Ionescu's face again.'

Daniel took me from the chapel into a daylight world where the sun was past its height and shadows had begun to lengthen. He was himself again, in human form. He gripped me by the wrist and led me across the yard.

'Don't!' I begged, twisting my arm and stumbling in an attempt to be free. 'Grace has got it all wrong.'

He walked past the arena, on up the mountain.

'You know how she is – she was confused. Please believe me.'

My words fell on deaf ears. Daniel's anger was cold and absolute. I'd been mistaken about the pitying glance.

'So I was scared. I wasn't quite sure what was going on. I misjudged the situation.' Terror invaded every inch of me. Now I would lie, cheat, deceive, do anything to save myself. 'Daniel, I'm sorry I was such a coward. Give me another chance, let me prove myself!'

A solitary red kite soared across the blue sky. It rose on an air current, tilted and veered, soared again over the summit of Black Rock. Daniel led me in silence under the lodge pole pines.

'Daniel, please!' I pulled, I twisted, I writhed.

He was strong and his face was set in grim, harsh lines. When he saw the telltale twist of smoke rising in the distance he didn't even break his stride. It was only the Forest Service team at work again, setting a new fireline by felling trees, digging ditches and burning scrub.

'What are you going to do to me?' I pleaded to know my fate, still struggled against it.

By now we were half a mile from Black Eagle Lodge, standing on a ledge of pink granite watching the smoke billow down the mountain towards us when he spoke at last. 'What's your biggest fear, Tania? Is it falling from a great height, or is it fire?'

I shook my head, tried to wrench free.

Daniel held me fast and gave a sardonic smile. 'In freefall with nothing to break your descent, just down and down into oblivion? Imagine that.'

'Give me another chance. Let me go, please!'

'Or watching the flames leap and dance all around you and closing in, feeling the intense heat on your skin, the choking smoke in your lungs? That's it, isn't it? Fire is what you dread the most.'

I groaned and felt my puny strength fail. I sank to my knees.

'Fire it is,' he muttered, dragging me to my feet and on up the mountain towards where the forest team worked.

I cried and sobbed, pictured myself devoured by flames, as Aimee had been before me. I said out loud and over and over that I was sorry, begged for mercy, for any reprieve.

White smoke drifted down Black Rock. It was already in my nostrils, in my throat when we heard a sound from the slopes below. There was a pounding in the distance, growing nearer, the thudding of hooves over rock and scree, the hard breathing of frightened horses.

'The mustangs,' Daniel muttered with a scowl and he turned to check.

Yes, mustangs free for a second time on the slopes of Black Rock, spooked by the smoke and thundering towards us, appearing on the ledge where we'd stood. They were bunched together. The lead stallion reared on to his hind legs as the smoke drifted and twisted at ground level.

Daniel frowned and hesitated. 'They broke out again. Or else somebody opened the gate.'

And they were heading our way, following our track, racing towards us and almost upon us. I felt Daniel flinch, saw him look for safety, out of the path of the fleeing horses. They were close – all twenty of them. I could make out the brown and white Appaloosa and Zoran's sorrel mare close behind, could see their tangled manes whipped back from their faces, their flattened ears and rolling eyes. And it was too late for Daniel and me to find refuge – the horses were here in the smoke and the dust, their hooves clashing against rock and sending up sparks. Sighting us ahead of them, they suddenly reared up and pawed the air with their flailing hooves. Wild horses surrounded us.

I heard the fatal blow – heavy and hard. I saw the sorrel mare rear up and thud down, threw myself to one side and knew that Daniel had gone under those hooves without a cry.

The mare reared again, came down a second time. Then the stallion broke away, cut back down the slope towards the green clearing where Maia had materialized earlier that morning. The others quickly followed, left the sorrel standing over Daniel, quivering and arching her neck to stare down at what lay beneath her hooves.

Daniel was face up in the dust. He was shrouded in smoke, but I could tell he was dead. The back of his skull was smashed; his blood stained the rock.

The mare raised her head. I believe the glance she gave me was one of total understanding before she took off after the herd. One glance, then those heavy hooves thundered away.

And I was hiding my face in my hands, staggering away from Daniel's body, losing my balance, sinking to the ground and blind to everything.

Arms caught me. I did not dare to look.

'Oh, Tania, I thought I'd lost you for good,' Orlando whispered. He held me close.

# 15

He hadn't left me for ever. He'd come back to find me.

'I opened the arena gate,' he confessed. 'It was me who let the horses out.'

'What made you come back to the lodge?' We were kneeling face to face under the trees. Orlando's arms were around me, my head was buried in his chest.

'I had a bad feeling,' he murmured. 'The more I thought about it, the more I knew something was wrong.'

'You didn't walk away,' I sighed with dawning realization. I can't tell you how good it felt.

'Before we even got home yesterday, I knew I had to come back.'

'It's bad here,' I rushed to explain. 'Jude is about to step over into something he can't control. Grace already made the move.'

Orlando stroked my hair. 'I didn't buy that crap about

Jude being too busy to see us yesterday. Jude's not like that. He always has time. And you and I had talked a lot about the weird way Grace was acting. I know we fought over it and you thought I didn't believe you, but it stayed with me and later, what you said began to make sense.'

'It takes a while – I know.'

'This is so huge, Tania. It has to do with stuff I never usually think of – forces we can't control.'

'Tell me about it.' I gave a small smile. 'In one way, and one way only, Grace is right. You have to dare to believe that this stuff exists. Ezra convinced her to join them and now Cristal has brainwashed Jude. But the point is – they're going to die. Unless we do something, they won't make it through the night.' I tell you – the joy of being able to say 'we' – 'unless we do something' – made me break down and sob again.

'Wait. Hear me out,' he insisted, his arms around me, still protecting me. 'One last thing, and it's the most important – about you and me. When Zoran and the other guys laid down the ultimatum – go home with him or stay here with us . . .'

'I was trying to get through to you but I couldn't spell it out in front of them. It almost killed me.'

'Listen. I saw the look in your eyes. I knew what you were trying to communicate.'

'So you acted mad at me, stormed off with Holly and Aaron just to fool them?' Bang, bang, bang – those three car doors still echoed in my head like gunshots.

'I'd like to say yes, clear and simple,' he told me, taking me by the shoulders and asking me to look straight at him while he explained the rest. 'But it was more complicated. Jealousy blinded me for a while, I guess.'

'I know. I understand.'

'And Holly was certain you'd lost it, totally freaked out, gone over to Daniel – whatever. She felt sorry for me.'

I sighed and shook my head. 'So part of you was angry with me?'

He nodded. 'You know how I am.'

'How *we* are,' I corrected. The 'we' word again. Both of us thin-skinned, hot-headed, still with a lot of growing to do. 'I don't blame you. In your position I would have reacted the same way.'

Orlando and I knelt there under the trees while thin smoke from the forest fire drifted around us, obscuring Daniel's corpse. I shivered when I thought of him lying there with his skull smashed into fragments like those antique Aztec masks on Zoran's wall. Only this time the pieces didn't slot back together and become whole.

'I did a lot of hard thinking way into the night,' Orlando admitted. 'Then I fell asleep and when I woke up this morning I knew what I needed to do.'

'And now you're here.' I drew him towards me and kissed him softly, feeling a calm stillness at the centre of all the pandemonium around us. 'So let me fill in some of the gaps. I don't expect you to believe all of it, but just try – OK?' It was the stuff about me being a medium, a link with the spiritual world, about Maia, my angel of light, and about Zoran and the whole warring cosmos.

I'd hardly got into it when Orlando shook his head. He looked as sorrowful as it's possible to be. Soulful and sad as he kissed me back and held me in his arms. 'I haven't finished,' he whispered hoarsely. 'I still haven't told you the most important part.'

'Go ahead,' I whispered. 'But why so sad?'

'I'm not sad, I'm serious.'

'OK, go ahead.'

'When I woke up this morning I knew this wasn't about Zoran, or Daniel, or Grace and Jude. It's about us. About you and me.'

For a split second I felt my familiar stab of panic. I thought Orlando would tell me this was it – we were through.

But he pulled me to my feet and held me close. 'Maybe we won't make it through this,' he sighed.

'We will,' I argued, stroking his cheek, stemming the flow of fear.

'Let's hope. But anyway I need you to know – you mean everything to me, Tania.'

I held him without speaking, my heart full.

'The first time ever I saw you, I knew we'd be together. It was like the sun on my face – the feeling I had when you looked at me and smiled. Really, the most amazing thing ever.'

'Stop. You're making me cry.' But I understood he had to get through to the end of what he'd stored up in his head, his heart.

'We went swimming in the lake at midnight,' he reminded me. 'Our first date – that's where we ended up.'

'I remember – every moment.' The moonlight and stars, the ice cold water on our skin.

'You were the most amazing thing that ever happened to me,' he whispered again. 'And I know you felt the same.' It wasn't a question, it was plain fact. 'We were meant to be.'

Silence, beautiful calm in the centre of chaos. I held him as he continued. 'Then we get into it and you know how it is – you have the most precious thing in this life and somewhere down the line you get scared you might lose it.'

'I know,' I sighed. 'It feels too good. Maybe you don't deserve it, or something bad will happen and it will all get blown away.' We sabotage love with doubt.

'So if – when – we get out of this, you know you're my sun, my moon, my midnight swimmer – everything and for ever?'

I looked up through my welling tears and nodded. I felt the steady beat of his heart.

His lips were against my cheek as he murmured, 'You can tell me any crazy stuff, ask me to do any stupid thing and I'll do it. I'll walk through fire and still feel the same way I do now.'

I didn't cry after all – I started to smile. 'I hear you,' I sighed.

'Love. This is what's happening between us, Tania.'

'That's it – you really do love me?' I whispered.

Orlando nodded. 'Love is what it's all about. You love me and I love you. What else is there to say?'


Love buoyed us up, boosted our courage, made us determined to go back for Grace and Jude.

'Grace let you down. She threw you under the bus,' Orlando pointed out, once I'd given him the lowdown on the latest events.

'We all know she's not the Grace we recognize and

now I think I understand why.' The 'rape' word stuck in my throat and I pussyfooted around it. 'She was— let's just say the worst thing happened to her with Ezra here at Black Eagle Lodge and now she's totally lost it.' Orlando and I were hand in hand, running down the mountain towards Zoran's house. By the time we reached the deserted arena where the gate swung open, smoke was still creeping down Black Rock and the whole sky to the west was pink over Carlsbad.

'Why the horses?' I asked as he hurriedly shut the gate.

'I'd parked my car where it wouldn't be spotted and was taking cover behind the barn. Daniel dragged you out of the chapel right past where I was hiding. I saw the mean look on his face and realized I had to act. Setting the mustangs free was a way of grabbing his attention.'

'It worked better than you could ever imagine,' I said quietly, aware that our voices would carry a long distance across the silent yard. But then I heard music from the chapel and began to understand why the barn, the arena and the yard were deserted – the sun was setting and it was time for Jude's ceremony to begin.

Listening to the slow, drawn-out notes, I recognized the tune to Zoran's old 'Love Hurts' song and soon made out the words. 'Our kisses taste of danger . . .'

'Maybe we're too late,' I breathed, pulling Orlando towards the chapel door, trying to prepare myself for whatever we found inside.

As Grace had forecast, it was exactly the same scene as twenty-four hours earlier – the guys in hunting dress, the girls as medieval maidens, plus the lean dogs, the shy woodland creatures. Orlando stopped dead in the entrance. 'What is this? Why is it happening all over again?' he hissed.

The guests' backs were turned, all eyes fixed on the platform at the far end of the chapel. Lights played over the scene, creating shadows, giving the illusion of sunlight through trees. The floor was sprinkled with meadow flowers, stately couples moved hand in hand in their fur-lined robes.

'They want Jude to step over and join them,' I whispered, drawing Orlando through the door and keeping to the darkest shadows. 'Zoran has set this up to trap him.'

The music changed. A new song began – 'Stardust', with its rapid beat and images of flying to the stars. Lights flickered on two figures already making their way to the platform – Cristal in virgin blue and Jude the condemned man in black, his face pale and passive. Among figures close to the platform I made out Grace in her black dress

372

with Ezra at her side. And then the bright white light fixed on Zoran at the centre of the platform. With small flames licking round his feet he spread his arms to welcome Jude, a look of eager triumph on his face. He had reached his goal – the moment had arrived.

'We have to stop him!' I told Orlando.

We saw foxes creep through long grass; deer hiding among trees. At Zoran's side the two lurchers sat with tongues lolling.

'I'm right here with you,' Orlando promised.

But for a while longer we were mesmerized and couldn't move.

Zoran stood in the light and spread his arms, his long black cape trailing behind him. Gold glinted at his neck, his face was deathly pale as he stepped forward to embrace Jude. The light intensified until it almost blinded.

'You are mine!' Zoran cried. 'You will walk with me. Where I go, you will go. You will not leave my side. I am your dark lord.' It was a man's voice but no longer a human face. The sharp features began to twist and morph and as he turned on the spot, the folds of his cape took on life, the black fur engulfed him, his hands became claws, his jaws opened and showed voracious, glistening teeth. His head was that of a bear.

'I am the dark power, I rise from the ashes!' The bear

roared and snarled, clutched Jude with arms too strong to resist. Deep in the forest, other huge creatures answered Death's cry.

*Catch the devil by the throat*. Don't turn, don't run, I told myself, though every instinct told me to flee. Zoran had shape-shifted and was ready to claim his victim but for the first time I held firm. I wasn't sucked in. I didn't become part of it.

'Evil rises and spreads throughout the world. It is everywhere and you are mine!' Zoran's voice crowed and Jude did not, could not resist. Cristal had beguiled him and her so-called love had trapped him like an insect in amber. Now Zoran sang out in triumph – fly with me through the dark cosmos; be mine!

Beside me I heard Orlando gasp and I was too slow to stop him from darting forward into the crowd. It was rash – exactly the wrong move, but all I could do was follow him through the crush.

Up on the platform, still unaware, Zoran released Jude into Cristal's arms then beckoned for Ezra to bring Grace on to the platform. Down on the floor, forest beasts roared, guests shed their cloaks and gowns, grew eagle talons or bared their fangs like dogs. Great shadowy birds rose into the blackness, black dogs yapped and bayed at the moon.

Orlando was just ahead of me, dogs biting at his heels. A wolf sprang from the shadows and snapped at me with deadly jaws.

'Jude, we're here for you!' Orlando's voice rose above the cacophony of animal cries.

The beast that was Zoran heard him and he swung round. He picked out Orlando and with a savage snarl he threw himself down from the platform, clawing the air, stamping on creatures that howled and yelped underfoot. I scrambled ahead of Orlando; stood between him and the devil beast.

I was face to face with Zoran without the physical strength to fight him, only the stubborn spark in my brain that kept on telling me not to give in. *Catch the devil by the throat*. I stood my ground, stared into the jaws of hell.

He glared down at me, saw that I had escaped from Daniel and recognized me for the powerful enemy I was.

I have never seen such dark and infinite anger. It overtook him, made him lash out at me with those lethal claws. But his blow missed its target and he overbalanced and crashed down on to all fours, a beast lumbering amongst the chaos of yapping dogs and howling wolves.

Seizing his chance, Orlando darted towards the platform and grabbed Jude's arm. Still in a daze, Jude let himself be dragged down among the writhing monsters and pulled towards the chapel door – the escape route. I stayed to see Cristal instantly shape-shift from virgin to wolf, her blue robe disintegrating into thick, stone-grey pelt, her green eyes fixed with hatred on the fleeing figures of Jude and Orlando.

She set off after them while Zoran raised himself on to his hind legs and advanced towards me a second time. Orlando still pushed his way towards the door with Jude in tow. Praying they would get out, I turned to face my enemy.

He lashed out, but I was alert, beyond fear and quick enough to jump clear of his lumbering, bear-claw swipe. He crashed down against the edge of the altar platform and for a time seemed winded, so now I seized my own chance to dart away to find Grace and get her out as well. Crouching low, I thrust myself forward between the shrieking beasts that tore into each other with claws and fangs. I smelled blood, heard the sound of pain.

'Traitor!' Suddenly the she-wolf Cristal was at my heels, she was snarling and leaping at my throat.

I dodged sideways then reached out and took hold of a sheaf of arrows flung away by a shape-shifting huntsman. Cristal leaped again, green eyes glaring from her beautiful beastly face. Time stood still. Her emerald eyes were outlined in black, the fur was silver, the pointed ears lined with pure white. I'll never forget.

I raised the arrow like a spear, aimed its tip between her eyes. I plunged it in deep.

Cristal stopped dead and fell at my feet. Blood poured from her mouth. Her eyes closed and the last breath left her body.

Blood, torn flesh, groans of agony – the universe in chaos. Bodies crashed through undergrowth, creatures writhed, rolled and slithered away in every direction. Only Zoran was upright, advancing again, roaring out curses, spewing his hot, putrid breath over me.

'Daniel is dead!' I cried, reaching for a second arrow.

Zoran faltered. His small black eyes flickered shut, then he opened them and lashed out, snatching the arrow from my grasp. 'He will rise again!' he swore. 'Cristal, Daniel – we will all rise!'

And at that moment of sudden despair, in the darkness of the chapel, a wind came. It blew with such power that the door was torn from its hinges and the windows high on the walls were shattered. Splinters of coloured glass rained down, sharper than arrows. Creatures howled as the wind raised them into the air, dashed them down then swept on.

I cowered defenceless under Zoran's hairy bulk. The

wind blasted him, made him stagger to one side. I stayed low, managed to crawl out of reach again. Then I was up and running, found that the wind had turned and was sweeping me clear through the door out into the night.

And out into the flames. Wind and fire had combined into a blowup – not imaginary but all too real. I'd escaped from shape-shifting hell into a natural disaster. High wind, smoke so dense I couldn't see my hand in front of me, air so hot it scorched my skin. After all this, wildfire would claim me.

'Tania, where are you?' Orlando was calling to me through the black smoke and swirls of orange sparks that rolled down the mountain.

'Over here. I'm OK.' But I saw flames sweep over the ridge towards me. It spread in many directions, even leaping down rocky ledges and eating up everything in its path. In the weird orange glow, I made out dark figures heading for the shelter of an overhanging ledge or towards the safety of the main house.

'Don't try the house – the door's locked!' I heard Orlando yell. 'Head for the barn.'

I spun around. Behind the black outline of the low barn I saw ponderosa pines explode into a wall of flame. The flames arched over the roof and raced across the arena. Orlando was right – the barn was the place to be.

If I could only fight my way across the yard and stick to the right direction I might survive. 'Where are you?'

'This way!' Orlando shouted. 'Follow the sound of my voice.'

Hot black smoke was burning my throat, my lungs were sucking it in. I was coughing as I staggered towards him. I crossed the yard under a thousand floating embers, ran slap into the arena fence, which brought me up short. I recovered, had my foot on the first rung, was about to climb over when a hand clutched my arm and dragged me down.

'That's far enough.' Zoran's voice was hoarse and cracked, his human face appeared skull-like through the smoke.

I didn't waste time pleading. I kicked and punched, bit and scratched but he refused to let go.

'Fire,' he hissed at me. 'The worst fate – borne on the wind, consuming everything.' Devil-face spitting malice – this was the real Zoran.

'Tania, I'm coming to get you!' Orlando cried from what seemed like a long way off.

'Don't! Stay where you are. I'm OK!' The smoke thickened, flames fizzed and crackled through the thorn bushes, leaped nearer.

'I'm coming anyway,' Orlando told me.

'Fire!' Zoran taunted. 'Nowhere to run. It lights up the sky, turns the world to ash. Look at it!' He held me fast, with Orlando's words in my ears.

Black Rock was alight. I could glimpse the dark angel's face through the smoke, could taste the flames on my tongue. 'Orlando, go back!' I pleaded.

The ground under my feet grew too hot to bear, the whole earth sighed in the wind.

'I win and you lose, Tania,' Zoran said. 'In the end you, Orlando, Grace, Jude – everyone will burn.'

I struggled, refused to give up the fight.

He laughed and said, 'There is nowhere to run.'

Another tree exploded in flames, the dark land burned. And then I felt the first drops of rain.

# 16

The heavens opened and the rain poured down.

I heard the drone of an engine overhead and looked up through the black smoke, heard more engines following on – a heavier tanker following the lead plane. No, this wasn't rain. I listened again and felt relief flood through me as I realized that the Carlsbad County firefighters had arrived.

They flew over the canyon, waiting until they were directly overhead before opening up their massive water tanks and releasing their cargo. Retardant fell like rain – thousands of gallons hit the ground. All around I heard the hiss and pop of flames as they died.

Flames hissed and steam rose. For a while the forest fire flickered and fought back, tried to regain its hold. Then another tanker flew low and did its job, killing the wall of flame in the tree canopy behind the barn.

'You lose!' I turned to Zoran in triumph but he was gone.

A figure ran from the barn swathed in hissing steam. More aircraft flew low, and now it was helicopters coming to help, chugging over the ridge above Black Eagle Lodge, blades churning, bringing more water to put out the fire. The figure raced towards me, emerging from the smoke and steam. 'You're safe, thank God!' Orlando said as he gathered me in his arms.

'Grace? Jude?' I asked.

'I got them both inside the barn. They're not hurt.' He dragged me back across the arena to join them. 'What happened to Zoran?'

'I don't know. He disappeared when the fire crew arrived.' Feeling the cold water on my skin, watching the flames die out, I was overwhelmed and sank against him.

Orlando hugged me back into action. 'OK, we don't stop to find out where he went. We collect Jude and Grace and we're out of here!'

I nodded. It was still hard to breathe and talk – the hot, moist air had turned the barn into a sauna – and everywhere was so dark that we had to grope our way forward and call out.

'Grace?' Orlando yelled above the drone of the choppers' engines.

'Here!' she called through the darkness. 'Hurry – Jude's not doing well!'

'Keep talking – we'll find you!' Orlando promised as we struggled through the clammy air.

'This way. Please hurry!'

We kept our heads down, stumbled into boxes stacked against a wall, sent them crashing.

'He can't breathe. You have to help me!' Grace pleaded.

At last we found them huddled in a corner – Jude slumped against the wall, Grace trying to revive him. She was bent over him in her torn black dress, loosening the collar of his robe, begging him to wake up. When she saw us appear out of the sweaty darkness, she broke down completely. 'Don't let him die!' she wept.

'No one's dying.' Straight away Orlando raised Jude's limp body from the ground. He slung one of his arms around his shoulder then told me to take the other. Then he ordered Grace to stay close behind as we made our way back towards the door. 'They have the fire under control, so we can head straight for my car, drive the hell out of here.'

Together we made it out of the barn and were halfway across the arena, still fighting for breath when a tall, terrifying figure confronted us. It emerged out of the clouds of white smoke, brandishing a flaming branch. It was Ezra, carrying fire. His face was blackened and burned, his eyes staring directly at Grace, who sank to her knees the moment she saw him.

Orlando and I saw her collapse. Jude was semiconscious, groaning and slumping forward, his arms still hooked around our shoulders. 'Grace, stand up!' I begged, trying to reach out for her.

But Ezra strode towards her, a hellish figure with his burned flesh and flaming brand shedding sparks as he came. He thrust it close to her face and with his free hand he seized her by the arm, his sooty fingers leaving marks on her pale skin. In the background the blades of the fire service choppers whirred and a mist of cold retardant hung in the air.

'Let her go!' I yelled as Ezra raised Grace to her feet.

'This isn't over. No one walks away,' he sneered, standing with his feet wide apart in the hissing dirt.

She winced then shuddered as sparks fell on her skin. But she didn't struggle.

'We're still strong,' Ezra vowed. The fire that had blistered his face hadn't weakened his willpower. 'We will always rise from the ashes.'

'No, no – you lose!' I raised my voice so that everyone could hear – those ghostly, unidentifiable figures in the distance who staggered through the smoke, bent double like soldiers gassed in the trenches, lungs shredded, coughing up blood. 'You can't take Grace with you. She's coming with us.'

He didn't loosen his grip and his hand was steady as he thrust the torch closer still. 'Who do you choose?' he snarled at her. 'Me or them?'

She was on her knees again, cowering away from the flame and from his mutilated face, trying to shield her eyes.

'Me or them?' he repeated, jerking her to her feet. Shadows flickered across his features. His eye sockets were dark and hollow.

I knew I had to act. 'Hold on to Jude,' I muttered to Orlando, stepping free and tugging at the chain around my neck. It broke easily but, before I could grasp it and give it to Grace, the gold crucifix slid away from me and dropped to the ground.

Out of the corner of his eye, Ezra saw where it landed. He gave a hollow laugh as he put his boot on it and stamped it into the dirt. 'You believe this can defeat me?' he sneered. 'The power of the cross – it's childish superstition!'

No – wrong! I kept to my first thought, gritted my teeth and ran at him, avoided the flaming branch as he swung it towards me, felt its heat against my cheek. And I charged into him with all the strength I could gather – enough to make him stagger backwards to reveal the gold cross in the dirt.

The power of the cross that my dad had given me, a gift from my great grandmother through the generations – the ancient power for good over evil.

I stooped to pick it up and give it to Grace, placed it in her palm and closed her trembling fingers over it.

'Go with Jude and Orlando!' I gasped at her as Ezra sprawled on the ground. His flaming torch had fallen against the arena fence. 'Go – now!' I meant everyone – Grace, Jude and Orlando. 'Get out of here!'

Orlando shook his head. He didn't seem able to take his eyes off Ezra rolling in the dirt, writhing there as if he was still burning in the flames that had disfigured him. He was visible in the guttering light of his torch, arms flailing, trying to beat back the invisible fire, rolling against the fence, gasping, shrieking, crying out to be saved.

'Make Grace keep hold of the cross,' I told Orlando. 'Ger her and Jude to the car.'

'I'm not leaving you!' Buckling under Jude's weight, he took Grace's hand and drew her away from Ezra.

'I'll be right behind you,' I promised above Ezra's

screams as the chopper blades whirred and a fresh bank of black smoke rolled off the mountain and hid Orlando, Grace and Jude from view.

The only thing visible in the dying light of the flaming torch was Ezra himself lying in the dirt. He fought an enemy he couldn't see, groaned and rolled on to his stomach, tried to crawl away, collapsed again. For as long as Grace held the cross in her hand he was powerless.

The smoke rolled on across the arena. Orlando had escaped with Jude and Grace but now a new force swept down from Black Rock. I felt it, I knew it in every atom of my being – dark angel Zoran had come back for me.

He swooped and gathered me up, lifted me from the ground and flew with me above the smoke, above the helicopters and the rising steam into the dark night. A million light years over our heads stars shone, while down on Black Rock sporadic fires still burned. I heard the beating of Zoran's great wings, up-down, up-down, glimpsed the sliver of moon in the sky, stared down on the dark western mountains, the white summits covered in snow – on and on.

I shivered in the dark lord's grasp, in his terrible airborne power, as he carried me away.

We came to rest in a white wilderness, high on a dizzying

slope – a place of ice-bound, violet crevasses, of shadows, sunset and silence, except for the thudding of my heart. This is where Zoran set me down.

He stood three paces away, his black wings spread wide – him and me alone on Carlsbad Mountain. Somewhere deep inside, I had known from the moment I first saw him that it would end like this, face to face.

'Now you have no one,' he said calmly.

I closed my eyes, opened them again. The ice crust creaked underfoot; my heart beat as though it would break out of my chest.

'No one will save you, Tania Ionescu. How does it feel to be alone?'

'Like I knew it would.'

'There is no power stronger than me,' he said slowly. 'You see now how it works?'

'You're weaker than you were,' I replied. Minus Ezra, Cristal and Daniel. And without Jude and Grace in your ranks. I held my head up – I could be proud of this at least.

'There will be other times, other places,' he said without blinking. 'A million other willing souls.'

I stood defenceless on the silent slope, my heart racing, my head held high. 'You didn't fool me,' I told him. 'You thought you did but you didn't.'

He smiled. 'Correct. I underestimated you.'

'You used Daniel to trap me. You wanted me to fall in love with him. It didn't work out.'

'Almost,' he said, still smiling. 'All I needed was one more day.'

'Never.' I trembled from the effort of standing tall in front of him. 'What do you know about love?' I challenged. 'For you it's all on the surface, skin deep.'

'That's the story for many others too. Remember Oliver, and Grace and Jude.'

'Not for me and Orlando.'

His smile mocked me, while the silence of the white mountain crowded in. 'Poor Tania. You held out longer than the others, but where did it get you? In the end, you suffer the most.'

I shook my head. In my mind I was saying goodbye. I saw the future – my mom and dad clearing my closet, packing away the paints and canvases in my studio then sitting in silence in an empty house. I saw Orlando cycling by Prayer River without me.

'The others go on with their lives.' Zoran's voice was scarcely more than a whisper and his dark eyes glittered.

I envisaged my last moments under those black, beating wings. And I saw everything like a drowning man, every detail right back to the first time Zoran came onstage at the Heavenly Bodies party – his rock-star strut under flashing lights, the way his voice soared and his lyrics carried their secret threat. 'You don't know me, you never will/ Shadows fall, voices kill.' The way he mesmerized us and grasped power – Zoran Brancusi, shape-shifting soul-stealer, brutal dealer in death.

'Here is where it ends,' he confirmed.

Black, nameless shapes rose from the blue crevasses. They flapped their wings and circled against the setting sun.

'You don't know me/ Though you see my face . . .' The haunting words flitted through my head like the black creatures in the blood-red sky. I remembered Maia's promise – knowledge is power – and I totally realized that I had nothing left to lose. 'I *know* you!' I said out loud and with all the defiant force I had left in my bruised and breathless body.

Zoran frowned as he took a step towards me. My words seemed to make him hesitate.

'I know that you're a fake. You're not who you pretend to be.' Keep in mind what Maia told me, then quickly, quickly deliver what I learned from Stefan. 'Zoran Brancusi is dead. He really did die in the hospital in Bucharest.' *Catch the devil by the throat.* 'What I say is true, and truth will bring you down.'

But no – it only made him falter then grow more angry. He knotted his brows, he spread his wings and drew down the creatures from the sky. They flitted through the darkening air, half-bat, half-bird with flapping, leathery wings. They would claw and peck at me, would cling to my face and smother me.

'You use Zoran's corpse,' I screamed, hitting out with words – the only weapon I had in my final armoury. 'You stole a dead man's life. I *know* you!'

'You don't know me/ Though you see my face/ My name is lost in time and space.'

The dark angel's lips stretched but no way was it a smile. It was arrogance on his face as he took the last steps. 'Who am I?' he taunted.

'My name is lost . . .'

Think. Drag it out of the recesses of memory. There was a guy at the Floreascu who claimed the body. He signed the form. Who was he? What was his name?

'Malach!' I cried. The answer sprang from me. I said it three times. 'Malach! Malach!'

'*Malach, angel of death. Brutal spirit of the underworld, creator of war, destroyer of infants.*' Maia's voice is in the *dying light, in the glistening ice beneath my feet.*

'Your name is Malach,' I repeated quietly.

In the end I find the key. You lose, I win.

The name entered his poisoned heart like a spear. Before my eyes it ripped him apart. He staggered backwards, fell with arms flailing, scattering the dark, flitting creatures in all directions. He sank into the snow.

*Angel of death. Destroyer of the innocents. Malach.*

I watched the demon die without pity. He sank, the flesh melted from his bones, he decayed. The dark eyes stayed alive until the end, glaring at me in rage. Calmly I witnessed this last transformation, saw him dissolve in torment. His eyes flashed in angry, bitter defeat until he was skull and skeleton, mouldering into the ice, returning to dust.

*'My child, my angel!' Maia lifts me and carries me from the mountain. Stars light our way. I don't see her but I hear her voice.*

*'He vanished. I looked and there was nothing left.'*

*'Back into darkness,' she murmurs. She bears me high through the heavens; we are one and the same, entwined.*

*I don't look down. I look up at the moon. A million souls rejoice and travel with us through the night.*

# 17

Orlando was the one who took longer to get over it. He said he couldn't forgive himself for leaving me alone on the mountain.

'You didn't,' I argued. 'I wasn't by myself up there.'

We were two days into the recovery period. Jude was out of hospital and we were at his house, courtesy of an invite from Dr and Mrs Medina, which in itself was a small miracle. It was meant to be a party to celebrate.

'I should have stayed,' Orlando said. He jutted out his bottom lip, hung his head.

'Then what?' Grace argued. 'No way would Jude have made it if you'd stayed to help Tania.'

'Yeah, thanks, buddy.' It was all Jude was able to say before he moved slowly out of the house on to the porch looking out on to Black Rock. There was a dark scar on the mountain – the burnout from the latest fire. We heard from the fire service that, despite their planes and helicopters, flames had totally wiped out Black Eagle Lodge and there were no survivors. The problem now was counting the dead – how many permanent residents had been at the commune, their identities, their next of kin.

'Good luck with that,' was my personal reaction.

'Luckily, there were no Bitterroot fatalities,' Ricki Suarez, the head of the hotshot team had told news journalists. 'Local families were not affected.'

'"Luckily!"' Holly had echoed as we'd watched the TV news. 'Hell's teeth – what did luck have to do with it?'

Quietly Grace followed Jude on to the porch and sat with him. Her mom had told my mom that since Tuesday night she'd never left his side.

'We need music,' Holly decided, and Aaron chose a dance CD though none of the rest of us felt up to dancing.

'It's a party,' Aaron reminded us. 'Everything worked out, didn't it?'

Orlando had got Jude to the hospital, Grace stayed with him all through the night. They didn't speak about events at Black Eagle Lodge – about Ezra and Cristal and the whole Zoran thing – and I don't suppose they ever will.

'It's like a black hole,' Grace had tried to explain to me before the party began. She was pale and edgy, snatching every opportunity to say thanks. And I have to say she still didn't look like the old gentle, generous, fun-loving Grace, but give her time. 'My memory has this giant hole and it scares the crap out of me.'

'Tell me about it,' I'd replied. I'd squeezed her hand.

Then Holly and Aaron had arrived to party. And now I stood inside the house looking out at Jude and Grace sitting hand in hand with Black Rock in the distance and a ragged, painful gap in their memories that would take a long time to heal, but I knew it would.

Orlando came to stand with me and hold my hand. 'Are we OK?' he checked.

'Hey, still Mister Insecure?' I smiled and slipped my hand in his.

'No, really. You don't hate me?'

I flashed him a look, told him not to be stupid, kissed him.

After a while we all got into the music and the party took off. Holly and Aaron danced, she blamed him for stepping on her foot, we laughed – same old, same old. Eventually Orlando and I smooched in a corner. Grace and Jude came in from the porch, ate snacks, drank beer. To look at us you would think that none of this had ever happened.

At around ten I told Orlando I was tired and would he drive me home. I asked him to stay over.

'Hey, you two,' Dad said when we walked into the house. 'Orlando, you want to come fishing with me tomorrow?'

'Dumb question,' Mom told him.

'Why dumb?'

'Because!'

'Tomorrow is Dallas,' I explained. 'Orlando's interview. While you're fishing I'll be driving him to the airport.' Me – not his mom, notice.

That night was special. We talked, we made love. I made sure Orlando knew how much I would miss him.

At the airport the next morning he almost wouldn't board his plane. They'd called his section and he was still standing at the gate, holding me tight.

'Go!' I whispered.

He shook his head, stayed exactly where he was. 'What if I changed my mind?'

'No. You can't. It's a great college – think Mimi Rossi, Julian Sellars. This is your future we're talking about.'

'What about our future, you and me?'

'This is our future,' I said. I leaned back to drink in those lovely features – the badly behaved sweep of dark hair, the blue Irish eyes and wide mouth. What a leap of faith, I thought as I eased out of his arms.

The desk attendant called his name. Immediate departure – all that.

'You know what you told me on Black Rock?' I reminded him. 'In the smoke, in the middle of everything.'

Orlando nodded. Slowly he bent down to pick up his bag.

'Whatever happens, wherever we are, what you said then is still true.'

He kissed my lips, waited for me to say it.

'This is about love,' I whispered, turning him towards the gate. 'Now go!'

*Tania's story continues in*

# TWISTED HEART

*coming soon . . .*

I sleep with a dream catcher above my bed. I use it to filter out bad dreams – I had enough of those earlier this summer. Flames eating up the forests, leaping across canyons, shooting firebrands through the night sky. Plus the dark angel voice slithering through my brain with a warning: 'We will all rise. There will be other times, other places, a million other willing souls!'

I travelled halfway across the world to get a break from all that flesh-creeping stuff and if my good angel isn't around any more to protect me, which she doesn't seem to be, I'm not too proud to rely on old superstitions, ancient beliefs, whatever.

My dream catcher is a circle of slender willow branches about thirty centimetres wide, wound with a narrow leather strip and with cotton threads woven across the centre in a geometric petal pattern. A pendulum of turquoise beads and white and black feathers hangs from the bottom of the hoop. Good dreams find their way through the net but bad ones can't get past. It works some of the time, I guess.

Since the last big burnout on Black Rock I also avoid going up on to the flame-seared slopes whenever possible – me and my best friend, Grace, and all the traumatized kids in Bitterroot if I'm honest.

I prefer valleys and water – cool streams, white-water rapids, Prayer River and Turner Lake.

I mean, I love the lake, totally adore the light sparkling on its surface and the way your feet and ankles turn pale and distort when you wade in from the pebble shore, the icy feel of the water between your toes. It's where Orlando and I fell in love.

It was midnight, and just remembering it makes my soul soar. The night sky was huge, the Milky Way streaming across it – a glittering banner made out of a million stars. We were tiny and unique. We took off our clothes and swam in the lake.

'You're my midnight swimmer,' he tells me even now.

Or he would do if he was here.

## Questions and Answers
# Eden Maguire

**Where do the ideas for your books come from?**

My ideas come from a mysterious region of the brain – the 'What if' part which must have a neurological label, but which works something like this: 'What if the world really is split between supernatural good and bad forces? What if we can all be tempted on to the side of shape-shifting, terrifying dark angels to fight against the angels of light?' With this basic idea, I can create a setting, a heroine and a whole cast of characters, plus a plot so full of twists and turns that even I don't know how it will end until I get there.

**Who would your dream cast be if *Dark Angel* was made into a film?**

Actors in a film of *Dark Angel*? Most of the ones I can think of are a few years too old (sorry!), but how about Natalie Portman for Tania (she's the right physical style and can play sensitive, tormented souls) and Robert Pattinson for Orlando (dream on!).

**What have you enjoyed writing the most – *Dark Angel* or the *Beautiful Dead*?**

The answer to which of my books I enjoy the most is always, 'The one I'm writing now.' So it has to be *Twisted Heart* (more on that later).

**Who do you relate to more – Darina from the *Beautiful Dead* or Tania in *Dark Angel*?**

I think Darina has more of the rebel in her – something I can relate to from my own teen years. I don't have Tania's psychic powers, but do share some of her thin-skinned sensitivity.

### If you could invite five people to dinner who would they be?

Top of my list for ideal dinner guests are: Marilyn Monroe, Shakespeare, Catherine Earnshaw from *Wuthering Heights*, John Lennon and Atticus Finch from *To Kill A Mocking Bird*.

### Where is your favourite place to write?

I can only write in one place and no other – it's my first storey office overlooking a river and a wooded hillside. No other room will do.

### Who is your favourite author and why?

Favourite author is so hard – this time I'll choose one who is alive – it's Annie Proulx who wrote the short story *Brokeback Mountain* which they turned into a great film. Everything she writes is strong and disturbing.

### What advice would you give to aspiring young writers?

People who really want to write don't need my advice. They're driven by some inner compulsion. It turns out right if they stick to the truth of their imaginations.

### What book do you wish you had written?

A book I totally admire is *The Kite Runner* by Khaled Hosseini. I wish I could write something so moving and powerful and true.

### How does it feel when you see your books in a bookshop?

When I see my own book on a bookshop shelf I have a mixed reaction. There's a big temptation to position it so that customers can see it more easily, but there's also an unexpected panic and a need to run and hide!

### Tell us one thing your readers won't already know about you.

I once fell off a horse high on a mountain with no other riders around. My horse didn't run off – he stayed and waited for me to get back on my feet, thank heavens. Not many people know that!

### What's next from Eden Maguire?

Next for Eden Maguire is the second book in the *Dark Angel* trilogy. It's called *Twisted Heart* and the strapline reads 'Nowhere to hide ...'

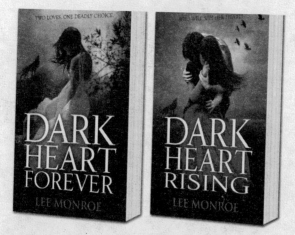